SHARK
TEETH

Also by Sherri Winston

Lotus Bloom and the Afro Revolution

SHARK TEETH

SHERRI WINSTON

BLOOMSBURY
CHILDREN'S BOOKS
NEW YORK LONDON OXFORD NEW DELHI SYDNEY

BLOOMSBURY CHILDREN'S BOOKS
Bloomsbury Publishing Inc., part of Bloomsbury Publishing Plc
1385 Broadway, New York, NY 10018

BLOOMSBURY, BLOOMSBURY CHILDREN'S BOOKS, and the Diana logo
are trademarks of Bloomsbury Publishing Plc

First published in the United States of America in January 2024
by Bloomsbury Children's Books

Bloomsbury books may be purchased for business or promotional use. For information on bulk purchases
please contact Macmillan Corporate and Premium Sales Department at
specialmarkets@macmillan.com

Library of Congress Cataloging-in-Publication Data
Names: Winston, Sherri, author.
Title: Shark teeth / by Sherri Winston.
Description: New York : Bloomsbury, 2024.
Summary: Seventh-grader Sharkita "Kita" embarks on a tumultuous journey
to keep her family together while handling the consequences of her mother's alcoholism.
Identifiers: LCCN 2023038049 (print) | LCCN 2023038050 (e-book)
ISBN 978-1-5476-0850-8 (hardcover) • ISBN 978-1-5476-0851-5 (e-book)
Subjects: CYAC: Family problems—Fiction. | Alcoholism—Fiction. | Middle schools—Fiction. |
Schools—Fiction. | African Americans—Fiction.
Classification: LCC PZ7.W7536 Sh 2024 (print) | LCC PZ7.W7536 (e-book) | DDC [Fic]—dc23
LC record available at https://lccn.loc.gov/2023038049

Book design by John Candell
Typeset by Westchester Publishing Services
Printed and bound in the U.S.A.
2 4 6 8 10 9 7 5 3 1

To find out more about our authors and books visit www.bloomsbury.com
and sign up for our newsletters.

Dedicated to my sister Janice, who spent decades working with children with broken lives, but not all had broken spirits. I love you, my Janny Bananny.

SHARK
TEETH

WE STUMBLED OVER MAMA'S best memories, like tripping on old bones, as we ran backward through time. All Mama's best memories lived in the Bruckner Orange Groves where her daddy worked as a manager, once upon a time.

"Right over there, that's where Daddy let me drive a tractor for the first time. I wasn't but this high," Mama said, balancing her palm even with her waist, parallel to the dusty ground. She let out a burst of laughter so bright it painted everything with joy. Never mind that the last time she pointed out the sacred site of her maiden tractor voyage it was nowhere near where we stood that morning. Who needs facts, right? She was riding a vibe.

My little sister turned a cartwheel; my little brother jumped up and down. Grinning, Mama went on, saying, "Daddy was good friends with his boss, the owner, back then, and he always showed me off and told me he was proud." I couldn't remember her ever saying she was proud of me, and I did way more than illegally drive a tractor.

But as usual, I gulped back my bitterness. Right now my mama's manner was as sweet and sticky as the juice in the oranges, and I was going to drink up as much of it as I could.

Our visits to Bruckner Groves often left me breathless. Mama brought us back here to relive good times from her past, times when she was her happiest. But sometimes the further Mama slipped back into time, the more kinks and knots formed in my belly. Because sometimes looking back on good times just made Mama look at how things were now and decide it wasn't good enough, not good enough at all. I'd ache from not knowing what the rest of the day would bring. I hated the feeling of not knowing what would happen next. It felt like that ride at the carnival that went around and around, speeding up until it threw you up against the wall and the floor fell away.

Yeah, with Mama, I never knew when the floor would fall right out from under us.

Several deep inhales and exhales later, I could finally feel my heart rate slow. But I still chewed on my lip.

I should have been grateful. Our little family was whole again. We'd spent several weeks torn apart—the worst weeks of my life. Even so, in that moment standing beside Mama, I didn't feel grateful. I felt frightened.

Granny once told me losing Granddaddy when she was four-teen pained Mama's soul so bad that something in her broke.

"She ain't been right since," Granny said.

Sometimes it felt like Mama thought the same about me—like somewhere along the way I'd been broken. Like my mind wasn't right.

2

On that sunny day, however, Mama drew herself back from the shadows of reality and shared her version of love equally. She shook her long black hair and smiled at the orange grove where she'd been daddy's little girl. She looked beautiful in her yellow sundress. Shades of green leaves, tree trunks straight as stripes, and drips of orange blobs like polka dots filled in the space around her.

"God, I love the way it smells out here. Oranges in the summer," Mama said.

I didn't roll my eyes this time, so I felt proud of myself. She never noticed what an effort that was.

Instead, I joined my siblings. We played and laughed, inhaling the thick, furry heat and lush scents.

Mama split open an orange with her nail and the juice ran down her arm, then she made her eyes go googly as she licked it off, and laughter poured from our hearts till we hurt from how good it felt. Just me, five-year-old Lillieana, and eight-year-old Lamar—and Mama. None of her hanging-out friends, none of the dudes she ran around with, just us.

For just a little while, we were enough.

My insides cramped with longing—could we be this way all the time?

I knew the answer, though. We couldn't.

Mama called out to me as Lamar growled like a monster and chased her, "Sharkita! Come on!"

I ran to catch up with her and the littles—my babies. I didn't want to think about how sometimes after Mama had a fun day in the sun remembering, she'd go home and swim into a black pool in her soul, thinking about all the good times she'd lost because of having a father who died unexpectedly; grieving the future she was cheated out of because of having a baby too young. Me. Sharkita.

The fear swelled up inside me. An awful feeling. Like being sucked into the jaws of a shark, squeezed in its belly. My nightmare. Well, my biggest nightmare. I had several.

All I wanted was to hold my family together. I didn't want to ever lose my brother and sister again. I wanted to keep us all together.

But sometimes . . . sometimes, no lie, I had to wonder if things were better without Mama.

(**2**)

BACK AT HOME INSIDE our town house, the AC unit blew icy air along my skin. The hair at the edge of my cornrows had curled into a tight fist. I sighed and let the coolness swim over me.

With the little ones covered in sand and dirt from running around outside all afternoon, I knew it would take less than sixty seconds to have everything in the house covered in sand and dirt, too.

"Bath time!" My voice was loud and cheery. Mama had started up to her room, but paused, looking back at me. I held her gaze before looking away.

"Come on, Lamar!" Mama said. That was the silent deal we made—I'd give Lilli her bath and Mama would bathe Lamar. She managed to hold on to her orange grove smile as she gathered his chubby fingers in hers.

Lilli took my hand and I couldn't help myself. Even though I knew better than to hope—I did. A lightness bubbled inside me as I glanced down the staircase, then back up at our walls.

As much as I'd loved living here the past two years, I couldn't help comparing it to houses I saw on design shows on TV. What would it be like to have a big house with a beautiful kitchen and a full walk-in pantry? Still a heck of a lot better than when we lived in the projects, though. You could barely sleep there sometimes. But even that was better than being in foster care this summer—at least in the projects we were together.

Lilli clasped my fingers. During bath time, the magic spell of having Mama back, us all being together again for the past few weeks, floated around us like the scent of fake citrus being pumped out from plug-in air fresheners. Mama had been borrowing her friends' cars, taking us out to eat at McDonald's, walking the little ones to the park, and most of all, helping me with the house chores. She did the laundry—folded it, too.

I was grateful her magic mojo had turned Lilli back into a little girl again. Normally, my sister acted more grown-up than most grown-ups. An "old soul," people called her.

Now, though, she was splashing around, talking about mermaids as she flipped onto her belly to float and pretend.

Neither of us spoke of the day back in June when social workers and police filled our downstairs. The only sound was Lilli making bubbles like a mermaid. The small bathroom smelled of chocolate.

"Lilli, how much candy did you have?" Her answer was a bunch of giggles that bounced off the sides of the tub and the walls. It made me laugh, too.

But the smell reminded me of the day when me, her, and

Lamar were yanked in different directions, our pain spilling like blood onto the floor. We'd landed in three separate homes all because Mama went out one night and decided not to come back for nine days. I wondered if, from time to time, she just got lost.

All things considered, the foster homes weren't bad—least not as bad as they could have been. None of us came back with the kind of horror stories you hear sometimes. But being away from my sibs—not knowing where they were or if they were okay—was torture.

"Kita, how come we can't take swimming lessons? How'm I gonna be a chocolate mermaid from the land of Chocotopia if you don't learn me how to swim?"

I reached into the bath water and playfully swatted her butt. "I can't 'learn' you something I don't know, silly goose!"

"But . . ." The thing about Lilli is she's too smart for her own good. "But I told you when I grow up I'm going to rule the land of Chocotopia and have giant squids as my bodyguards. And I can't go unless you go, too." Chocotopia? Giant squids? Where does she come up with this stuff?

For the past year, Lilli has been pushing me to sign up for swim classes at the community center. So we can be mermaids.

"They don't have sharks in the community center pool," she says. Immediately I want to ask: *How do you know!*

Lilli knew my fear of water. More importantly, my fear of sharks. She knew that even thinking about getting in the ocean, a lake, or even a large pool was enough to send me over the edge.

Mustering up as much playful attitude as I could, I tickled her tummy. "Girl, boo!" I said. "I know there are no sharks in the community center pool. Know what else isn't there? No Kita, either!"

Once Lilli finished swimming with mermaids, I kept her busy with chatter as I dried her off, careful to steer clear of her question about me joining her in the pool. Then she wrapped her arms around me. They were thin, like reeds. She held on tight as she whispered, "You think she means it this time?"

After a beat of surprise, I nodded wordlessly, not looking at her. All day long orange-grove mama had been promising us more road trips and pizzas and burgers, trips to the science museum. Plans for the future. When mama spoke about *The Future* she made it sound like Oz, a shiny new world where the refrigerators stayed full and the mamas were always home, full of love. A place without late-night clubbing or liquor or empty bottles in the kitchen trash.

A magical place where twelve-year-old girls didn't have to be responsible for younger siblings all on their own.

"Did you hear her at McDonald's?" Lilli whispered. I was applying lotion and baby oil to her skin while it was still damp. Lilli had a tendency to break out in itchy patches. Eczema. I had to stay on top of her ointments and creams. I shook my head at her question. "She promised my mermaid birthday party again. Then I'll really be queen of Chocotopia! I'll be six!" She held up six fingers. "She promised this time it's gonna happen."

My scalp bulged from the pressure starting inside my head. What could I say to her? Nobody wanted Mama to get right more than me. Lilli deserved her shimmering mermaid party with lots of bubbles, balloons, friends, cake, family, and most of all— a mama.

I tried to shake off the birthday question as we went into our room and she chose her favorite, a picture book called *Pearl*, from her bookshelf. Her birthday wasn't until March. Months away. In Mama days, that was a lifetime; too far away to be sure of anything.

Lilli dropped onto her bed, looking right at home in her pink palace. We shared the room, but it was designed by Lilli, one hundred percent. I lay beside her with the book flat in front of us. Lilli was old enough for chapter books, but she had been reading this book her whole life, it seemed like, and it was her favorite.

"Look how pretty she is," Lilli said, pointing to the opening picture for the millionth time. She tried to read the words aloud and I concentrated on the images, which were amazing. I wondered if I'd ever be able to paint something like that. I loved to draw, but probably I'd never be as good as that. The soft pastel colors and the swirling, gentle movement of the images was hypnotic.

We could still hear Lamar down the hall in Mama's bathroom. She was singing funny songs to him like she used to. Me and Lilli laughed, but the silent kind where our shoulders bumped up and down but we didn't make a sound. We couldn't risk breaking the spell.

Lamar's mind didn't work like other kids. I thought he was hilarious, and I loved everything about him. Well, almost. I didn't like the fact that his favorite animal was the one I hated most—*sharks!*

I had hated sharks since I was little, when my granny sat there and watched *Jaws* and *Jaws 2* with me right next to her. I had nightmares for weeks. Ever since then, they gave me the creeps. Not just because they were killers who could eat you alive, either. I hated them for what we had in common.

After we'd been kicked out of our first apartment because Mama didn't pay the rent, we wound up in a housing project where nobody went if they could afford better. It was first grade, and I had changed schools. Mama took me there my first day. The teacher let her introduce me to the class.

She said, "This is Sharkita, like 'shark' and 'ita.' You can remember it 'cause my baby got teeth stacked up like a shark's!"

Kids laughed and I couldn't stop the tears leaking out of my eyes. They started calling me "Crybaby Shark"; then it changed to "Baby Shark." By fourth grade, after all the other kids had shed their baby teeth but I was stuck with a double row resembling the mouth of a great white, they started calling me "Shark Teeth."

Now just thinking about sharks made me shiver all over. I had gale-o-phobia, a fear of sharks that could lead to fast heart rate, shaking, sweating, and dizziness. *It's a real thing, look it up!*

Like I said, me and sharks were not friends. Seeing them made me feel ugly—feel like that was what people saw when they looked at me.

Lamar was constantly watching specials about sharks, TV

shows, even cartoons. It kept him calm, though, so I didn't mind much.

Like I said, his brain didn't work like other kids'. Something that happened before he was born. So he needed special attention, which was fine with me—I'd do anything for the littles. Except sometimes Mama was the only one who could calm him down. And she wasn't always around.

I tried not to think any more about my brother's fits. Not now. Not when everything was going well. Okay, maybe not well, but better. I couldn't help smiling as Mama and Lamar breezed past Lilli's room holding hands and dancing. He loved to dance. Or try to dance. He really didn't have much coordination.

We listened to Lamar's giggles, which brought back the happiness of our day. Even the walls seemed to stretch and sigh with his joy. He was so happy it could break your heart.

The tear on my cheek went unchecked until Lilli's little fingers rubbed it away. "It'll be okay," she said. "If she don't do right this time, they'll take us for good and find real homes, right?"

Her matter-of-fact words and sweet little girl voice stung like a slap. The older, wiser five-year-old had replaced the carefree girl from the tub again. She seemed so ready to move on, but if that happened, it would mean I'd failed. My stomach twisted. While she floated amid a bed of seaweed kelp in her mermaid daydreams, I felt like fish food being sucked into the belly of a beastly shark.

"Nobody is taking us anywhere, baby girl," I said softly. I tried to hug her, but she pulled away.

11

"Yes, they will, Kita. Mama better act right 'cause I don't like this. I don't want to keep going through this," she said.

I pulled her to me, and this time I held her tight against my body. If I tried to speak, my words might break apart and blow away.

We stayed like that for a while. Then eventually Lilli fell asleep. Once I made it out of our room, I was nearly panting from the effort to keep calm.

I wanted to march into Lamar's room and demand to know if Mama was done running around, acting stupid. I wanted to know if she was ready to be the mama so I could be the kid.

But saying the wrong thing was dangerous. Mama had a temper like lightning, and my words were attached to live wires. Say the wrong thing, and I never knew where she might strike. She wasn't a whooping kind of mama, other than a slap here and there, but her words had fire in them. I'd been burned too many times.

Down the hallway, Mama kept singing, making my brother happy and sounding happy, too. *God, let this time be different. Let the change be real.* She sounded so full of joy.

Life really was so much better when Mama was happy.

EVENINGS WITH ME AND Mama felt so awkward after Lilli and Lamar were in bed. Since we'd been back together, it felt even weirder. Our Saturday today hadn't included any other citrus trips. Although Mama did take the littles to the park for an hour or so.

We sat across from each other in the town-house dining room, which was really just a table and chairs between the kitchen and living room. She had her MacBook out. I was drawing. As much as Mama liked looking at herself, I knew she wasn't on social media.

"What're you doing?" I asked.

"Touching up my résumé," she said, glancing over the top of her laptop. My eyes widened but my mouth stayed shut.

"You don't have to act shocked," she said. "You know I'll work, and get good jobs, too."

Yeah, when you want to!

I shrugged. Then she did something I didn't remember her

doing for a long, long time. She cocked her head to one side and asked, "Can I wash your hair?"

I went rigid, but shrugged. "Okay. If you want to."

Mama gathered her hair-doin' supplies, the good stuff she usually kept for her and Lilli. My mama knew she was beautiful, like movie-star beautiful. She felt the same way about Lilli. Not me, though. Not me.

She took me to the sink in the kitchen.

"Run the water, Kita. Make sure it's not too hot," she said. Even as she was talking, I could feel her heartbeat against my back as I bent forward and she lowered me down, down, down until warm water whooshed past my face.

Was I holding my breath?

Waiting for something to happen? Mama said I was paranoid. Said I had a "negative soul." She could never understand why I was so untrusting. *Hmm . . .* I couldn't imagine why.

She kept talking. "This shampoo is amazing. Even though your hair isn't nearly as thick as mine or Lilli's, it should work well on you." Her voice echoed through my body as she massaged my scalp, trailing her fingers down the lines my cornrows left after she took them out.

"Did . . . the foster mom braid your hair? I know you can't braid."

Small shoulder shrug from me. Head nod. Mama was on her tiptoes. I was taller than her now.

"She didn't do a bad job," Mama said. "Dang, Kita! You grew so much in such a little amount of time."

Sixty-six days. My knees turned to jelly. I melted. Felt myself washed down the drain. Two months of going to bed wondering if Lilli was okay or if Lamar was being mistreated.

He didn't do well with new places and new people didn't know what to do about it. Mama knew, though.

When he was still a baby, they realized something wasn't right. Doctor's appointments, tests, lots of sleepless nights and worry, but Mama finally got answers.

Mama wanted the hospital people to say he had Down syndrome. I looked it up later—it was a condition you couldn't control, something that just happened based on your genes. He didn't have that, though. What he had was alcohol poisoning. Fetal alcohol syndrome. Mama drank so much when she was pregnant that she hurt her baby.

She fought the diagnosis.

"I read all about Down syndrome," she'd said. "I'm sure that's what's happening to my baby." She argued with the hospital people and social worker. Threw a fit. Said they were ganging up on her. I sat right next to her. Only four years old. Not understanding then.

But I understood now.

"Girl, your mind is a million miles away," Mama said to me now. Her touch, having her so close to me, it set off a thousand different feelings. Joy, sadness, rage, glee, relief . . . Mama had never been affectionate with me. Feeling her heartbeat on my back made me want to cry. Or slap her. Or both.

Had she changed? Really changed? A small part of my brain whispered, *Don't let your guard drop.*

"You know we're still partners, right? You're still my ride or die, right?"

I sucked in a breath. My whole body flinched. The question hung above my head like an anvil in those really old cartoons. Lamar loves those old *Looney Tunes*.

My stomach cramped. She used "ride or die" when she needed me to cover for her shady parenting. But I was tired of being her ride or die when she wouldn't do the same for me.

The warmth of her heartbeat against me vanished. Was it me? Was there something wrong with me that I felt like so much of our history—mine and hers—tasted like ashes on my tongue? Probably from a lifetime of burning bridges. Only I wasn't sure who'd set the fires.

Once when I was little, Mama did something that ticked me off. She tried to make it better by hugging me. When I refused and pulled away, she asked, "What's wrong with you?"

Like a little kid, I was honest:

"I'm mad at you!"

It could've turned out to be a funny moment, only it was Mama I was dealing with. She grabbed my wrist and pinched me, hard. As the tears filled my eyes, she practically spat out:

"You don't have a right to be angry! If anyone has a right to be angry, it's me! Everything I sacrificed just to bring you into this world. Everything I do for you. If you knew like I knew, you'd be grateful!"

"Baby, relax!" Mama said, cutting into another ugly memory. "I've told you, holding on to old stuff . . . it'll make you sick.

16

And the last thing you need is to wind up in somebody's mental ward."

"Mental ward." I cringed. My heart hammered. The way she said it. So casual. Mama made going to see a psychologist seem like the worst thing in the world. Didn't want me telling a stranger all our business, probably. Sometimes I wish I did have someone I could talk to about . . . *everything*.

Sometimes I thought Mama liked making me think something was wrong with me so I wouldn't ask questions or stand up to her.

Mama squeezed water from my hair, then lathered it with slick conditioner, massaging it into my scalp. The sound of the water, the smell of mint and lavender in the conditioner, it all made me drowsy. I could feel myself relaxing.

"I know you didn't mean to let what happened in June, happen. It's okay, I understand. You were scared. We'll both just need to try harder now." Her tone sounded so normal. Matter of fact. She seemed as floaty as a mermaid.

Then her words and meanings wrapped around me like the tentacles on an octopus. Squeezing me until my eyes bulged. *Is she serious?* Blaming me for us getting sent into foster care?

Mama shifted gears.

"This looks good," she said, slowly detangling my hair with her fingers, "especially for your hair. You remember how thin and scraggly it used to be. It's not like that anymore. I might actually be able to style this." Even her praise held razor blades.

She squeezed water from my hair after rinsing the conditioner. She handed me a towel to dry my hair, then led me into the living room. Mama positioned me on the floor between her knees and began blow-drying my hair.

When she was done, I could feel her playing with it. I hardly ever blew out my hair. My head felt lighter.

"We should look into getting you a relaxer. You'd look really good with straight hair," she said.

I hated how much that compliment filled me up. I hate even more how much I wanted to believe it.

"I never thought about it much, really," I lied. I wished I was upstairs, in the tiny room I shared with Lilli. Mama was wearing me out, keeping me on edge.

Then she drew a deep breath and went in a whole other direction. My emotions struggled to keep up.

"I'm sorry, Kita. I'm so sorry I have been . . . that I've missed out on a lot. But I love you. I love all my babies. I don't want anyone trying to tear us apart ever again. I mean that!"

Just like that, the anger that had inflated inside my chest, my head, my whole self, turned into uncertainty. Mama apologized. To me. How many times had I fantasized about that? Maybe what she said before, about us being "good" as in okay with each other, was true.

Take a breath!

Please, give her a chance.

I wanted to obey that little voice in my head. Breathe deep, exhale, and throw my arms around Mama and believe her when she said everything would be all right. But my heart, my brain, my soul resisted. We'd all been on this carnival ride before—where everything is fun until the floor comes out from under us and the screaming begins.

Music from the early 2000s bumped across the carpet as some passing car stereo shook our quiet street with bass. Mama let loose a deep sigh and without looking I could feel her smile work through her body as she patted her foot and swayed her whole body.

"Ooo, baby girl! This song takes me back!" she said. Then she shared memories she'd tucked behind each lyric and bass beat.

She dug out her phone and went into her photos. "This song was playing on the radio when I went to the hospital to have you. Look at my baby," she said. It was a picture of me right after I was born. She was sitting in the hospital bed. I was wrapped up in a baby blanket tucked perfectly in her arms.

"I was so scared," Mama said. "There you were, so pale. Even then you had this same reddish-brown hair. I loved you so much, no matter what my mama said."

She dragged the comb through my hair, separating it into sections to put a little oil on my scalp. I craned my head around and frowned. She nodded. Mama almost never talked about me with words that glowed.

Once I found my voice, I asked, "Mama. Was it hard? Having me?"

"You mean giving birth or having to be a fifteen-year-old mom?" she said on a laugh. My knuckles whitened from squeezing my fist so tight.

"Being a mom?" I asked.

19

Mama was quiet a long time. Finally, sighing, she answered, "Yeah. It was hard. Trying to figure everything out. Your granny nagging me constantly, always quick to tell me what I was doing wrong. Sometimes . . ." Mama's voice snagged, like a sweater caught on a nail. When I tilted my head upward, I saw the pain glazing her eyes.

"Sometimes I think I'd have had a better chance if I'd raised you on the streets, by myself." I felt her fingers tighten their grip on my hair. "She ruins everything. No matter how much she fronts like the reliable grandmother, my mama was incapable of giving a damn about me!"

She sounded so sad and lost, and when I twisted around to look into her face, I spotted the glint of a tear.

Back when I was three, before Lamar and Lilli were born, Mama and me lived with Granny. She and Mama fought about everything—from how to fix my hair to what kind of job Mama should get.

One night Mama wanted to go out. Granny said she wasn't going to babysit me. Mama went out anyway and left me alone because she thought Granny was coming right back. Next thing I know, the police and a social worker are on the doorstep. That was the first time I was put in foster care.

Granny called them to report that Mama had left me alone. To this day, I still couldn't believe my own grandmother could do something like that.

When I looked at Mama again, her pained expression jabbed at my heart.

"Show me some more pictures, Mama," I said. She might be the Queen of Diversions, but I'd been a good apprentice. Time to shift gears.

Mama shook herself free of the memory, then began flipping through timelines in her photos. I was reminded of old friends she had growing up—friends who would later babysit me. Friends who kicked her to the curb when she didn't show up to get me one too many times.

"This is my favorite picture of you," she said. Her voice became sunny and carefree. The scent of orange blossoms and green grass filled me.

"I've never seen this," I said, my heart hammering. I must have been three or four. Definitely four.

"Girl, you *was* Miss Fancy that day. Do you remember?" I shook my head slowly. I didn't remember it at all. Mama kept on, "My friend girl back then, Mercedes, her little girl was your age. Do you remember? I think her daughter's name was Freya. Remember?"

I didn't remember little Freya.

I *did* remember Miss Mercedes.

Mama had once left me with her for "a few hours." When my mama came back three days later, the two of them came to blows.

"No, Mama, I can't quite remember her," I said.

"Hmm? I thought for sure you'd remember her. Wonder what ol' Mercedes is up to these days?"

Like she had no memory of their fight that awful day. Me? I'd seen too many and remembered them all. Couldn't help it.

She finished blow-drying and curling my hair.

Two twists on opposite sides of my face. Then she wound each into a bun. The hair in back hung past my shoulders, almost to my bra strap. She wrapped the hair around the curling iron and made spiral curls. They felt springy and light.

Finally, she spun me around. For a long moment, she just held my shoulders and looked at me. Looked at me like maybe she was really seeing me. My insides waged a silent battle—do we believe her, or should we be on super-high alert?

"Go look! Look!" Mama pointed to the mirror in the living room. When I turned and saw myself, I gasped. "Looks good, doesn't it?" Mama laughed, and I wanted to wrap myself in her joy. I wanted to run and hide.

But what I really wanted was to believe her. Could I take the risk?

At the same time, the creeping sensation of a shark inhaling and sucking me into its darkness, past rows of knifelike teeth, filled me with dread. While Mama was laughing, still on Memory Lane, I felt like I was about to be digested by a shark.

One thought fighting through the fog of my emotions:

Would she still be here in the morning?

(**4**)

LILLI SLEPT SOUNDLY. HER bed had a white frame, like the kind little white girls on Disney shows slept in. Mine was a foldout sofa with Lilli's Minnie and Mickey Mouse pillows on it. The sleeper was in an L-shape to Lilli's bed. Space was tight. The third drawer in the white dresser didn't close all the way. I always had to remember to step around it because otherwise I'd hit my leg. It really hurt when that happened.

Folding my new blow-out do against my head, I slipped on my satin sleep bonnet. Gotta protect yourself from frizz. Lilli made another soft snort, the only light came from the night-light beside her bed. I inched across the shadowy floor carefully—not carefully enough, though.

I slammed my leg bone against the drawer, almost falling over.

"Kita?" Lilli's tiny sleep-thickened voice came out like a cloud. Still hopping on one leg, I turned and saw her little hands reaching out for me.

"It's okay, Lil, it's just me," I said. I went over and took her hand.

"Don't leave me," she said. She took my hand and pulled me to the edge of her bed. I grabbed my Minnie Mouse pillow, curled up on the floor beside her, and fell asleep holding her hand.

It was two or three hours later when I woke. No longer holding her fingers. Body curled into a tight ball.

Couldn't move. My body curled to one side. Feeling somewhere between pain and numbness. A weight pressed into me.

Trying to get up was useless. Nothing moved, except my eyes. And my mind. My brain kept shouting signals, but my limbs didn't work.

Ears ringing, breaths coming louder and faster. Sweat trickling down my neckline. Tightness clawing at my throat.

I hate this! I hate this! I hate this!

When . . . this happened—this eerie, weird, creepy thing that held on to my body like a bully with a grudge.

Times like this, I'd wake up unable to move. My own personal shark attack. I read that sharks swallowed prey whole and let their stomach juices break them down. And that's what it felt like. Like I was trapped, stuck, being slowly eaten away at.

Mama and the uncertainty that came from living with her, it was breaking me down.

My mind screamed into my skull. *Why couldn't I move?* A moan pulsed in my throat.

Everything that worried me bubbled up inside my head.

What if Mama started drinking again? What if we went back

into foster care? I felt afraid of losing my family. Afraid of what a future with Mama would be like. Terrified I didn't know which was worse—a life with her or one without.

~⁓

When I woke up on Monday morning, I could hear her somewhere in the distance, already cooing at Lamar. My sleepy brain made a quiet checkmark—Day Sixteen since coming home from foster care, Mama's still here.

I drew a deep inhale when Lilli kissed my cheek. I'd made it back to my bed.

Despite it being well before seven in the morning, bright light flooded the bedroom. My head was pounding. My eyes were grainy with sleep. It had taken me half an hour to wriggle free of the vise grip of the squeezing that had pinned me to the floor.

"I love you, Kita!" Lilli sang. "It's time to go to school!"

Mama helped me get the littles ready for the first day of school—which had quit happening long before we were taken from her in June. We were busy doing what needed doing, then my brother and sister started asking me for help:

"Where're my shoes at, Kita?" "Can I wear this, Kita?" Mama got a little salty, I could tell, but she tried to make a joke out of it.

"Y'all leave Kita alone," she said, wearing a wide smile that looked like it had been pinned on crooked. "I'm yo' mama. I can help you!" Mama managed to graduate high school early despite missing time from having me. She was scary smart—when she wanted to be.

Lilli looked at me but didn't say anything. Lamar, though, that boy didn't know no better.

"Mama you be gone a lot, s'pecially when it's morning time. Kita always is the one who makes us breakfast and—" Mama shushed him and hugged him until he forgot what he was saying. But I was holding my breath, waiting, because he was right.

Mama must have guessed what I was thinking. She said: "Girl, don't go looking at me like you think I'm some kind of bad mama." She did a little dance move and snapped her fingers still trying to make it all seem so happy-happy, good-good. "I know you're the one who's been here for them, but sometimes Mama needs a break. That's why we're partners, right?"

Partners. That word again. My whole body tensed.

I said, "Sorry, Mama," because I always felt sorry for something. It came out automatic.

She kept the fake smile on her face, but darkness slithered behind her eyes. I swallowed hard and took Lilli by the hand.

"I need to help Lil find her shoes. It's almost time to go," I said, voice as normal as I could make it.

"You do that," she said, putting steel in her everything-is-fine voice. "Yo' butt don't like it when I take charge of my own kids. You're as controlling as your granny. Now you go on," she made her voice extra syrupy, "with those crooked teeth just like your daddy!" That was her way of putting me in my place, letting me know who was in charge. She barked out a laugh and threw her head back. Lamar laughed because she was laughing. Me and Lilli didn't laugh.

26

A heat, like anger, rose under the neckline of my black *Wakanda Forever* tee. Seventh grade was starting just like sixth grade ended—full of uncertainty.

I ushered Lilli to the stairs. Mama's dark-eyed gaze followed. She was watching me.

And even with my back turned, I was watching her right back.

GROVE MIDDLE WAS ONLY a few blocks from where I lived. My pace slowed. Feet feeling heavier the closer I got. I liked school and wanted to do well. Really, I did. But it was hard being a good student when you struggled to stay awake after a night of taking care of your little siblings.

I thought about all the clubs and activities I'd longed to try over the years. All the friendships I had missed out on. Because Mama needed me home. So she didn't have to be.

"Sharkita! Sharkita Lloyd! Girl, it sho' is good to see you." The loud voice jarred me. I jumped just in time to hear a big, hearty laugh. "Dang, girl! You about came out of your skin . . . *outta yo' skin! . . . outta yo' skin . . . !*"

The only person at Grove Middle I had been truly looking forward to seeing, Shaniece "Niecy" Hall.

"Hey, girl!" I said, trying to get my wind back. "Still singing everything?"

Her loud self hopped side to side, singing a high-pitched *wooo-hooo-hooo.* "*My girl is back! My girl is back! My girl is back!*" She was like a cartoon character. She struck one pose. Then another.

We both broke out laughing and I found myself exhaling as we held on to each other, rocking together.

"You grew!" said. She was as short and curvy as I was long and straight.

"Where you been girl? I ain't seen you since . . ." Her voice trickled away, and her smile fell tragically over a cliff.

She hadn't seen me since our birthdays. We were born one day apart—June second and June third. She was a day older but years bossier. We'd been twirling garage sale batons out back, like always, and stopped to share a Hostess CupCake. I was licking icing off my fingers watching the sunset, not knowing the storm that was coming.

"How's Lamar?" She wasn't singing now. Her voice fell soft and low.

"He's all right," I said softly, too.

"And Miss Lilli? How's she doing with her grown behind?"

Now we'd both cracked smiles. I told her Lilli was doing good. "Still trying to be a mermaid. Girl, now she says she's a chocolate mermaid in the land of Chocotopia! Already trying to take over the world—or at least her made-up one."

We walked in the morning heat, not exactly forcing laughter.

"Good, I'm glad to hear it," she said. "That was a bad day, last time I saw y'all. Really bad." Now her tone had slipped into grimness. My heart thudded in my rib cage. My breath came in short bursts. The day in June rushing at me like a huge wave.

Lilli's scream.

It still rang in my ears. The chill that skirted through my blood, all the way inside my skull until I felt light-headed, leaving my fingertips bloodless.

I had raced inside the house. Niecy raced after me. The sight of my little brother brought us both skidding to a halt.

He was sitting on the kitchen floor. His head banging over and over against the cabinets. A skinny ribbon of blood trickled down his face. His eyes held no focus. He was looking at me but it was like he didn't see me.

"Here," said Niecy. Her tone was a gentle tap on the shoulder, bringing me back to the sidewalk with my friend. "I never got a chance to give you your birthday present."

My stomach tightened like it was being screwed shut. Something inside twisted. I'd had a gift for her, too. We always celebrated our birthdays together. Her mama would make a cake for both of us. I never got to eat my cake this year, though.

While my fingers shook trying to open the gift bag, Niecy reached up and touched a spot on my forehead.

"You don't have a scar, at least."

I shrugged.

More memory came hurtling at me. Lamar so out of control he'd smacked me, me hitting my head on the corner of the counter.

"I'm just glad you're okay and you're back, girl!" Niecy's beautiful soprano voice, high and sweet, brought a sting of tears.

"Me too!" I said. My voice a whisper as I fought down the emotions. I stopped, undid the wrapping, and took out a small handmade book.

"You like it? It's a friendship book!" She grinned at me as I thumbed through pages she had hand-cut and filled with little drawings, photos of us, our faces pressed together—her grinning, mugging for the camera; me shyly tucking my lips around my teeth to keep my killer shark mouth hidden.

"Niecy! I love it!"

She beamed and did a little dance, and we laughed some more. We were beneath a blanket of shade from trees in the park. The air felt cooler, sweeter. Yet, the future felt the same.

After a few more steps, Niecy asked, "You ready for this year?"

My hand shook. She squeezed it in hers. "I just . . . I hope I don't have problems," I said.

"Kita, you're so smart! I mean, you'd have a lot more friends if you weren't so quiet, but you don't have anything to worry about. My mama threatened me. If my grades aren't 'good enough,' she won't let me do theater or any other clubs," she said. "You have a brain, girl. And talent with your art. Teachers love you!"

"Not all of them. You remember Mrs. Wilcher, right?"

A shadow moved behind my friend's dark eyes. "Yeah, I remember," Niecy said. "But don't let one bitter old *b*— I mean 'witch' matter more than all the other teachers."

Wilcher's witchy face appeared in my mind, and I shuddered. She was the teacher of nightmares. Wilcher the Witch. Her

superpower was figuring out which kid couldn't solve the problem, then calling on them. I had been her favorite victim.

"She was so mean," Niecy said, sensing my thoughts. "Good
ol' Mrs. Wilcher. You'd think she'd have a better name, but I guess
Satan was taken."

"She told me if I couldn't manage simple math I'd 'never
amount to anything.' Who says that to someone?" Truth was I
didn't have a problem with the math—I was just wiped out from
a night of wondering where Mama was, and other shark tales.

Niecy nudged me, then nudged me again. When I looked
down at her, she bounced her eyebrows up and down. She wanted
me to "let it go," to "move on," or "forget about it." Mama always
told me that, too. She said I hung on to things too much and didn't
know how to let go. With Mama, the past never truly passed.

"Stop biting your lip. You're worrying about stuff that don't
matter, baby girl! Wilcher was sixth grade. We are officially
seventh-grade honeys!"

"Honeys?" That cracked me up. The more I laughed, the
smaller the image of Wilcher became, shrinking to almost nothing. Shrinking—but still there.

Niecy's arm reached around and squeezed me into a hug. "No
matter what that mean old bat Wilcher says, you are a smart, cute,
fun woman of power and together we will become butterflies,
breaking free of our sixth-grade cocoons!"

I snorted a laugh as she fluttered her fingers into the sky, and
I noticed my feet felt less heavy as we moved across the side lawn
to school.

Niecy asked, "Are you up for some twirling this week?"

"*Yaaaas!*" I said. "It's a date!" She linked her arm in mine and we did a whole *Wizard of Oz* thing, skipping the rest of the way. I told myself to remember to do something nice for Niecy. Not just because of the birthday present, but for being my friend.

We stopped on the bottom front step, Niecy holding up her cell phone. She sang, "*Uh, TikTok we don't stop, TikTok we won't stop!*"

"You know you've got issues, right?" I pushed her away.

"I'm gonna be a star!" she said, bowing deeply. Seeing myself in videos was not my thing. Niecy, on the other hand . . . that girl had her mother subscribe to the Sunday *New York Times* so she could keep up with what was happening on Broadway. ON BROADWAY! IN NEW YORK CITY. She actually believed a future onstage was possible. I wish I had her confidence.

Niecy dreamed about a grown-up future where she'd be a star of stage and screen. Maybe crank out a pop album or two.

Me? I dreamed of waking up and not feeling afraid. I dreamed of trust and honesty. What was the word the social workers liked to use? Oh, yeah, *stability*.

Almost to the door. My stomach tensed up. I tried to play it off. Niecy, not noticing, said, "So, how's it going with you and ol' Britt?"

I stopped moving. She was on the step above me so it was my turn to look up. Niecy always referred to Mama as "ol' Britt." Short for Brittany.

"*Really?*" I said.

"Well, you know, I'd call her 'Miss So-And-So' but it's hard to remember her last name," she said. We both let out dry unfunny laughs. Mama did like letting folks know her last name was not the same as mine. She had Lilli and Lamar's daddy's last name, even though he bounced years ago.

Niecy shrugged and turned back to the door, reaching for the handle. *Almost there*, my body whispered. My muscles grew tighter.

I wanted the year to be better. *I* wanted to be better—more friends, more activities, good grades.

The wrench twisting my insides turned into a jackhammer.

At the threshold between the world and the world of middle school, two voices yelled right in my face, "Shark Teeth! You got taller!"

Dumb One and Dumb Two. That was my name for them. So dumb they had to co-bully me. Guess it was too much for one.

Dumb Two started fake-instrument humming the theme for *Jaws*.

Even though he had the talent of a toenail, hearing that tune gave me the shivers. I pictured a great white, with teeth like a chain saw. Rows and rows. They could have over thirty thousand in a lifetime.

Dumb One and Dumb Two had been in my elementary class that day Mama gave the whole world permission to torment me about my teeth. And they never forgot it.

Self-consciously, I dragged my tongue over my teeth.

All the teasing, pointing, name-calling—it used to hurt so bad.

Luckily, the body had a way of building tolerance for cruelty.

Between Mama and people like Dumb One and Two, all the places that used to boil and sting from the pain had gone numb.

I started to open my mouth but felt more like a shark than ever.

Dumb One, aka Durell Lampkin—I swear to goodness that was his real name—burst into this jeering, ugly laugh. Dumb Two is his boy, Chester Dunbar.

"Get on outta here! Before I tell the police who broke Mr. Johnson's window!" Niecy's voice rose—loud—and Dumb One turned green, opened his mouth to say something, then ran inside with Two running after him.

"Stop chewing on your lip!" Niecy scolded, throwing the door open and holding it for me.

Dumb One, Dumb Two—their teasing didn't hurt me as much as it used to, but the memories did. The bullying had got so bad I came home crying one day and begged for braces. Mama laughed in my face, saying: "Like I'd spend that kind of money to fix *your* teeth!" That was how she'd said it—*your* teeth! Like maybe she would do it for someone else, but not me. Your soul remembers a thing like that.

So yeah. Even a hundred Durells couldn't hurt me. Not anymore.

INSIDE, THE FRONT HALLWAY felt wide and vast. Cement and concrete and stone. Bodies, so many bodies—students wriggling, giggling, jeering, and leering moving in uneven masses of jeans and T-shirts' emblazoned logos. Sneakers squeaked on linoleum, maybe mine, too, as Niecy yanked me from one bulletin board to another in search of, well, destiny. I made my feet move, following Niecy as she tugged me along, all while wondering what each of those faces that looked my way knew or thought they knew about my life. I felt both ignored and observed like a bug on a petri dish.

Niecy left a trail of her "Ooos!" and "Ahhhs!" as we stopped at sign-up sheets for cooking club (already do enough of that at home, thank you very much) and anime club, even Spanish club, until Niecy stopped in her tracks. Drama club.

"We have to do it!" Her tone went soft and raspy. I heard her heart in her words.

I gave her the head tilt like, *Chile, please!* "That's fine for you but . . ."

"For you, too. Studying theater can help you get over your shyness." She was ready for a fight, but I wasn't playing.

"Girl, get to class!" I said, giving her a push. Truth was, I'd really like to do an afterschool activity. Probably not drama—that was Niecy's territory—but maybe something with art? There wasn't much time for stuff like that, though. My only extra-curricular was babysitting.

Still, my eyes lingered on the sign-up sheets. If Mama kept her promise, maybe I wouldn't need to be home right after school. Maybe I could make this work. Maybe.

～～

English class was first on my schedule. I had Mrs. Bailey, which was awesome because she had a reputation for being super sweet, and when we filled out the forms last spring for who we wanted, I'd requested her.

She took us through our syllabus, outlining books we were going to read. Everything went normal till she passed out this questionnaire.

"The great thing about literature," she said, "is its ability to take us on a journey of self-discovery. As part of that journey and growth, I want to help each of you grow in your own personal way. To do that, you have to get to know yourself. What do you stand for? What are you all about? Themes we'll explore in your reading and writing."

The bell rang, but not before I'd read through the questions and had a mild heart attack. Okay, not mild. My heart thumped like war drums pounded in my ears.

One question stopped me cold:

12. "What is your biggest mistake?"

Tiny alarms went off in my skull. My eyes shut tight.

My biggest mistake?

A scene from my endless supply of "Mama's greatest hits" blurred my eyes. A memory as fresh as a new haircut. The disaster that led to us spending the summer at Camp Foster Care.

How that disappearance act started was like this:

It was Memorial Day weekend. Mama flounced her behind into my bedroom that Friday and announced she was going to Miami with friends.

She was like, "You're twelve now, you can handle things a few days." She promised we'd celebrate my birthday when she got back. Then, because she was Mama, she had to throw in, "Remember, you're my ride or die. I'm counting on you to hold it down till I get back."

By that point, it wasn't unusual for her to up and leave for a few days. Only this time, Lamar wasn't having it. He started acting up, getting worse and worse. The day of my birthday, June 3—a Saturday—his bad spell became the worst I'd ever seen.

He'd been banging his head on the cabinets when me and Niecy ran into the kitchen. He started kicking and yelling, balling his fists, pounding the floor. Then he slid down, whacking his head against the tile of the kitchen floor, screaming, "No! No! No! No! No!"

When I rushed over to try and calm him down, he swung at me, causing me to fall backward into the corner of the counter. A milky way of bright stars shattered my vision. Tears flooded my eyes and my mind felt muddy as I wondered if I was okay.

After that, it was obvious no matter what I'd promised Mama about being her ride or die, I had to call 9-1-1 for help.

RIIIIING!

The bell!

It felt loud and painful in my head.

The room was noisy, and fist bumps and finger popping played like background music as everyone got up to go to their next class, but my heart still pounded from the memory of seeing the cops handcuff Mama after she staggered in through the back door. They were already putting Lamar in the ambulance.

No longer was I in Mrs. Bailey's class holding the piece of paper. I was back there. Right there in the kitchen. I could smell the leftover spaghetti I'd warmed up for the littles for lunch. Felt the warm trickle of blood on my forehead; felt the swelling bloom in my lip. "How long has your mama been gone?" the lady cop asked.

Lilli had spoken up first. "She been gone nine days!" She had tears in her eyes and her thumb in her mouth. Lilli hadn't sucked her thumb since she was two.

Mama hadn't responded to any of my calls and texts. She didn't even wish me a happy birthday. But leave it to her to waltz back in after I felt like I'd had no other choice, when everything was falling apart.

She took it out on me.

"I knew you were messed up in the head. How could you do

this to us, Kita?" she spat the words at me, struggling against the policewoman's grip. "I was coming back, Kita. You know that! I always come back. You're worthless, girl! You were supposed to be my ride or die!"

"But Mama, I . . ." Tears dripped off my chin and cheek. The policewoman had started dragging her toward the door. Still, Mama wasn't having it.

"I knew something was wrong with you, Sharkita Lashay Lloyd," Mama growled, baring her fangs.

She had blamed *me*. Slinging knives in the dark, not caring about the damage, the cuts, the pain. What person could unhear all that? Her blaming me scorched my soul.

Me blaming *myself* felt even worse.

"Miss Lloyd? Sharkita? Are you all right?" I look up and instantly cringe. The class had almost cleared out, except for me and one other girl. Mrs. Bailey stared at me, ocean-blue eyes filled with concern.

I can't look at her. Can't. "Sorry, yeah, I'm fine," I mumble. I feel like an idiot and race from the room before she can ask anything else.

~⌒~

After two more classes it was finally lunchtime, and Niecy was holding court in the cafeteria when I found her. Swishing her hips around in her new denim capris, tossing her hair, and posing up a storm. I didn't know why she needed drama club. Sis was already the star of her own show.

"Look at you," Niecy cooed at me, movie star dramatic. I half expected her to blow me a kiss.

Oh, wait. She did blow me a kiss. I shook my head. Then she snatched up my arm and gave me a twirl, looking toward my backside, which, no lie, kinda freaked me out. Oh god, what now? My thoughts went to the darkest, most humiliating what-ifs.

"What?" I demanded, a thousand personal imperfections flashing before my eyes.

"Kita got a booty over the summer!" she announced, making me her beloved costar.

"Niecy! Dang! Shut up!" I said, before covering my mouth with my hand. An automatic reflex when you have shark teeth and bullies nearby are waiting to pounce. By the way, the thing I have with my teeth being in two rows—the fancy word for it is "hyperdontia," but informally, dentists really did refer to it as "shark teeth."

With no idea of the fun facts swimming through my brain, Niecy started laughing so hard her shoulders began shaking—so hard, I couldn't help laughing, too.

It took a full minute for me to realize that along with being red-faced with embarrassment and laughter, I also felt a weird ripple of something unfamiliar to me—*pride*? Niecy had had curves since fourth grade. This was new for me. I smiled in secret.

We found a table in the back, dropping our food trays onto the surface. Niecy invited three girls to sit with us. Chasity Wright. Trinity Robertson. Octavia Meadows. Faces and names I knew from classes, but I'd never hung out with any of them.

They all smiled and said hi as they sat down. I held my breath, bracing myself. Spending time with people I didn't know well always set my nerves on end, and middle school made it worse. Which one would ask me what's wrong with my teeth? Which one would say "no offense" before saying something that could only be seen as offensive? Or what hurt the most—which one would look at me and pretend I wasn't there?

We all did that thing, sizing each other up, looking for flaws, weaknesses—measuring who was prettiest or smartest or had the best clothes. We were learning how to judge each other to make us feel better or worse about ourselves. Some lessons didn't need a classroom.

Chasity squinted at me, and how she was looking made my insides sweat.

"I know you," she said, still smiling wide. I sucked in air, braced my body for the impact of words wrapped in cinder blocks. Mama taught me well. "We had language arts together last year, at least until they split up our class after Mrs. Neal went on maternity leave. You wrote that poem. What was it called again? Ugh, it was so good!"

A cinder block–sized lump squeezed down my throat. The poem. I remembered it. All of them, even Niecy, began staring at me. Tiny needles of embarrassment poked at my cheeks, my scalp, my fingertips. Not the humiliation, just extreme embarrassment.

Niecy pulled a face. "Don't start chewing on your lip, Kita, just 'cause you don't like being the center of attention."

Being ignored I could handle. It was familiar. But getting attention—I didn't get a lot of practice with that, especially not for anything good.

"The . . ." My voice cracked. I cleared my throat. "Glass berries, broken dreams."

I wish I'd never written that poem. Wish the teacher hadn't liked it so much she had me read it out in front of the class. It put too much on display. Put too much of *me* on display.

Last year, Mama was up to her late-night fooling around, and I got up earlier than the sun. When my nerves were bad, I cleaned. It was one of those mornings.

Anyway, I was straightening up the kitchen a second time because Mama came home, messed it up, then I had to send her to bed like she was the child. After cleaning up the cellophane wrapper from the cheese slices and scraps of bologna and paper towels with smears of mustard, I took out the trash.

The wind was blowing and a rattling noise came from behind a bush beneath our kitchen window. I looked and saw a paper bag full of empty wine bottles.

It was April. Poetry month. Our teacher had us doing an assignment and something about those bottles got my pen flying.

"Do you still have it?" asked Chasity now. "Or do you know it by heart?"

"I want to hear it!" said Trinity.

"Me too," chimed in Niecy. "This whole time my best friend was a poet and I didn't even know it!"

Now I really felt like I had swallowed a brick. Niecy prodded me with her elbow and said, "C'mon, Kita. Time to set your butterfly free. Fly, butterfly, fly!"

I was about tired of her butterfly. I was even more tired of them staring at me like magic was about to come out my nose. I sighed. Then, not looking at anyone, I began:

Beneath the kitchen
window its berries bright
red its deep green
leaves sprout jagged
fruit made of secrets.

Bottles hold the liquid
shining in her eyes;
she hides her sips in
darkness. The vessels
split like souls without
dreams.

Unspoken wishes
swallowed, jagged and
dangerous as shards
of glass.

"That was excellent," said a voice too deep to be any of the girls.

I hadn't realized I'd closed my eyes. I opened them slowly and saw everyone all staring wide-eyed. A woman I didn't know stood beside the table, looking right at me. Even though she was smiling, I couldn't help feeling guilty. For some reason, I couldn't help wondering, *What have I done now?*

(**7**)

THE WOMAN WAS TALL, curvy. What Granny would call "hippy." She wore a brightly printed dress—black and white polka dots on bottom and big yellow and pink flowers on top—beneath a hot pink blazer. She topped it off with one of those purses they keep chained up in department stores.

Niecy went bug-eyed and I bit my lip. We call women like this "Macy's Mamas." Because that outfit had to come from some-where like Macy's. It did not come from Walmart like most of our clothes did.

She looked elegant. Classy and sophisticated. Was she a teacher? If so, she could be the kind who acted like she was better than us. Mrs. Wilcher dressed okay, and she for sure thought she was better than us. Or at least, me.

"I'm sorry, I didn't mean to eavesdrop," she said, her smile warm. "That poem was beautiful. Just beautiful. You are very talented."

"That's what I said!" Chasity chimed in. "I remembered it from our class last year and asked her to say it again. It is so good. Are you the new assistant principal? I saw you in the office. Someone said you were new. I—"

"Dang! Chasity, let the woman answer!" Niecy scolded.

My eyebrows rose into my hairline. I felt frozen. I felt—exposed. I wasn't sure why that word popped into my head, but there it was. Exposed. Like I'd been caught in the locker room naked and couldn't find my towel.

"Yes, I'm Dr. Sapperstein, the new assistant principal. I'm walking around taking the time to meet students and introduce myself. May I ask what your names are?"

We all introduced ourselves, and the AP continued to smile at us. She had dark eyes that contrasted with her light brown skin. Her coloring was similar to mine but her eyes were dark like Mama's and Lilli's.

"Well, it's great to meet you all. I've told a few students already, but I'm starting a dance team and dance club here. Don't suppose I have any twirlers or dancers at this table, do I?"

Her words were like magnets, practically pulling Niecy out of her seat.

"Yes!" Niecy shouted. "I love to dance, and twirl. And me and Kita twirl with each other all the time. We're starting up again, right, Kita?"

The groan rumbled from my soul. Before I could answer, Chasity cut in.

"Dr. Sapperstein, no offense, but why do you have a white

lady name? I never met a Black person with a name like 'Sapperstein' before," she said.

"Goodness, Chasity! Don't be rude," Octavia said.

Luckily, Dr. Sapperstein just laughed. She told us she married a Jewish man, took his last name, The End. That made us laugh, even me.

"Well, if you don't mind having a coach with a white lady name, tryouts are next Monday, a week from today. We're also doing some workshops starting this Wednesday. You should come, get some practice, and learn the routine for tryouts. I hope to see all of you soon," she said, looking at me with a smile. "I'd love to have a poet on the team."

She said goodbye then and walked to the next group of students.

Niecy's eyes had gone from hard-boiled to sunny-side up. "Kita! C'mon y'all. We've got to do this!"

"I can dance, but I can't twirl nobody's baton," Trinity said.

I said, not thinking, "She did say dancers *and* twirlers. You probably don't need to be able to twirl if you're a good dancer."

"Exactly!" Niecy said to Trinity before turning to me. "So, Kita, will you do it? Please, please, please!" Me and my big mouth. I knew me saying anything would make her think I wanted to do this.

But before she even finished talking, I was already shaking my head.

"You know I can't try out," I said.

"Why not?! Come on, *please?*"

"I'm doing it! I'm trying out," said Chasity. Now it was both Niecy and Trinity squealing.

"Yeah, come on, Kita, it'll be fun," Octavia said. "I could use the exercise!"

"And I could use the excuse not to have to watch my baby brother after school!" Chasity said with a fake shudder.

A year ago, the answer would've been a hard no.

Could I do this?

I want to.

Am I good enough?

Am I good enough?

Am I good enough?

Muscles squeezed stiff in my neck. My jaw felt tight as a fist. I fought off the feeling of being pulled deeper into the shark.

Could this year be different? Could I?

No more rushing home to be a mama. No more struggling to keep up in math or wishing my Bs in English and history and art could be the As I would've earned if I'd had time.

No more feeling scared all the time.

Still, because I did feel afraid, I said, "I don't know about taking on that kind of commitment."

Niecy, her silly self, she got up out of her seat, put her hand on her hip, and did her imitation of a proper white lady being fancy. The British kind.

"Oh, excuse me," she mimicked, pinching her index finger and thumb together like she was holding a teacup, raising her voice high and shaky. "I don't know about making that kind of commitment."

Oh, so that's how I sound? Really?

The girls at our table were almost on the floor laughing. Other kids who had no idea what she was doing were falling out of their seats laughing, too. Then a cafeteria lady came over shaking her head, but Niecy wasn't thinking 'bout her. Pretty soon, even the cafeteria worker was laughing. Niecy was something else.

Meanwhile, I was over there turning ninety-nine shades of red!

I tugged her back into her seat. She said, "Dang, Kita, just once, can you do something for you?"

Could I start doing things like other kids? Being like other kids? Niecy seemed to think so. So did Chasity, Trinity, and Octavia. All of them were waiting on an answer from me.

"I'll think about it, okay?"

The whole group cheered and Niecy gave me a hug. I wished I could do it just for Niecy, because she was such a good friend. I smiled, closed-lip, but there was a big hurdle I had to get over before I could celebrate, too.

I'd have to tell Mama.

I WENT THE LONG way home, passing my block to walk with Niecy to hers. Stalling. I knew the littles' bus didn't arrive until four, so I didn't have to rush. I wasn't ready to be home yet, anyway.

"Should I come over to practice today?" Niecy asked. She'd been talking a mile a minute since we left school.

I felt my teeth chew my bottom lip. "I think so. Text me before you come."

Niecy was already planning her award acceptance speech in case middle school girls twirling with a high school band received lifetime achievement awards. My thoughts tumbled inside my head, trying to make sense of my day.

Finally, she started talking about something else, "And Miss Lady, the AP, her drip was straight fire!"

"Dr. Sapperstein's fit was poppin'," I agreed. Then we looked at each other at the same time and yelled, "Macy's Mama!" That got us laughing again.

"You know, it wasn't just that the dress was pretty or the heels were, like, *everything*, it was how she put it all together. The jewelry. The hair. The way she held herself, too."

"I know, right? Miss Lady got that vibe. Like, she talks proper and everything, but you can tell she's got a little spice to her."

Dr. Sapperstein looked like someone from a TV show. Not a real person. More like an image of someone you might want to be.

When I looked up, other middle schoolers with backpacks slung over their shoulders heading home dotted the streets around us. It felt like I'd been gone a week. Sweat pooled in the collar of my shirt.

"What about your classes. What did you think?" Niecy said.

I filled her in on the classes I had after lunch. Mr. Gavin, my science teacher, happened to be a freak for sharks. He had posters and pictures of them all over, even had a stuffed animal version on his desk. That was going to be so much fun—not. And of course I told her about art.

"Art class was AMAZING. Mr. Sanders is very strict, but strict like he won't take any messing around in his class. Last year's art class was fun, but it was arts and crafts. Mr. Sanders is dropping knowledge. Real art."

Niecy told me all about her classes—too bad we didn't have any together—until we made it to her house. She waved goodbye and told me she'd text me before heading over later.

Once she was inside, I had no choice but to turn toward home. Like earlier going to school, the closer I got to home, the heavier my feet got. Tiny punches in my chest. Breath caught in my throat. What would be waiting for me at home?

The town house came into view. I sucked in some air. Then I saw Mama unloading Walmart bags from a friend's car. Knots kinked in my stomach. I froze, watching as she disappeared inside our front door.

After several deep breaths and another long sigh, I followed in her footsteps, pulled open our front door, and stepped inside.

Mama stood in the kitchen, dropping plastic bags onto the table and floor. Amber, one of her friends from high school, dropped a bunch of bags, too.

"Hey, Kita!" Amber called out, looking me up and down. I stood there, frozen. Mama's friends made me nervous. Since I was a little kid, I never quite knew what to do with myself when they were around. This was the first time Amber was visiting us here in University Village, though, so it'd been a while since I'd seen her. I always liked her best of all Mama's friends.

She looked the same, basically. She was still a little rounder and softer than Mama, pale brown skin with yellow undertones and a sprinkling of freckles across her round cheeks and small nose.

Now, she held her arms out and said, "Come here, baby! Look at you!"

Amber liked to hug. As self-conscious as I felt around EVERY-BODY, soon as she pulled me to her, I remembered how much I loved feeling her warmth. I even let myself snuggle into her a little bit. Two hugs in one day—first Niecy, then Amber. It really was turning into a good day.

"Look at you, baby! You're growing like a weed!" she said, grinning. "And this place is immaculate. Look how clean it is."

She had released me and was taking a slow turn. I followed her gaze trying not to cringe. The kitchen was small but modern, and I loved cleaning it until it sparkled. "Chile, I remember you at five and six years old, carrying around that old broom twice your size. I never met anyone who loves polishing furniture more than you!"

She let out one of her big laughs, and dimples deep as a well creased her warm, freckled cheeks. I shrugged shyly.

"I still like to polish things," I said, smiling.

"All the time," Mama mumbled, like polishing furniture, floors, or countertops was dumb or weird.

Was it weird? Was I weird? Even now, seeing the gray Walmart bags all over the counters made me cringe. I could see where Lamar had been fooling around with the kitchen towels and messed them up before he left. Mama's slouchy leather bag hung from the back of a chair when it should be on a hook by the door. When I looked up, I saw Mama's gaze following mine.

"She can be a big help," Mama said to Amber, her hard eyes following me. "But you know Kita. If everything's not perfect, she falls apart."

Amber slid me a sideways glance, then looked away, trying to laugh off the awkward Mama was sprinkling around. My face reddened, skin hot. *Perfect?* Was she serious? I learned a long time ago to keep my expectations *waaaaaaay* below "perfect"!

Amber's gaze touched mine before I could look away. She had been around during some of Mama's bad scenes. She leaned over and gave me a quick kiss on the cheek. She knew what Mama could be like.

"I just hope Christina is as mature and organized when she gets to be Kita's age," said Amber.

Mama's only reply was, "*Mmmhmmm!*"

Not long after, she walked Amber to the door and thanked her for the ride to the market. I braced myself, uncertain of what to expect once we were alone. Just like when I was little, I stood still, stuck in one place, waiting to know what mood I needed to react to.

"Why're you looking like that?" Mama said when she came bouncing back into the kitchen.

"Like what?"

"I don't know. Like a little kid who about to get spanked." Her voice held amusement, like she wanted to laugh. That made me cringe more than the messed-up towels. Then she cleared her throat. When I looked at her, her expression grew softer.

She grabbed a few bags and moved toward me. "Here," she said, pushing the bag toward me. "I was out picking up a few things today and stopped and got some stuff for you. Art supplies. Pens and paper. I thought you'd like it."

Much as she got on my nerves, seeing her happy to give me a gift, a gift she knew I'd love, made me smile.

Then she said, "Look, I know . . . well, you didn't have a good birthday. And I know how you are about your art . . ."

"It's perfect, Mama. Thank you," I said.

I ran my fingers over the new drawing pads and colored pen

and pencil sets in the bag. I felt truly grateful, and when I hugged her and she hugged me back, I almost didn't flinch.

We pulled apart like people not accustomed to holding each other. Guilt swept over me. I always felt so guilty around her. One minute I was mad enough at her to start screaming. The next— she was giving me art supplies and I felt guilty for all the bad thoughts and memories I couldn't let go of.

Never knowing what to expect made my head ache. The ground around Mama was constantly shifting.

MR. SANDERS, MY ART TEACHER, had a beard like sandpaper, rough-looking stubble on his cheeks and chin. Color from paint-projects-past stained his stubby fingers. He was wide, like a football player, but not very tall. He wasn't known as a "nice" teacher.

As soon as we walked in Tuesday afternoon, he told us to take out our drawing pads. He said, "I want you to turn to the person next to you and sketch them. That is your assignment for the entire period, so I expect to see some effort put in."

Everybody moaned and groaned. He smirked.

Gotta admit, I was a part of the groaning. I didn't like the idea of someone staring at my face for so long, thinking of all the things wrong with it. Luckily, my neighbor was Chasity.

As we drew, his tone grew soothing. He told us to concentrate on the lines and shapes.

"Let your eyes move over the shape of muscle and bone and skin that makes up your model. Take turns doing an outline sketch and tomorrow we'll discuss them," he said. "We are not hoping for masterpieces in the first week. I won't expect perfection until week two!" Art teacher humor.

I turned to Chasity. My hands had already started to shake. I said, "I'm not very good. I'm sorry."

She pulled a face.

"Girl, please! You've got to be better than me. I just hope you're not mad when my drawing of you looks like a tree. No offense, but I'm awful at drawing faces!" she said.

We both laughed, which helped with my nerves. A little. Mr. Sanders wandered around the room glancing over students' shoulders. Chasity decided to draw me first; then I would draw her.

She leaned over and whispered, "You and Niecy were talking about practicing your twirling today after school, right? Can I meet up with y'all?"

I looked left and right. If we got caught whispering, we might get in trouble. I'd die if I got in trouble with the teacher on the second day. Soon as I nodded and said, "It's fine with me," my stomach began to swirl and knot.

Niecy had been worked up since she came over after school yesterday. "We're going to the tryout workshop. We're gonna kill it. We need to practice . . ." And on and on. Which was great. Except for one thing:

I hadn't asked Mama. After she gave me the art supplies, it wasn't long until Lilli and Lamar came home. They both talked a mile a minute about their first days at school, and to be honest, I kept them talking so I would have an excuse not to ask Mama about tryouts. My siblings needed me, anyway, and I couldn't make sure they were okay if I wasn't home.

If our family was going to stand a chance of staying together, I had to stay focused.

Chasity nudged me, breaking my thoughts. She was holding her sketch pad toward me. "See? What did I tell you? I can't draw people," she said.

What in the world? The drawing looked like a bunch of lines smooshing together. With eyeballs. I couldn't hold back—I burst out laughing.

"It looks like . . . a turtle with really huge eyes," I said, catching my breath. "I love it!" Chasity giggled.

"You're a cute turtle. And look, I gave you some hot fashion!" She pointed toward some scribbles that were meant to be my collar. We both laughed, almost falling into each other. I realized I was exhaling. I'd been holding my breath. Part of my brain had been afraid Chasity would draw something really ugly just to make fun of me. I'd laughed so hard, it made me forget about my teeth.

Chasity saw inside my mouth. Instantly, I slapped a hand over it.

"You've got a lot of teeth," she said in that way she had. "Girl, don't be shy about it. At least yours aren't full of cavities like mine. I love SweeTARTS just too, too much!"

We busted out laughing again and Mr. Sanders sent us a warning look.

Not wanting to cause trouble, we got ourselves together for the rest of the class. I managed to focus on drawing Chasity, putting aside my worries about how I hadn't asked Mama for permission to try out yet.

"You've got a good eye," a male voice said into my ear. I jumped and dropped my sketch pad, which made a loud thud and got everyone in class looking at me.

"Apologies, Miss Lloyd. I didn't mean to startle you," Mr. Sanders said, picking up my sketch book and handing it back.

"It's okay," I mumbled, inhaling a bellyful of air. "I'm sorry, I didn't mean to . . ."

My voice trailed off.

"I was saying you have a good eye for proportions, light. It's a tough assignment. I'm glad to see you took it seriously. You did a good job allowing your pencil to follow the line of her jaw, the curve of her chin. Great line work. I'm impressed."

"Thank you," I mumbled, feeling wobbly from his praise.

"Don't thank me yet," he said. I froze, looking up at him from my seat at the table. "I'll expect more from you because I can already see what you're capable of."

When he moved on, Chasity grinned. "I thought you told me you were bad at drawing faces!"

My blushing was so deep, you could almost hear it. I looked down at the paper. I saw a million things wrong with the drawing. But I had to give myself props. It wasn't completely bad.

What would it be like to get really good at something? To practice and practice and see yourself getting better?

In that moment, I decided to talk to Mama after school.

I didn't want to.

I really didn't.

But I had to. If not for Niecy and my friends, then for me.

~⌣~

Our backyard was a perfect rectangle. Two elbow-patches of lawn sat on either side of a narrow walkway that dead-ended at a larger rectangle of grass. Thanks to the homeowners' association, the lawn was well cared for, even the huge, blooming fire bush, with its bright red shoots and dark green leaves. I liked how having the lawn cared for made me feel. Like the people who lived here were worth the effort.

It was also the perfect spot for twirling. Used to be me and Niecy hung out here mostly because I had to look after Lamar and Lilli because Mama was gone. With Mama home, it felt sort of strange. I kept stealing glances at the window, wondering if I needed to go check on anything, wondering if she was watching.

"What do you think our uniforms will look like? How're y'all gonna wear your hair for tryouts?" Niecy was buzzing around, twirling her baton, singing. Chasity egged her on, laughing at how extra Niecy was.

Neither me nor Chasity had given much thought to our hair-styles for tryouts. I didn't think it mattered much. I was more worried about not throwing up during a cartwheel.

"You tell your mama yet?" Chasity asked me instead of answering Niecy.

"Tell her mama what?" came a voice from behind us.

Have mercy. I about jumped out of my skin. I'd never even

heard the backdoor open. Niecy must've been having such a fantasy moment about her future glory that she hadn't seen her, either.

"Miss Brittany! How are you!" Niecy's voice rose to super soprano as she smiled wide at Mama. I stared straight ahead. Mama knew what Niecy was doing, trying to distract her. My mama wasn't having it.

"Hey, Miss Niecy, good to see you. I'm fine. Tell your mama I said hello," Mama said before turning full-on to me. "Tell me what, Kita?"

My mouth felt dry. Already hot from being outside for the past hour, I suddenly felt weak, heart racing, knees wobbly, and a dull ache in my head.

Never knowing which version of Mama was showing up was nerve-racking. Would she bless us all with her smile or start screaming at me right in front of everyone?

Even though I kept going back and forth about it, allowing myself to dream about being on a dance team, having friends, feeling normal—it felt good. I wanted that feeling to last.

"Kita? You hear me talking to you. What did you need to tell me?"

I finally met her gaze. She didn't look angry. But I knew that could change in a second.

"Um . . . we . . . um . . . at our school . . ." My tongue stuck to the roof of my mouth, and to my great horror, tears began to well in my eyes. Now I was looking straight at the ground again. No, I wasn't looking at the ground because I had squeezed shut my stupid eyes.

Roasted chicken and frozen vegetables cooking inside painted the area with their warm, rich scents. Calming. I took a breath. Cleared my throat.

"Our school has a new assistant principal, and she's starting a majorette squad and a club, which is super cool you know because Grove Middle needs something like that, but, anyway, they're holding tryouts next week and workshops starting on Wednesday. Um, I . . . I want to try out."

I bit down on my lips, which had rolled up like shades, tucked neatly in my mouth. Meanwhile, a slow smile crept across Mama's face.

"*Guuuuurl*, you go ahead and try out! I'd be so proud if you made the team," Mama said, pulling me into another awkward hug. When she released me and stepped back, she turned to Niecy and Chasity and said, "You know I used to twirl back in the day, right?"

I could feel Chasity and Niecy looking at me. I nodded. "I know, Mama."

"*Mmm-huh!* I was good, too," she said, rocking her head back and forth, being . . . what? The cool mom? What a horrifying thought.

"Are you sure?" I said on a rush of air and pure nerves. "I mean, we'll probably have practice four nights a week."

"We're performing with the high school band and major-ettes," Chasity added.

"I'm pretty sure I will be a star!" Niecy said with a twirl. "Kita too."

Mom clicked her tongue. "Yes, go ahead and try out. It's about time you did something other than sitting around here with the kids. A girl your age needs to be out, making friends, having fun, all that," she said. We all hear the musical tone of a timer— dinner's done cooking. Mama waved 'bye to the girls and me and raced back inside to save her chicken.

"She seems nice!" Chasity said. "I don't know why you were so nervous to ask." Me and Niecy exchanged looks. Niecy knew all too well what Mama was really like. One time, Mama came home drunk in the middle of the afternoon. We were twirling in the backyard, smiling and laughing. Then here comes Mama.

"Your little friend is getting fatter," she said about Niecy. "The two of you side by side look like the number ten—and you're the one." She did not whisper.

So, yeah. Mama could be nice when she wanted to be. The question was always, Does she want to be?

(**10**)

THE AFTERNOON OF OUR first majorette workshop I had wobbly knees and a sick feeling in the pit of my stomach. I was so excited to be there, but nervous about leaving Mama in charge of the sibs. She had been doing good the past few days. Sure, I still had to pay the bills, check her balances, remind her how much we had left before her next settlement check deposited.

Back when I was eight, a soda company truck ran a red light and slammed into us. It took forever, but we finally got a settlement. A pretty large one, too. Mama bought the whole town house with that money. No more of the projects. No more rent.

Two years ago, I thought that settlement was going to save our lives. But all it did was give Mama more drinking money.

She was doing better now, though. Better than she had been in a long time, and for way longer than ever before, too. I still did most of the housekeeping, but she cooked, helped with the baths, and was there when the littles got home.

Each day, though, the horrible thought tangles in my head:

What if this is the day she doesn't show up?

What if Lamar and Lilli wound up at home alone?

What if one of her low-life exes came back?

That was life with Mama. No matter how good things seemed, I was always *waiting . . . waiting . . . waiting . . .* for the next catastrophe. Because with her, there was just no telling.

Tightness pulled at my scalp, my face—pulled so hard I started to itch. Loving Mama, being her ride or die, sometimes it hurt.

Excited chatter of other dance team hopefuls brought me back to the present moment. All the other students, mostly girls but a few boys, circled around the tryout area. Excitement dripped from their pores. A lot of giggles and bad jokes and nervous energy. With me, that was mixed with good old-fashioned terror from not knowing what was going on at home.

Dr. Sapperstein clapped her hands twice to get everyone's attention and the chatter died down. "I'm so glad all of you have decided to join us today," she began. She wore her hair wavy on top with a swingy ponytail in back. Since my blowout, my hair was long enough for a ponytail, too.

Miss Lady's warm-up suit, which fit her body like a glove, was the color of midnight, trimmed in double stripes the color of a summer ocean. One day, would I be able to give back to the community while dripping in the best gear money could buy?

Niecy leaned into me and whispered, "Are you ready for this?"

I nodded, unable to find the right words.

"I like my dudes and all, but I think I've got a girl crush on Dr. Sapperstein!" Niecy said with a laugh.

A voice from behind us said, "I like my dudes, too!"

Without looking, we knew who it was.

"Get away from me, Saint! You know you're too silly!" Niecy play-scolded the boy. We knew Saint had been gay long before we knew what gay was. Nobody really made a big deal out of it. That was just Saint being Saint.

He batted his eyes. "I'm just saying, Miss Kadejah, definitely got a little somethin'-somethin' going on."

Dr. Sapperstein told everyone we could call her Kadejah or Miss Kadejah or just Coach after school hours, which I thought was dope. "Now, I have a few members of the high school dance team here to help me show you some basic skills."

We all dropped to the hard cafeteria floor—the tables were folded and pushed away—sitting crisscross.

Watching Miss Kadejah walk us through everything, little by little the nerves faded. The idea of looking like a fool in front of everybody still had me shook, though. The little voice in my head, the doubt whisperer, had been in overdrive, warning me I was walking into the shark's belly. Still, it didn't take long to realize almost everybody felt the same way.

After going through all the basics, the high school girls split us into groups—twirlers and dancers. Me, Niecy, and Chasity went one way, while Trinity went the other. Miss Kadejah moved back and forth between us, offering guidance and suggestions. Throughout the day, she was like the big sister anybody would want. She had a way of making everybody feel good about themselves.

By the time she tooted her final whistle, sweat poured off me and my throat was dry and scratchy.

"Young ladies and gentlemen," she said, "we're going to call it quits today. You all are talented and worthy and wonderful. I see great things in all of your futures. But it's not all about skill or potential. Success comes down to who is willing to work hard enough, long enough. And having the guts to keep going even when everyone doubts you. We have a limited number of spots available on the team, but do not despair. If you do not make the team, we would love to have you in our ongoing dance and twirl club—you unfortunately won't perform at games, but will still be very much a part of everything else. I want you to know that I appreciate each and every one of you. Now give yourselves a round of applause."

We did and some of us slapped high fives or bumped knuckles. After a minute, Miss Kadejah patted the air, letting us know she wanted our attention again.

"If I can get you all to settle before I let you go," she began. We all turned back to her. She was standing at the edge of the cafeteria stage. She took a moment before she began speaking.

"I am truly looking forward to starting this process with you all. I grew up in this community and went to school here. I know what it means to attend a school like Grove, where we might not get all the funding or respect, but we have a lot of pride.

"I twirled at the high school and was a majorette all four years at FAMU. I hope I can inspire all of you to do more, want more, be more than you ever imagined. Talk to me, get to know me, and if I can help you, I am here for you."

Another round of applause followed, and it continued to ring in my ears as we all packed up.

"Can I help with anything? Do you need help putting away the equipment?" I asked Miss Kadejah, almost out of breath. Just being here, having a good time, being happy—it was almost over-whelming. I felt the least I could do was pitch in during cleanup since I'd had such a great time.

"We've got it, but thank you for offering! You did good today, poet." She laughed. "Go home and soak your aching muscles."

Dr. Sapperstein was right about the aching body parts. My legs felt heavy on the walk home, but not because I was dragging my feet. It was because of what Dr. Sapperstein said. About want-ing us to "want more, be more . . ." than we'd ever imagined. Niecy imagined all the time about what she wanted to be.

Not me.

The question of who did I want to be still tugged at me as I pushed through our front door. Lilli yelled:

"Hey, Kita! I learned a new word. Fas-cin-at-ing. It means a person who is interesting, and smart and kind and beautiful . . ."

I didn't think that was exactly the definition, but hey, nobody said it could have only one meaning. Mama sat across from Lilli. "She's very proud," Mama said, cheesing hard like someone had said *she* was fas-cin-at-ing.

"Lilli," I said, crossing the room and dropping my gym bag

and book bag on the floor, "you are the most fascinating person, ever!"

She giggled and hugged me. Beside her, Lamar was playing with a puzzle. His attention was intense, and brows knitted over his wide-set eyes. I kissed his cheek.

It was a calm, peaceful moment, so naturally Mama had to muck it up.

She said, "My Lilli is beautiful and smart and fascinating. She's like you, Kita." Then in a lower voice, "Well, the smart part, anyway." Oh, she knew I heard her. The fake smile she threw at me told me everything.

"Just kidding," she cooed. The way she looked at me, I knew she was trying to get under my skin.

"I'm going to shower," I said, ignoring her little taunt and hoisting my school bags off the floor. Practice really did have me sweating, but actually I just wanted to get away from Mama.

"Oh, Kita! Wait!"

Mama sprang up with the biggest smile on her face. And she was like, "Guess what?"

Really?

I didn't even answer. Just looked at her, letting my gaze shift toward the stairs, like "hurry up and say whatever messed-up thing you're going to say!" But I didn't say it out loud.

"I got a job!" she squealed.

"Job-job-job-job!" Lamar banged on his gameboard as he repeated the word again and again.

Once again, I was off-balance.

"What? Where, Mama? What kind of job?" Horrible as it might've been to admit, my first thought was, *Uh-oh! No more baton twirling for me.*

"Don't worry," Mama said, striking a sassy pose, "it's not going to affect your after-school activities. I made sure of that." And she was part witch, reading my thoughts—but only when I don't want her to.

She kept standing there, in front of me, like she was waiting on something. Finally, I reached out and hugged her. "Congratulations, Mama."

That seemed like the magic word because she spent the next ten minutes chattering at me like Lilli.

"You know how I have my paralegal certificate? I'm going to work part-time in a judge's office. Make some extra money so I can put some away and we can take trips and do more stuff."

"How much are they paying you?" The math part of my brain switched on. Extra money would be nice. The settlement covered our bills for the most part, but it was always tight. Mama hesitated, pulled her head back, then seemed too excited to stay quiet.

"I'll get twenty-two dollars an hour to start!" she said. That worked out to four-hundred-forty a week; seventeen-hundred-sixty a month. I felt my shoulders loosen, not even realizing how tense they'd been. That kind of money would take so many of my worries away. Maybe I could even get an allowance to spend on art supplies.

Mama went on, saying the office was in walking distance,

right around the corner. "I won't even have to worry about trans-portation," she said.

Lamar started cheering again—"Job! Job! Job!"—and Mama and Lilli joined in, dancing and being silly. I smiled, watching, before heading up to my room.

Upstairs, I fell back against the bedroom door and drew a deep breath. Exhaled. For a few glorious moments, I imagined every day could be like this. Happy. Normal. No sign of the shark drifting along in the shadows, waiting to swallow me. No feelings of being dragged under, fighting and fighting, with the force pulling me under.

In the cool pinkness of Lilli's room, I smiled to myself, then tucked that smile in my heart.

Our little family, the four of us, we really did have a chance.

(11)

LATE THAT NIGHT, THE small, tidy community known as University Village sparkled beneath me. My neighborhood. Rows and rows of neatly planted town houses painted in soft shades of pink, yellow, peach, and blue. Perfectly spaced streetlamps with old-fashioned globes that bent the light and gave the world a hazy glow. It was a little past midnight. Everybody was asleep. I had been, too, but woke up and couldn't go back to sleep.

Popping open the window at the end of the hall was easy.

I liked to sneak out onto the roof sometimes. The room I shared with my sister felt so much more like hers than mine—pink everywhere, unicorn posters, and a village of stuffed animals. There were times I needed a space that was just mine.

The roof below the windowsill was flat for about four feet. Plenty of room for me. I was leaning back against the frame of the house. I loved how quiet it was at night. Peaceful, and the night air felt silky after the angry heat of the day.

I held my new sketchbook and had a portable LED light clipped to the edges. I loved drawing. I read stories with my sister and stared at the artwork, wishing I could do something that good one day.

Could I?

My thoughts shifted from the lines on the paper. I'd sketched Lilli from memory. A cartoon version. Now my brain churned on the question of the day:

Would I be trying out with Niecy and the others?

Practice had been amazing. Dr. Sapperstein was amazing, too. Hearing her talk about her dreams for our futures, you couldn't help but wonder what our futures could be.

Did I have the guts to do that? To keep pushing, harder and harder, until I achieved a goal? I wasn't sure. I wasn't even sure I had a goal—unless my goal was to keep our family together. But more than anything, I think, I wanted to be normal.

I'd never known my dad. He and Mama had been teenagers and I guess teenage boys run faster. I wasn't sure. So, I didn't crave that mommy-and-daddy scene. One parent was fine, as long as she showed up.

Normal for me would just mean not having to worry about money (which reminds me—gotta pay the pest control people) or parenting my siblings. Normal for me was just . . . simple stuff. Being-a-kid stuff. Thinking about the future like Miss Kadejah said instead of worrying about the day-to-day of caring for a family.

One of the books I read with Lilli at night was one she'd checked out of her school library. It was called *The Lion & the*

Mouse. The pictures were so gorgeous. It was amazing. And in back, I saw that it was painted by this Black man named Jerry Pinkney. It made me wonder, when he was growing up, what was his life like? When did he know he wanted to be a painter? An artist? A book illustrator? It made me wonder, could I be those things, too?

Then I glanced at the few lines I'd drawn to recreate Lilli's likeness. If that Mr. Pinkney man could see this sketchbook he'd probably take my pencils away!

Imagine. Me? A famous book illustrator?

As soon as the thought entered into my head, I shook it off. No way in a million years I'd ever be as good as that Pinkney dude. The way his colors and images filled the page and came alive. No way. No way I could do that.

But could I get close one day? With practice, maybe?

I was tiptoeing my way into normal. With Mama acting like it was something I should've done long ago and Niecy telling me it was, I made a decision:

I'm going to do my best to make it work.

Instead of feeling joy, however, my body felt like too much was packed under my skin. Like I had too many emotions and thoughts and ideas for one person to hold them all.

Did any of that make sense?

A throbbing pain pulsed in a rhythm inside my skull. I didn't like admitting it, but the more I thought about it, the more I wanted to make the twirling squad so bad. Like, I hadn't even realized how much I'd want it.

But what if I got it and Mama decided to do her usual? Then what?

I could look on the bright side—maybe I wouldn't make it at all!

~

That Friday we turned in our questionnaires for Mrs. Bailey's class. I had been dreading filling it out, but something about our practice sessions with Miss Kadejah—er, Dr. Sapperstein during school hours—made it seem less scary. Made me feel . . . braver, somehow. Dr. Sapperstein's speeches were working on me! Here was how I filled mine out:

1. What are my strengths? *I am good at helping others, good at taking care of my brother and sister.*
2. If I could have one wish, it would be? *I wish my mama could really like her job and keep it and be happy. I wish Lilli, my sister, could have the big birthday party of her dreams. I wish my brother Lamar could get the extra help he needs.*
3. Who matters most to me? *Lilli and Lamar matter most to me in this world. And Mama too.*
4. What does the little voice in my head say about me? *Sometimes the voice in my head is very negative. It makes me sad. I want to do good and the little voice makes me feel like maybe I can't be good at anything.*

5. What do I like to do for fun? *I love to draw because art is one of my favorite things. I like to dance and twirl baton, too.*

6. What am I worried about? *I worry about a lot of things but that doesn't mean there's something wrong with me because worrying is normal.*

7. What do I believe in? *I believe parents shouldn't lie to their kids and should try their hardest to be good people. I believe everybody should try their hardest to be good at life.*

8. What am I ashamed of? *I am ashamed that we got taken from Mama and had to go to foster care because I couldn't handle my brother's tantrum. I wish I could've done better.*

9. Where do I feel safest? *I don't know.*

10. If I wasn't afraid, I would _____ *If I wasn't afraid, I would tell people what's really on my mind and not be scared.*

11. What is my proudest accomplishment? *I don't know.*

12. What is my biggest mistake? *Not being able to keep my brother and sister and myself out of foster care.*

13. What do I like about school? What do I dislike? *I like being friends with Niecy. I like this class and art and math. I don't like when kids tease me and call me Shark Teeth.*

14. What do I do to show myself self-compassion and self-care? *I'm not sure.*

15. Am I an introvert or an extrovert? Am I energized being around others or being by myself? *I like being around other people as long as they're not trying to get in my business. But I am kind of shy.*

16. What am I passionate about? *I am passionate about keeping my family together.*

17. What is my happiest memory? *My happiest memory is when I drew a picture of a bird in first grade and it won a prize.*

18. What is my favorite book? *PLANET MIDDLE SCHOOL* Movie? *BLACK PANTHER* Band? *KEHLANI* Food? *CHINESE DUMPLINGS* Color? *OCEAN BLUE* Possession? *A photo of Mama when she was my age. She is so beautiful.*

19. What am I grateful for? *MY FAMILY*

20. I know I'm stressed when I _____ *When I am stressed I close my eyes and try to hold my breath until the squeezing feeling goes away.*

Mrs. Bailey had us drop them on her desk at the end of class. "Don't forget your book," Mrs. Bailey had called to me, book in hand. She'd given us a reading assignment, and when I couldn't decide on a book, she chose one for me.

The book was called *Speak*. I'd never heard of it, but I figured it would be fine, maybe over the weekend it would help me not think about tryouts or any of that. All day my mind had been asking *what if . . . what if . . . what if . . .*

I took the book and said thank you.

Mrs. Bailey said, "Have a great weekend." I tried to smile, but felt a fresh case of shudders ripple through me.

Then I pulled myself together and wished her the same.

The weekend turned out to be me and Mama—or, Mama and I, according to Kadejah, who'd corrected about ten different girls in practice—doing our best to make everything all right. Lilli and Lamar were being real handfuls. Saturday night, after the little bits fell asleep in the living room watching their movie, Mama asked if there was anything I wanted to watch instead. That almost never happened.

"I think I'm going to the room to do some reading for my English class before I go to bed," I said, forever wary whenever she did something nice.

Mama shrugged. "You don't want to hang out with me?" I froze, not knowing what to say. Then she smiled and yawned. "Boo, I'm just playing. Go on. Read your book."

I thought reading the book Mrs. Bailey gave me would take my mind off everything. I wished I'd known what it was about ahead of time.

Speak, by Laurie Halse Anderson, was about this girl, Melinda. She was narrating the story, so it felt like she was talking right to me. The book was separated into marking periods—first period, second, third, like that. In the story, something bad had happened to Melinda, but she couldn't tell anyone. And when her grades started to suffer, her parents were so focused on how her classes were going, they couldn't see what was really going on. Each time

I tried to put the book down, something would be revealed, and I'd get pulled deeper and deeper into Melinda's world.

I was going to read only a few chapters, I'd told myself, but read all the way to "Third Marking Period" when I realized how quiet our house had gotten. Mama had put the kids to bed a long time ago. Lilli slept on her tummy, her sweet little breathing noises as comforting as a lullaby. Mama must have gone to sleep, too, because I didn't hear the TV playing or anything.

A cramp squeezed my neck muscles from lying on the sleeper with my head against the wall. My fantasy of having my own room, walls covered in artwork, prints, and posters, pale walls and fluffy rugs flitted through my mind.

Quietly, I stepped into the hall, then tiptoed down the stairs. It felt cool, empty, and quiet. I used my little LED light, clipping it to the edge of the book, and I flopped onto the sofa.

Well, at some point I must've fallen asleep because I woke up feeling like I was dying.

The living room was shadowy. I thought the LED light must've fallen over inside the book. When I tried to twist my neck or move my body, I couldn't. I swallowed hard, feeling my heart pace quicken. Feeling the sharks from my nightmares clamp their jaws, slowly squeezing me to death. Swallowed by a great white.

If I could have controlled my body at all, I would've been screaming. But when my mind tried to tell my mouth to open, only a pitiful sputter spilled over my lips.

Another reason Mama told me I had a mental problem was these episodes. The way my body would freeze up, how my muscles couldn't move, and I couldn't speak. All of it was terrifying. And according to my mama, it all pointed to me being crazy.

Shh . . . tell no one!

Skin on my face pulled tight. Fear knifed through. My throat closed tighter and tighter. I couldn't talk. And I couldn't move.

Then came the pressure. It was like being crushed. The shark was digesting me. My whole body ached.

Before waking up in this half-dead, half-alive state, I'd been having a bad dream. Lilli and Lamar were in danger. I was running to them, reaching for them, straining to scream but no scream would come out. I couldn't save them.

Heartbeats like hoofbeats pounded in my ears.

Spasms coiled my muscles. It hurt so bad. I was terrified.

Was it a heart attack? Would I die this time?

I want to be normal.

I want to be strong.

I want to feel . . . free.

A tear trembled down my cheek. Why couldn't I move my body? Was I really awake? Or was I still sleeping?

It felt like hours passed, but probably only minutes. I heard a door open. A voice, light and low. Mama. She was saying something to Lamar. He was saying something back. They sounded so far away.

Then came the footsteps. Soft on carpeted stairs. Mama coming down to get juice for Lamar. Normal functions in my mind scrambled. Even though she sounded so far away, I could tell she was walking right past the sofa. I felt her stop and look down at me, probably wondering why I wasn't upstairs with Lilli.

My body was rolled to one side. Inside I was trying to move myself, to turn, to look at her. But she never stopped. She never said anything.

The fridge opened. Bottles rattled. Then she was gone.

Slowly . . .

Blood slogged through me. Thick and heavy.

Feeling gradually returned. Numbness slowly disappeared.

I realized I could move my foot, then my leg, then my whole body. I dropped off the side of the sofa and hit the floor with a thump. Relief rolled through me like sweet rain. I was gasping for the release.

Then my relief turned to shame.

I knew exactly how Melinda in the book felt. The way her mind and body must've been fighting with both guilt and shame.

How on earth could I be a majorette? What if they had a slumber party or we were on a long bus ride where I fell asleep? What if I woke up looking wild-eyed and unable to move?

They'd lock me up and throw away the key.

I could never tell anyone about this. It was so embarrassing. Whatever it was, feeling like a mummy, unable to move.

What if something *really* was wrong with me?

(**12**)

MONDAY WAS THE LONGEST day ever. It might as well have been a hundred years. By the time classes were over, I felt more nervous than ever. There was no way I could go to tryouts.

"Don't just stand there, get moving!" barked Niecy behind me, hooking my arm as she came around to my side.

"Niecy, wait," I said, hating the whine in my voice. "I don't . . ." She wasn't trying to hear it.

"Un-uh, Miss Sharkita. You are not backing out," Niecy pulled harder.

"But . . ." I didn't realize my feet were digging into the concrete.

"No buts!" She snatched me so hard my shoes almost came off. When we were outside the locker room, she pulled me until I spun around to face her.

My breath came in short, fast bursts. A crazy sense of panic began clawing at me.

Niecy put her hands on her hips and narrowed her eyes at me. She said:

"Look, little Miss. You have had to be a mama, daddy, brother, and sister to the little bits. You keep the house clean, the laundry done, and most of the time find a way to put food on the table. That's a beautiful thing. Now, Mama is back to being a mama. Woo-hoo for her. It's time for you to do something for YOU. Be . . . *young*, like the rest of us!"

"I just . . . I worry all the time—about Mar-Mar, Lilli, even Mama." My voice was a tiny, sorry thing, almost too flimsy to be real. Even more quietly, I said, "Not sure I know how to act young or be like everybody else."

Silence pooled around our feet, sharp and dangerous as gasoline. When Niecy spoke again, her tone was softer.

"Lucky for you, I know all about being young and single and ready to mingle. Besides, I'm not sure you're aware of this, but I can be too much for some people."

I hiccupped a laugh. She smirked.

"Seriously," she said. "You are my best friend. I need you."

At first, her head tilted downward, then she dropped an arm over my shoulder before steering my sorry behind to the locker room door. I changed without another peep. Miss Kadejah soon came in and told us it was time to meet in front of the gym door.

"Miss Kadejah!" Niecy called out, loud and proud. I groaned. I felt sick. Weak. What was Niecy doing? "Miss Kadejah, would you tell Kita not to drop out because she's really good? She's getting cold feet."

I tried to melt into the floor. She was right—my feet weren't just cold, they were pure ice!

"Is this true, Sharkita?" asked Miss Kadejah. She stopped in front of me. She was wearing fancy blue sneakers with bright yellow and pink stripes. I could tell they were expensive. Her workout suit, too.

Somebody like her, would she ever understand somebody like me? A girl with my problems. It was hard looking at her, so I stared at the ground.

"Sharkita, you have nothing to worry about. Everyone says how great you're doing and what a great asset you would be to our squad," Kadejah said.

"Yes, ma'am, sorry," I said because I didn't know what else to say.

Kadejah smiled wide, then laughed. "Baby girl, we're going to have to teach you how to have fun."

For the next forty-five minutes, majorette dancers tried out first.

"Alyssa Aaron, you're first!" Nikki, one of the high schoolers who'd been helping with practice, called from the doorway. Alyssa entered the gym. They'd covered the windows with construction paper. Tryouts were private.

My chest was getting tighter. My breathing felt choked. My hands felt twitchy. I spun around, grabbed Niecy, and pulled her down the hall.

I gasped, voice low and hoarse, "I don't think I can do this. I mean, I really don't think I can!"

Now, I was panting.

Who was I trying to kid? It was beyond ridiculous for me to even think I'd have the nerve to go through with this. I could feel the sharks circling.

Niecy frowned.

"Kita, you have to calm down. You're sweating," she said. "Deep breath!" She made me inhale and exhale with her.

After a few seconds, my chest did feel less tight. Panic slid away—a little.

"I don't know," I said. "I just don't think I can do it."

"Yes, Kita, you can!" she said. Her nose flaring.

We stared at each other for several seconds. Before I could answer, the gym doors opened, and Nikki called out again.

"Sharkita Lloyd? Kita?"

Niecy mouthed, "You've got this!"

I wordlessly walked through the gym doors.

Nikki explained, "Okay, Kita, we're going to take you through a series of basic baton movements. Everyone gets a little nervous when they come in here so we're giving you two minutes to get your mind right, then we'll start calling out commands."

I nodded, unable to fully look at the faces behind the judge's table anymore.

It took eight minutes to get through all the commands. Heart drumming in an eight-count. The music started, and I had to perform the routine. I thought about Miss Kadejah's instructions to have fun.

Then I realized, all week I'd been having fun. Maybe I could do this, I wanted it so bad . . . so, so bad.

At some point, I stopped thinking. I leaned into the music and thought about the butterfly Niecy had teased me with on the first day of school.

"Fly, little butterfly, fly!"

My tryout ended. I'd done it! Joy filled me up like a milkshake after a cheeseburger, and I savored it the whole rest of the day.

Once Niecy's audition was over, me and Niecy—I mean, Niecy and I—walked home replaying the afternoon's events. I didn't even have room to feel nervous about when we'd hear back with the results.

I really wanted to be a butterfly, like Niecy said, fluttering fast and free. I was tired of feeling like shark bait! And this tryout felt like my first step out of the water and into the sky.

(**13**)

WHEN I GOT HOME, Mama was excited to talk about her first day
at work. She didn't ask about tryouts yet, which was good. I was
still coming down off the bubbly feeling from earlier. I had really
tried out. Me! It was a weird tangle of feelings, mostly good feelings, mixed with a stab of fear. I kept thinking I felt my phone
vibrating with the text from Kadejah that would tell me whether
I'd made the team or not. So far, I hadn't.

We ate at the dining room table, a square of black fake wood
surrounded by repainted black chairs—I repainted them.

Lamar clapped his chubby hands, picking up on Mama's excitement. Princess Lilli sat prim and proper as I cut her chicken because
she "don't like cutting it 'cause it might make the chicken sad."
Never stopped her from chowing down on my chicken parm,
coated in breadcrumbs with a layer of shredded mozzarella and
marinara sauce. I'd cooked dinner that night while Mama went on
and on.

"I think it's going to be a good fit," Mama was saying. "Already, the judge said I showed real promise."

A judge, huh? Mama chittered and chattered on and on. I couldn't blame her. She was proud of herself, getting a part-time gig working at the courthouse, getting friendly with a judge. Mama had ways of working her magic.

By the time Lamar was finishing his second helping and Lilli was eating her cup of Jell-O chocolate pudding, Mama looked at me and asked, "Oh my goodness, Kita. I forgot, how was the try-out? Please tell me you didn't chicken out?"

"No, I didn't chicken out," I said, smiling. "I think I did a good job, but I don't know. They're going to text us with the results tonight."

"Well, that's good," Mama said. We were both standing, collecting dishes from the dinner table, moving into the kitchen. Scraping food off the dishes into the trash, we began stacking the dirty dishes on the counter.

"I've got it, Mama," I said, nodding to the dishes. I had a lot of nervous energy. I needed to keep moving. I'd expected Mama to go do something else, but she stood there, one hand propped on the kitchen counter and the other on her hip.

She cocked her head to one side and looked me up and down. Then she said, "You know what? You aren't a bad-looking little mama. Thin, but starting to fill out some . . ."

"Mama, no!" I shouted. I wanted to cover myself, my body. I didn't want her looking at me, talking to me about my body. Why did grown-ups do that?

She laughed. "I'm your mother. Of course I'm going to notice how you're changing. It's all part of growing up. Here, I got something for you!"

Two gifts in two weeks? For me? This really was a new Mama.

She went inside the pantry and returned with something long and shiny.

A *baton*.

When I held it, I couldn't believe how heavy, weighted it felt. It had to be one of the real kind from the music store, not the cheap toy department kind me and Niecy had been using.

"What if I don't make it?" I said, frowning.

"You will." She said it so surely. Then she added, "You have a chance to be part of something normal and make friends. Don't mess it up being weird and paranoid. You have a knack for seeing problems where they don't exist." I felt my cheeks go red. "And for God's sake don't start obsessing over little things the way you do with me. It will turn those kids off. Trust me. I'm just looking out for you."

Her tone was perfectly normal. She'd even reached out and tugged at my ponytail. Our faces had been so close, I could smell the lemon scent of her soap. She spun around with a finality that said she was done. I stood there shaking.

See, that was what she did! One minute she was building you up; and the next, she was chopping you down.

Naturally, after that pep talk, I was a nervous wreck. The worst thing in the world would be not making it and having that shiny new baton lying around to remind me every day.

I started checking my phone every five seconds. Convincing myself there was no way I was going to make the team. Praying to God about the good deeds I would do if he just let me have this one thing. Then praying I didn't make it in case anyone else found out about my "mental problems." Thanks to Mama, it was a lose-lose for me.

"Kita, it's time to take my bath," Lilli said, breaking my pathetic train of thought. She was already scrubbing at her eyes with one hand, which meant bath time would be quick. Bedtime was so necessary.

Once she was finished splish-splashing and dried off, she yawned. "Only one book, Kita," she said. "I'm sleepy." Her little sleepy face made me giggle. No matter how badly I felt, Lilli and Mar-Mar always could make me feel better.

She pulled an oldie but goodie off the shelf, *Rainbow Fish*, by somebody named Marcus Pfister. I didn't think the author was Black, but I did know that book was in the library when I was in elementary. I checked it out a lot. Lilli had her own copy.

My sister climbed over me and into bed. She propped herself on her elbow and stared at me with a look that made my heart flip.

She said, "Mama acting real good most of the time, Kita. But what's going to happen next?"

I frowned. "Next?"

Lilli let out this big sigh. Then her voice got soft as she looked around before pinning me with her large, dark eyes.

"Kita, you know! When is she gonna start," she dropped her voice to a whisper, "you know what again?"

I was really confused. We stared at each other a minute. Finally, I said, "You mean," I dropped my voice, too, "drinking?" Lilli nodded her head, slow and serious. I didn't even realize Lilli knew Mama had a drinking problem. She knew something was wrong before, sure, but I had thought . . . Well, I thought I'd protected her a little better than that.

Lilli whispered, "What's gonna happen when she starts again? What happens next?"

"Mama's not drinking now. She's doing much better," I said, feeling my heart rate kick up. Was Lilli being paranoid? Seeing problems that weren't there like Mama said I did? Did I cause that?

I pulled her into a hug.

"It's going to be all right," I said. I rubbed her thin back and tried hard to make her feel safe. When we pulled away, I picked up the *Rainbow Fish* book. I'd always loved it. The same way Lilli was in love with the idea of being a mermaid, I'd been that way, too, once upon a time.

The purple-and-silvery colors swirling across the pages were perfect for making you feel like you were underwater. I remembered going through every purple crayon in the box to try and draw the beautiful, colorful fish on the cover.

Lilli barely made it to the end of the book before passing out asleep. I slipped out of the room soon after. I felt too amped up to stay in the tiny space of ours. Mama was still up, moving around downstairs. I wasn't ready for more awkward. The window at the end of the hall, overlooking the roof, was calling me.

Cool night air greeted me on the rooftop. Soon as I settled back against the wall, I felt a buzzing in my back pocket for real this time. I took out my phone.

Dr. Sapperstein's name appeared on the screen. My gut clenched. This was it. The Text. Every insecurity I'd ever had bunched up in my stomach like old license plates in a shark's belly. (Sharks can swallow cars whole. They often had car parts in their guts. I saw it one time on *Shark Week*!)

A million years passed on that roof before I finally opened the text.

Hi Miss Kita, I would like to personally welcome you to our baton twirler squad. Official practice starts on Wednesday. Congratulations!

My hand dropped and my head fell backward. It was like a hundred-pound weight had lifted off me.

I made it.

I made it.

A lightness filled me, and I wanted to giggle and laugh and hug somebody. Before I could text her, Niecy had already texted me. She made it, too!

And so did Chasity.

Much as I tried to fight it, I felt so happy. So, so happy.

Then . . . Ma's words whispered in my ears:

Don't mess it up . . . don't mess it up . . . don't mess it up!

(**14**)

THE SCHOOL'S FRONT OFFICE buzzed with activity. I was waiting for Dr. Charles, the school's new counselor. I had to spend thirty minutes with him—everyone in the school did. It was a new thing they were doing this year. Something about making sure each student felt "supported" and "equipped for the future." Definitely sounded like something Dr. Sapperstein would say—I had a feeling she was behind the whole thing as assistant principal. She was the one who spoke about it on the morning announcements Tuesday, saying we'd get our appointment date and time during our homeroom classes. I got mine from Mrs. Bailey and almost passed out seeing I'd be meeting with him so soon. Mama wouldn't have been very happy about it.

I didn't want to be here. Sitting in an uncomfortable chair, I tapped my foot and bounced my leg up and down like crazy.

Oh, wait! How could this situation get more tense? My old math teacher, of course.

Since sixth, seventh, and eighth grades are in different sections of the building, it was the first time I'd seen Wilcher the Witch since school began. The minute I saw her, the burning anger I'd felt that day last year came rushing back.

I'd wanted to turn away, but I was too late. Our gazes locked. I was sitting in one of those hard orange plastic chairs that dotted the school like overripened oranges. She came and stood right over me. Arms crossed over her body. A smug look on her face.

"Well, Miss Lloyd, I see you made it out of sixth grade despite your questionable study habits." She looked down her nose at me. My hands started to shake. I chewed on my lip so hard, I tasted blood.

My head sank into my shoulders. Mrs. Wilcher's witchy spell was turning me into a turtle, retreating into its shell. She frowned. "I hope you're not still sleeping in class—"

"Can I help you with something?" a man asked. Wilcher almost jumped out of her pointy pumps. He stood, a curious expression in his soft brown eyes. "I'm Dr. Charles. I believe Sharkita Lloyd"—he looked at me and I nodded—"is here to see me."

"Of course! Of course! I'm Eileen Wilcher," she said, reaching her hand out to shake his. "I teach sixth-grade math. Miss Lloyd had my class last year. I was just saying I hope she's putting forth more effort this year."

It was as if something inside me exploded. Tears flooded my eyes. My insides had that inflated feeling again, like I might burst out of my own skin. Dr. Charles must have picked up on it. He moved between Wilcher and me.

She was still talking, but he cut her off. "I'm afraid we have an appointment now and this is cutting into our time. Come along, Sharkita. Let's get you settled. Nice to meet you, Mrs. Wilson." Mrs. Wilson! Ha! Sad as I was, I could have kissed him for that.

He was closing the door to his office while she was sputtering, "It's Wilcher." The door shut. All the noise from the waiting area, which really was just a carpeted hallway where multiple offices sat, vanished. Silence made it impossible to hide the fact that I was sniffling back tears.

He motioned at a chair for me to sit in. Once seated, I looked at the floor, crossed my ankles and arms. I wiped my eyes. My body felt so tight it was a wonder oxygen could pass through my blood cells.

"So . . . Mrs. Wilcher," he said. He did know her name! I looked up at him after dropping into the chair he'd been pointing at. "Not your biggest fan, huh?"

I shook my head, too overwhelmed with emotion to trust myself to speak.

"You know, you don't have to be afraid in here. I almost never cut open students' brains anymore," he said. My head snapped up.

My mouth dropped open. Then I saw his face. He threw his head back and let out a roaring laugh.

I felt like a wild deer that had wandered into a petting zoo.

Or an orange grove.

Dr. Charles wasn't a tall guy, but he did remind me of a talking teddy bear, wearing a Florida A&M polo shirt, deep green with orange lettering. His bright red St. Louis Cardinals baseball cap clashed. In white script, it read World Champions 2011.

"It's just a joke, Sharkita. So stop all that shaking and squinting. You're making me nervous!" he said.

He suggested I take a few deep breaths, which I did.

While I calmed myself down, he fixed a cup of tea. I'd never had hot tea, so when he asked if I wanted one, I said, "Sure."

It was way too hot and tasted like grass with honey on it. *Bleh!*

But it was nice to hold on to while we chitchatted for a minute or two. Enough time for me to look around the office. Mini college football helmets—Tennessee, Michigan State, Texas Tech, North Carolina A&T—none of them matching the logo on his shirt.

"Ka—um—Dr. Sapperstein went to FAMU. Did you go there, too?" I asked, glad I had found my voice.

"Alcorn State," he said looking proud.

I shrugged. "I've never heard of it."

He made his eyes get as round as pool balls. "What? You ain't never heard of it? *Lawwd*, have mercy. What are they teaching the youth today?" His words didn't punch me in the stomach the way Wilcher's had. He was kidding.

"Why are you wearing a FAMU shirt then?" I asked, feeling myself get a little more comfortable.

"My daughter and son go there. Two years from now, they'll both be graduating, and I'll be the happiest papa in the South!" He let out another big laugh.

"Because you'll be proud of them?" My voice was soft but clear.

"Heck no! I'll be happy because I can take all the money I've been using on tuition and buy myself a boat!"

He roared with laughter at his own silly joke. I couldn't help myself. I laughed, too.

He wiped his eyes with the backs of his bear paw hands. When he looked at me, his laughter faded into a warm, comfortable smile.

"You know, we never properly introduced ourselves. You are Sharkita, right?"

I nodded.

"Do you like to be called . . ."

"Um, Kita. Everybody calls me Kita."

Dr. Charles drained his cup and sat it down.

"Okay, Kita. Listen, I am a psychologist, not a psychic. I have my own practice downtown across from the hospital. However, I'm working at a few schools in the county. I'm not here to trick you or judge you. Not here to gossip or spread your business. I help people. Believe it or not, I'm good at it. And if you feel nervous or unsure or upset about anything—or if you just need to work out a plan, we can talk it out."

I flinched. He noticed. Didn't mean to, but I did. I had to bite my tongue to stop myself from spilling my life story. My whole life felt like an unbearable weight pressing down on my shoulders—worrying about Mama, the kids, going back to foster care, losing touch with my brother and sister, trying to be normal.

The fear that something inside me had broken—mentally, emotionally. I had to suck in a breath to keep it all in.

He frowned at me before going on.

"Now, somebody told me you are going to be a baton twirler. Is that true? My daughter twirled all four years of high school."

"Yeah, uh, I mean, yes. Yes, sir. Our first game where they're letting us perform is a few weeks from now."

"You nervous?"

I nodded. "A little."

"When you found out you made it did you run to your phone and call your friends and were you like, 'Oh my god, girl! Ooo-weee! I made it! Isn't that wonderful'!" His voice was high and girlish. I had to laugh.

But I covered my mouth with my hand because I didn't want him looking at my teeth.

"No, it wasn't even like that," I said, smiling, hand still covering my mouth.

"You want some techniques to help you not be so nervous come game time?"

My face answered before my mouth could get a word out. I felt my eyes widen and an uncertain smile touch my lips.

"Really?" I said.

"Of course." He sat forward, staring at me for a moment. Then he asked, "Who's your best friend?"

Not sure what this had to do with not being nervous, but I answered, anyway. "Niecy."

"Shaniece!" he said. We both paused, then we both laughed. Of course he remembered Niecy. "She's a cool kid."

I nodded.

"And she's a twirl girl, too, right?"

I said, "Yes."

He asked me what Niecy thought of my twirling, whether or not she thought I was any good. When I told him she was very supportive and thought I was the best between the three of us—me, her, and Chasity—he said, "Good. Do you trust her?"

"Niecy?" I thought about how she always had my back; how she didn't go blabbing all over the neighborhood about what went on in our house. "Yes, I trust her."

"And do you think she's a good baton twirler?"

I nodded.

"Good. So here's what you do. When you're at the game about to strut out there and the negative, scary thoughts try to take over, think about Niecy."

I frowned. "Really?"

"Really. I want you to focus on Niecy. Not watch her but focus on her with your mind. Think about how she's a great friend and y'girl wouldn't steer you wrong. Then think about how good she is. You might feel like everybody's watching you but if Niecy is as good as you think, they'll probably be watching her, too. And the band. And the other dancers. You get what I'm saying?"

"I think so. Maybe everyone won't be focused on me," I said.

"Exactly! And with that, young lady, I think that's all the time we have today."

He stood and walked me to the door. He held out his hand to shake. I reached out and took it as he opened the door. "It was nice meeting you, Kita. I'm here a few times a week. I'll be working through all the other kids' appointments for a while, but I always try to accommodate students, no matter what. You can come talk informally or you can set something up with Vickie."

The lady at the desk in the far-right corner looked up and waved. I waved back.

"What if I wanted to just ask some questions about things? Could I do that?" I don't even know where the question comes from before it's out of my mouth.

"Yes, but I'd have to set you up with the other secretary. She handles all the questions."

I looked at him curiously, then he smiled.

"Kidding! Go talk to Vickie, she'll help you set something it up."

I'd taken a few steps toward Vickie before turning back and asking, "Coming in here to talk doesn't mean you have a problem, right?"

He gave me a gentle push in my back toward Vickie. He raised his hands and said easily, "It could just mean you have questions that need answering. Nothing wrong with that, right?"

Right!

(15)

THE NEXT FEW WEEKS passed in a blur. Miss Kadejah wanted us to be ready for our first game. We practiced three times a week: Tuesday, Wednesday, and Thursday.

We grew more and more comfortable with one another—and our coach. Me and Niecy thought Miss Kadejah's workout-wear game was fire. Each day when we spent time with her, I wondered what it must be like to be her. Wondered if I could ever *be* like her.

Between practicing and going to class, I started looking for reasons to go past Miss Kadejah's office. She would wave or smile if she saw me. Something about seeing her and her seeing me made me happy inside. I was happy. It felt strange.

Strange but good.

On the Thursday before our first performance, she sat us down about fifteen minutes before practice ended. She told us again how she'd been a twirler at FAMU, telling us all about her first game there, trying to make us feel better about ours tomorrow.

"Those were some of the best years of my life," she said.

"I hope all of you get to experience college. It's truly an amazing time in your life."

Chasity couldn't help herself. "Um, no offense Miss Kadejah, but yo' girl right here won't need college when I'm the Number One influencer on Insta!" The rest of us dropped our heads. Chas should have been embarrassed by her own ridiculousness, but she wasn't.

Coach moved until she was standing right over Chas, and stared down at her for so long, even Chasity understood she should be quiet.

"You might be amazed by what you learn," she said, turning to look back down at Chasity.

I tried to picture it. Me. On a college campus. It never felt like that would be my thing. All of a sudden, I felt desperate to visit one. Did I have a chance same as everybody else?

A familiar knot pulled at my scalp, my stomach—a drawstring tied to my emotions. I imagined myself in college, hanging with my friends. I would love to study art. The idea ran over me. A runaway train of possibilities.

Then came the shadow.

Mama!

"Kita? You okay?" Miss Kadejah's voice came from across a frozen lake. A distance. The whole scene, from idea to enrollment to present had appeared swiftly, burning out just as fast. "Kita?"

"Yes, ma'am," I said, coming back to the present moment. Kadejah looked at me—really looked at me—before continuing on with reminders for tomorrow. Finally, she dismissed us.

"Kita, can you hang back a sec?" Kadejah called for me. Oh god, what had I done wrong?

Niecy said she'd meet me outside, and I walked over to Miss Kadejah. "I'm sorry for zoning out while you were talking, Miss, I didn't mean—"

"Kita, sweetie, you're not in trouble," she interrupted me. "I just wanted to check in. You feeling good about tomorrow?"

My stomach churned, but I nodded.

"Well, you should feel good. I've been really impressed with you," Miss Kadejah said. My surprise must have shown on my face, because she continued, "Don't look so shocked! You're a great twirler, and between you and me, you have a little something extra in you. You're disciplined. A leader. You're always helping your peers learn moves they're struggling with and you clearly care a lot about this team. I can see you being a captain once you get to high school."

I can barely understand the words she's saying. Me? A leader? A captain? It never even occurred to me. "Wow," I manage. "Thank you." I don't know what else to say.

Miss Kadejah gives my arm a squeeze. "I believe in you, Kita. I hope soon you can learn to believe in yourself, too."

With Kadejah as my coach, I think I just might.

～～

The next day, uniforms spilled from brown cardboard boxes, protected by rectangles of cellophane slippery to the touch. We all got to *ooo*-ing and *ahhh*-ing.

It was time for our first performance. A Friday night football game at the high school. Me and my friends—my squad—dancing under the lights. I wasn't used to the feelings rippling through me. Pride. Joy. Amazement. How could I feel so scared and happy at the same time?

Miss Kadejah said anybody who'd built up "day funk" should hit the showers before trying on their dance costume. That meant most of us, so we raced for the showers and dried off quickly.

My twirl costume was unbelievably beautiful. Lilli would love it. I was gonna look like a mermaid in a gold-and-icy-blue two-piece—shiny, golden scaled leggings on bottom and matching, one-sleeved leotard on top. I couldn't wait for her to see. I had reminded Mama that morning about the game, and she said she'd come with the littles. Performing in front of Mama added to my nerves, but I wanted to show her everything I'd been working on. Everything I could do when I wasn't doing her job of being a mama.

It took a few minutes of carefully inching it up my body, but I finally got on the costume. I held my breath. How did I look? I had my back to the mirror, afraid to see my reflection.

"Girl, you look good," Niecy said, coming alongside me, "or at least you will when you put some color on them lips!"

I avoided lipstick or lip gloss. No way I wanted to draw attention to my mouth and teeth. I said, "Didn't Miss Kadejah say we should keep our faces clean and clear?"

"No, she didn't, Sharkita Lashay Lloyd! A little mascara, eyeliner, and some gloss are fine!"

It was always easier to go along with Niecy when she got like this. She opened up her bag and spilled shiny tubes of doodads into a nearby sink basin.

"Close your eyes," she commanded. I obeyed. The nerves were beginning to swell and swell inside my belly.

"All right," Niecy said after painting on my face, "behold! My masterpiece!"

When I looked in the mirror, I saw the pinkish-red shade she'd applied to my lips. I didn't have full lips like a lot of the girls at our school. Mine were kind of thin, with a little plumpness in the bottom lip. Mama used to say my bottom lip was that way because I chewed it so much.

"Now do like this," Niecy said, making her lips pop. I did as she said. "You good, girl. Gorgeous!"

When she walked away and I was alone, I smiled at the mirror. I closed my mouth and stared at a reflection that was me, but not quite. I prayed to God one day I could look at myself in a mirror and see "gorgeous" like Niecy said.

Not long after, we were lining up to take the field. I took deep breaths like Dr. Charles had me do in our session, and focused my mind on Niecy like he told me to. Weirdly, it did help.

"All right, girls, it's your time to shine!" Kadejah announced before we marched onto the field. As she passed by me, she gave my arm a quick squeeze. "You're gonna do great." She was saying it to the whole group, but it felt like she was saying it straight to me.

The band started to play, and our eight-count marches were on and poppin'. A swell of something like pride—or maybe terror—blossomed inside me. March, march, march, march . . . *five, six, seven, eight*. It was going down.

I was praying not to lose step and mess up, but of course, I messed up. My heart sank into my belly for like a second. Then I remembered what Kadejah told us: "If you make a mistake, keep on performing."

So, that was what I did. I kept on doing my thing and before I knew it, it was over.

All of us were jumping and cheering and celebrating our first performance when Kadejah came up to us.

"I'm sorry I missed that step," I blurted out.

She said, "Nonsense, girl! You handled yourself like a pro. Very good. All of you did a fantastic job!"

"Sharkita!" I was still smiling when I heard my name being called. I thought it might be Mama with Lilli and Lamar, but I didn't see their faces in the crowd. Instead, I saw Granny.

My breath caught in my chest. I hadn't seen or spoken with her since . . . since June!

How did she even know I was here?

I walked over, unsure what to expect.

"Granny?"

"Baby, you sure looked good out there. I'm really proud of you," she said, reaching out, pulling me into a hug. Grandma hugs are supposed to feel like the best things in the world, but mine always felt a little cold, stiff. Especially after everything that had gone down.

"Thanks, Granny. But . . . how . . . ?"

Granny flicks her wrist. "You think I don't keep up with my grandbabies?" It was clear that was as much of an explanation as I was gonna get.

She glanced around behind me. I knew she was looking for Mama and the kids, but she just said, "Where everybody at?"

"Mama," I croaked, cleared my throat, started again. "She said they were coming, but I think Lamar wasn't having such a good day," I lied. I didn't know why Mama hadn't shown up. I was a little disappointed but hardly surprised.

Granny recognized the lie, but for once she let it go.

"Well, you keep up with your schoolwork, you hear? I know you're doing good. Those teachers talk when they're down at the beauty parlor. Granny keeps up with all y'all. Now you be good, and call me if you need me," she said, talking about herself the same way Niecy did.

Granny was a thin woman with a thin face. When she wrapped her arms around me, her hug felt as if she were made of wires. She squeezed me hard, patting my back clumsily before letting go.

I watched as her little head-rag, brightly colored like the Pan-African flag, disappeared into a sea of chanting, loud people.

"KITA!" Niecy waved wildly, calling me over to keep celebrating with the rest of the squad.

"Hey, um, you're Sharkita, right?" a different voice said, catching me off guard. I waved to Niecy before turning to see who was behind me.

It was the most beautiful boy in the whole wide world. Breath caught in my throat. *Did I just gasp?* My mouth would have dropped open, except, you know? Not with my teeth. I didn't dare.

"Um . . . um-uh, yes, I, um, me . . . I'm Sharkita," I said, sounding like I was just plain dumb. Oh, man! My face was so red. I could feel it. But when he looked down, his cheeks were turning bright, too.

"I'm, uh, Quintin Downs. I just started here this year. I think I've seen you around at lunch." I felt like I was in one of those Netflix movies. The romantic comedies. Like the one that lady wrote, *To All the Boys I've Loved Before*. My heart was pounding super fast. And my mouth was so dry. I just nodded.

Right then, Niecy, who I'd completely forgotten, roared into view.

"Kita!" she sang out. Like I said—LOUD. I knew she was going to embarrass me, pooching out her lips 'n' stuff.

"Niecy," I said in a whisper, "this is Quintin Downs." I felt shook, plain and simple. Why was this hot boy talking to me?

"Girl, I know who he is," said Niecy. "Why do you think he's over here? He was asking about you and I told him to go get you so we can all walk home together!" **Loud, loud, loud.**

Poor Quintin. He looked as scared as I felt. Come on, Kita. Pull yourself together. This IS your first rodeo. *Don't blow it!*

"You live over by us at University Village?" I asked.

"Sixteen, seven, eighty-five!" Niecy said, sticking her tongue out as she rattled off my address. "Commons Boulevard. I live right around the corner. You should come check us out!"

Well, I died. Right there. On the pavement between the hot

dog stand and the big old-fashioned grill where Big Luther was flipping burgers. Dead.

Quintin turned his attention back to me, but even as he spoke, I kept my head down. "I'm in Village East," he said.

When I finally lifted my eyes, I saw he was smiling. A funny feeling danced in my stomach. My cheeks were hot and I could feel them staining red. Then we both just stood there, looking goofy.

Niecy: "We just gonna' stand here? Or can we get a move on? Mama's making lasagna for dinner. I do not want to miss out, you *huuur*!" Yes, we "hear." Everybody *hears*. She needs a volume control button.

By the time we reached our neighborhood, I'd learned that Quintin lived with his mom and dad, had a younger brother and sister, and sometimes he had to babysit, just like me.

"Yeah, I'm on sibling duty a lot. But I love them. Only time I mind it is when my mom is gone all night," I say.

"Oh, uh, my parents don't really stay out that long," Quintin said. Oh, that was right. That was just my mama who didn't come back.

Quintin talked some more (for once Niecy was quiet, though the look on her face was saying plenty). When we got to my house, he walked me all the way to my front door. From the sidewalk, Niecy was batting her eyes at me and blowing kisses. I turned my back on her.

"See you around," he said. "Maybe we can sit together at lunch sometime?"

"Sounds good," I answered without hesitation.

Quintin smiled. "That's what's up. Okay, well, I'll see you later."

He trotted down to his friend, whose name I didn't get, and Niecy. They all waved and I stood there, watching them vanish into the dusky purples and grays of evening.

Truth was, I didn't even care Mama hadn't come to see me perform. This was one of the best nights of my life.

(16)

THE FIRST CRACK IN New Mama's image came five days later, on the last Wednesday of the month—roughly fifty-two days since New Mama rode in on her humble horse of promises.

She'd gotten home at her usual time. Handled the littles and gave them a snack. I'd come home late from practice, which was part of our new normal.

Mama seemed in a good enough mood, at first. Without alcohol, sometimes her personality was flat—not all the time, of course. Mama always sparkled. But it was like, when she drank, it lit her up from the inside out. For a while, at least. Until all the hurt and pain of her life rose up on a wine-soaked wave.

That night we were making tacos, opening the little yellow seasoning packets to go on the ground beef. The meat was simmering. Mama asked, "You've got a game Friday?"

I'd never asked why she hadn't shown at last week's game. Wasn't worth the fight. She was already putting Lamar and Lilli to bed by the time I'd gotten home and went straight to her room afterward, and I was still riding high on my first performance and conversation with Quintin.

But now, words tumbled out of me.

"Friday. Well, it's not a game, technically. It's a performance across town at that arts school. They're having some kind of show and invited us. Niecy actually got permission from her mama to have a sleepover with some of the other dancers afterward. Can I go, too?" I didn't know how to ask because I didn't have a lot of experience asking to go anywhere. I chopped as I chattered. Bright red tomatoes split into tiny rectangles.

Then I saw my mistake. I'd been so caught up in what I was doing, running my mouth about all the fun I was fixing to have, I didn't even notice how Mama was looking.

Then she let out one of those long sighs like only Mama could do—like the whole world was wearing her down. I twisted around to look at her, but she had her back to me at the stove stirring the ground beef.

"Must be nice," she muttered, "still being young enough to have fun and go out. No kids to hold you back. Enjoy it while you can." Bitterness dripped off her words like sweat on a prisoner's forehead.

No kids to hold you back!

Right after that punch to the stomach, Lamar came running into the kitchen clanging a pot lid against a metal pot.

CLANG! CLANG! CLANG!

"I'm in a marching band! I'm like Kita! Look, Kita, look!" he practically shouted. He looked so goofy and sweet, I wanted to hug and squeeze him and blow raspberries on his fat cheeks. But Mama spun around and the ugly in her eyes dried up all the good feelings in the air.

She looked at him with such a mean face.

The worst part was when she raised the wooden spoon she'd been stirring the meat with. She was holding that spoon like a club, and when she spoke, she looked like an angry ghost towering over him.

"Boy, if you don't cut out all that noise, I'm gonna make you wish you did!" she said, grating out the words.

The whole world went silent. Even the meat didn't sizzle. A few seconds passed, then Lamar's big eyes filled with tears, and he burst out crying. I felt like such an idiot. I should have known, soon as he started clanging on those pots and pans, that he would push her too far and she'd get mad.

"Why Mama mad at me? Why Mama mad at me? Why she mad at me?" Said it over and over. Flung himself on the floor and started thrashing around, hitting his head against the floor again. It was awful. But I'd seen him do worse.

I was used to Lamar's spells. Without even having to think or talk about it, I got on the floor on my knees. I took one of his hands and gently rubbed his fingers.

"Laaaa-ma-rrrr," I sang softly, breaking his name into three pieces, trying to make my singing like Mama's but not doing a very good job, "it's gonna be all right. Mama didn't mean it. She's not mad."

It took several minutes, but Lamar calmed down and I helped him up. When I looked around, I realized Mama had taken the meat off the burner and left the kitchen.

"She in her room," Lilli said from the sofa. "I wonder what she got in there that she likes more than us?" I had nothing to say to that. Inside my head, I felt something angry bumping around like a marble in a jar.

You don't have a right to be angry! If anyone has a right to be angry it's me!

Mama had said it so many times. So many. I believed it even when I knew it wasn't true.

We ate without her—the three of us, like usual. After dinner, I was clearing the table when I smelled something faint—*burning*? I turned around and Lamar was standing at the stove lighting a piece of paper towel on fire.

"Oh, no, Mar-Mar!" I yelled out. Lilli's eyes got all big and round.

I ran around the counter and took the paper from him, sticking it in the sink and turning the water on.

My heart pounded wildly. I could hardly speak. The flame died swiftly under the water. After taking a huge gulp of air to calm myself, I wrapped Lamar in a huge hug.

"Lamar, sweetie, playing with fire is dangerous," I said, rubbing his face. "Fire is bad. No fire, okay?" My voice shook. If I sounded mad, he could spin out of control, but would sounding too sweet make him think it's a game?

He finally raised his head. Tears welled in the corners of his eyes, and he said, "Okay, sister, I sorry." He laid his head on my shoulder. "But if I cook, Mama won't be so mad."

A flash of anger lit my belly—not at Lamar, but at Mama. She knows how easy it is to set him off.

"Mama's not mad. She is tired, okay? Now, promise me, Lamar, you will never touch the stove. It's dangerous. Okay?"

"Me have some ju-ju?" he answered. He wanted juice. Sometimes it was impossible to know if he understood, or not.

Lilli had returned to her spot on the sofa in front of the TV. Steve Harvey. Now how you gonna be five years old and be in love with the host of *Family Feud*? That was crazy, right?

When I glanced at her, grinning at the television, cooing at Steve Harvey, for just a second, I felt a flicker of anger. At Lilli. The voice in my head said, *Why do you get to go over there and sit down, tee-heeing at your favorite show while I'm over here struggling?*

Then, as I filled his cup and sank to the floor, cleaning up pieces of burnt paper towel, a flood of tears filled my eyes.

What was I thinking? Angry that a five-year-old girl wasn't doing more to help her older brother? Now, who did that bag of crazy sound like?

One guess—dear old Mama!

Was I turning into her—on the inside?

No.

Add another goal: Never become HER!

Later, Mama came down while I was doing my homework. "I'm going out for a while. Just up the block to Mavis's place. Call if you need me. I'll be back."

Just like that. She was gone. Tension squeezed my belly. I distracted myself with laundry, then filling the dishwasher, and taking out the garbage. That was one of my tricks. You had to keep busy. Besides, I was determined that if social services dropped in one day, they wouldn't catch us living in filth. That would be tragic.

She came back a few hours later to a clean, silent house. I heard her come in, but I had nothing to say to her. Nothing at all.

(17)

THE NEXT DAY AFTER practice, I was walking home alone. Niecy had a church thing to go to, so her mama had picked her up early. Honestly, it was nice to have a little peace and quiet for once. Not that I didn't love my girl! But she said it herself—she was a lot sometimes.

In the silence, I let my thoughts drift to lunch. And Quintin. He'd stopped by our table. He was even more beautiful than he'd been last Friday. Since the game, he and I waved in the hallway or hung out in groups with his friends and mine.

It felt wonderful.

That warm sparkly feeling danced in my belly again as I thought about him. He seemed to like me. When I said that to Niecy, that girl punched me in the thigh.

"That's because he does like you, fool!" Niecy was all about that tough love.

I passed by a Walgreens and decided to stop in to buy Sour

Punch straws, maybe some chocolate for Lilli and Lamar. Mama left money for me in the kitchen this morning with a smiley face note. Her way of apologizing, I guessed.

Shiny packages of brightly colored candies filled my vision as I moved along the candy aisle.

Someone called my name.

"Kita! Girl, is that you? You growing like a weed!" I turned and saw Miss Rose. She drove our elementary school bus route, so I used to see her every day. Now she drives Lilli and Lamar.

Miss Rose was a woman with wide hips and a wider smile. But her waist was teeny-tiny. She wore lashes out to here and four-inch heels that still only brought her up to my neck.

When she made her way over to me, her hips swung atop her strappy pink-and-white heels, and she wrapped me in her arms and squeezed till my feet lifted off the floor. Miss Rose had balance for days!

"Hi, Miss Rose," I squeaked.

"You sure have grown, baby, since you rode my bus two years ago," she said. She asked about my practices and told me she'd seen me perform. Her son was in the high school marching band. "You're so good with that baton. I never knew you could do all that twirling."

I blushed. "Thank you."

Then she cocked her eyebrow and went on. "You know, I thought you might already be home. I didn't see your mama at the bus stop earlier like she been doing the past few weeks . . ."

A bag of candy dropped from my hand.

"Mama wasn't at the bus stop?" My eyes bugged. My hands started to sweat, closing into fists of knotted anxiety.

"Well, no, sugar. But I saw Lamar open the door, I figured, you know, you or your mama was probably right inside . . ."

Maybe she was.

But what if she wasn't?

I started running toward the door, checking Find My Friends on my phone. Mama was nowhere to be seen—she had turned hers off. My heart flopped, then dropped into my belly.

"I gotta go, Miss Rose," I called over my shoulder.

I was already running . . . running . . . running!

I ran three blocks, fast as I could. A disaster movie played in my head—kidnappers; Chester the Molester hiding in the bushes; Lamar with somebody's matches; Lilli calling 9-1-1; social services showing up again.

My legs pumped harder, faster.

The sun was starting to melt in the sky, a hundred shades of orange and yellow and red like wax crayons melting together, sticky in the heat.

When I reached our town house, I burst through the front door like the Kool-Aid Man. Lamar sat on the floor playing with a little car. Lilli was on the sofa, a doll in her lap, and holding a book like she'd been reading to the doll. Mama was in the kitchen, her back to the front door. She was cooking. She turned, looked at me quick, but didn't say anything.

No disaster film. No fires or weirdos or kidnappers. No reason for panic.

"Kita, Kita, Kita," sang Lamar, "Kita is home! Kita is home! Kita is home!"

I collapsed onto the couch, my heart still running even though my body had stopped.

Mama must have just been waiting inside like Miss Rose said. Her phone probably died—that's why I couldn't see her location. Everything is fine. I tried to reassure myself, reason with myself.

It was like I was swimming in a shark's belly, being swallowed and squeezed. I was exhausted and felt too old for my twelve years on earth.

It was fine. Everything was fine. Normal.

We ate dinner.

Bedtime and all its rituals came.

Lilli chose a new book. When I finished reading, I expected her to be asleep. She wasn't. She was staring right at me.

"Kita. Mama wasn't home when we got here. She told me not to say nothing to you," Lilli said. Something in her little eyes, even in the soft lighting of the room, was heartbreaking. She didn't look sad or mad—she looked as tired as I'd felt. Now, how you gonna be five years old and already be tired of life?

"She gonna go back to how she was, isn't she?" Her voice was real quiet.

It hurt, looking at her, feeling her disappointment.

"She's trying really hard, Lil. And I'm helping. We're fine," I said.

She looked at me, sighed, and rolled over. I clicked on her little pink night-light. In the fairy-tale darkness she said, "I wish she would just go away. I wish we didn't have to live with her. I'm tired of not knowing what's going to happen every day."

I couldn't think of anything to say to that, so I just let it hang in between us.

After I was sure Lilli was asleep, that night with my phone wedged into the back pocket of my denim shorts, I climbed out my bedroom window and lay on the slanted roof beneath the stars.

Construction on I-4 had shifted the highway lanes even closer to our neighborhood. The sound of traffic at night was like listening to a concrete waterfall.

This day had been a roller coaster. I'd been so stupidly happy about Quintin, had so much fun at practice, all for it to come crashing down again.

A little voice in my head whispered, "Faker!" It hit me like a hammer wrapped in velvet. Who was I kidding? Thinking I could be one of the cute, happy, popular girls. A normal girl. Thinking Mama could be the adult we needed her to be.

Anger burned in my belly. Anger at myself for believing Niecy's hype. Anger at thinking I could be like everybody else—like I didn't have responsibilities. Lilli and Lamar needed me.

My heart hammered so that my body shook.

Look how I'd been acting lately—wearing lip gloss, smiling at people even though I knew better than to laugh with my jagged, ugly, crooked, disgusting teeth.

Fear threaded through me like a virus. My insides felt hot. I shut my eyes, trying to get a grip. Then I heard the soft thump in the night.

Thinking one of the littles had gotten up, I shrank into the shadows. Letting the littles see me would be a disaster. If Lamar saw me on the roof, it would be over.

I looked down to the street. A pool of purple violets shimmered beneath the streetlamp below.

Next, I saw something approaching. Black and silent as any predator, a car gleamed in the lamplight. Footsteps echoed beneath me. Quick. But soft, too.

Mama?

Mama!

The panther-black car opened its mouth and swallowed her whole. Before I even had time to breathe, she was rolling silently away. I crept back inside, locked my window, and checked on my siblings. Mama's room was empty, and the house instantly felt empty without her. I felt empty, too.

That night I lay with my cheek pressed against the carpet on our bedroom floor. I slept without sleeping at all.

(18)

THE SUBWAY SANDWICH IN front of me was my favorite—tuna with provolone. It was especially good because I was in Miss Kadejah's office. She invited me, Niecy, and Chasity to eat lunch with her. She called us her "Twirl Girls." We'd eaten with her a few times since school started. Sometimes we brought lunch or grabbed it from the cafeteria, but today Miss Kadejah offered to order us sandwiches.

"Thank you, girls, for letting me buy you lunch," she said, "this is fun."

I took another tiny bite of my sandwich. I didn't want to look greedy or anything, even though at home I'd have been tearing that sub up!

We chatted about our last performance, our upcoming performance, and our classes. It was very mellow and chill. I needed chill. My brain did not want to replay last night.

"Are you okay, Kita?" Miss Kadejah asked, and I realized she was looking at me. "Seems like you're clenching your jaw. Is your sandwich not what you wanted?"

"No, no, no! The sandwich is great," I said.

"What's on your mind?" She turned and looked at me. Niecy and Chasity, too. I gulped. No way I was going to tell her what was really on my mind.

How angry I was at Mama for going back to her old ways.

How much I wished, like Lilli kept whispering, that she would just go away.

"Kita? You're crying, girl. What's wrong?" Niecy said. I quickly reached up and swiped at the tear. Where had my mind gone? I didn't even realize I'd been crying.

"I'm fine, really!" I tried to laugh.

You're messed up . . .

"Dang, Sharkita. I know you're not upset about nothing in art class because you're killing it in there. And now that you have a *boo-thang*!" Chasity's big mouth said.

"What's a *boo-thing*?" Miss Kadejah asked.

"*Thang!*" Chasity corrected. "Quintin Downs. She likes him, he likes her." God! Chasity was worse than Niecy. She was dancing around in her seat, eyes bright and sparkly. Miss Kadejah smiled at me, but her eyes still held a sorrowful look.

"Baby girl, what's really going on with your emotions today? It's not this boo-thing person, is it?" she asked.

I shook my head. "No, I am not crying over that boy. And we're just friends!" I snapped off to Chasity.

Okay, I knew I better come up with something—*quick*! The truth was not an option.

Maybe I could tell a different truth. I drew in a deep breath and made a big show of exhaling.

"Mr. Gavin is making us go to that aquarium next week," I said, managing to sound sad and shook. I mean, I didn't want to go—not one bit. Still, I had bigger things on my mind.

Miss Kadejah and the girls argued that the field trip to the Florida Aquarium next Friday would be fun, and I told them about my fear of sharks and how Mr. Gavin was in love with them, and we had to do this project on them.

"I'm sorry," Miss Kadejah said at one point, cutting me off. "What's your problem with sharks?"

"They're scary!" I said, then took a big bite of my sub so they would stop talking to me. The door opened then, and Dr. Charles stuck his head inside.

"I didn't know you were having a party, Dr. Sapperstein," he said, with a grin. He looked over at the rest of us and added, "Hey, girls. What are we talking about today?"

"Sharkita and her fear of sharks!" Chasity said. Then, if that wasn't humiliating enough, she went on. "Shark-ita? You know, your name almost sounds like shark. Do you hate your name? Is that why you don't like sharks?"

"I'm gon' pray for you, girl!" Niecy said, staring Chasity dead in her eyes.

Now my heart was pounding. They were all looking at me. I just wanted to sit here and enjoy my Subway. Thank you, Lord, the warning bell rang. I jumped up and started clearing away my stuff without looking at anybody.

Somehow, Niecy and Chasity managed to get out of the room

ahead of me. Of course, Miss Kadejah touched my elbow, stopping me.

"I'm sorry you're nervous about the trip to the aquarium. It should be an enjoyable day away from school for both of Mr. Gavin's classes. If visiting the shark tank is really going to be that disturbing, I can speak with your teacher and have you excused from that part of the tour," she said.

I shook my head. That would only draw more attention to me, which was exactly what I didn't want.

"If you have time after regular school hours, you could come and talk to me," Dr. Charles said. "I've got some time this afternoon."

The way they were looking at me, I just wanted the moment to end. So, I said, "Sure, I mean, thank you."

I'd never run so fast in a school hallway in my life!

(19)

WHAT DO YOU CALL it when you wind up in counseling kinda against your will? Would it be a hostage situation? I'm asking for a friend . . .

After school, Miss Kadejah told me I could miss the first thirty minutes of practice to see Dr. Charles. She'd taken it upon herself to set up the appointment for me. I'd sighed but knew she was just trying to be helpful.

Dr. Charles was waiting for me when I dragged into his office. He'd traded his college gear for pros. He wore a Miami Dolphins jersey with jeans and a pair of J's. He saw me looking at his shoes and grinned.

"You like my old-school Jordans, right?" He laughed and it was so goofy sounding, I couldn't help smiling.

He directed me to a seat. Soon as he sat, he asked, "So let's talk about what's really going on with you. There's more behind those sad, tired eyes than fearing a shark in a tank. What's up?"

All I could do, at first, was blink. I'd hoped he'd jump in and say something else, but he just sat there, silent. Waiting.

What I heard myself say next came as a surprise even to me.

"You can't tell anybody what I say, right?"

He sat back in his chair. The humorous gleam in his eyes gone. He was one hundred percent professional.

"Nope, not unless you're admitting to being a threat to yourself or others. Then I am bound by law to say something for your protection and the protection of others. Is what you want to tell me something of that nature?"

"No," I said quickly. "No, no, no." I blew out another sigh, tried to find my words. This time he did cut in.

"Let's talk, then. What's on your mind? How are things at home? You live with your mom, right? Tell me about her."

The word flew out before I could stop it:

"No!" Instantly, my cheeks heated. "Not Mama."

He nodded at me.

"Then you start wherever you want to. Maybe I can help."

We talked for a little while. I danced around what I'd been feeling, downplaying that shark attack sensation so it sounded like it was just normal stress about school. Dr. Charles listened. Told me it was normal to feel anxiety (that's the word he used for it). He gave me some tips like he had during our first session, and before I knew it, I was heading back to twirl practice.

"Feeling better?" Miss Kadejah asked.

I smiled softly and nodded. I did almost feel better when I left Dr. Charles's office.

It didn't last long.

When I got home, Mama was in her closet. Packing.

"Hey!" she yelled too loud. Her fake smile as crooked as a shelf in a hurricane.

"Mama! Where are you going?"

"Don't you have a game tonight?" she said, trying to distract me while she returned to her closet.

"Tomorrow," I said.

Then I caught sight of the half-open suitcase on her bed. "I'll be back first thing tomorrow morning, don't worry about that," she said. And when I asked who she was going away with, she told me to "stay outta grown-folks' business!"

She kept up her weak smile until I said, "You know how Lamar gets when you start running the streets."

The weak smile slid off her face. Hard eyes glittered at me like eight balls. *There she is!* I thought to myself. The mama I knew best.

She shoved her hands on her hips. "I said I was coming back in the morning. You have stayed here plenty of times with these kids, you know you can handle it. Besides, I've been working hard. I deserve a break, too."

A break? New Mama had been here for barely two months and already she was overwhelmed?

The crushing feeling swallowed me whole. The ugly shark sliding me deeper into its belly.

Mama leapt around the foot of her bed. Eyes hard as flat stones.

"Look here, little girl," she was leaning into me, finger pointed, "you don't tell me what to do, okay? I tell you! I'm the mama. I'm the one in charge. Just because I *let* you help me don't mean you get to call the shots."

Teamwork really did make the dream work. If I left right now, she wouldn't know how to pay the light bill to save her soul. At my sides, fingers curled into sweaty fists.

Dr. Charles's techniques to control my stress popped into my head. But everything was happening so fast. I couldn't wrap my mind around the doctor's advice. Didn't think I'd need it so soon.

"I'm not trying to tell you what to do, Mama, but Lamar . . ."

She frowned, then turned back to her packing. "Don't you use Lamar to guilt-trip me."

Anger bubbled inside me.

Mama flashed her beautiful, Princess Jasmine smile, and I remembered its impact when I was four years old and believed she really could take me on a magic carpet ride. Now it looked hollow and dangerous.

"Tomorrow morning, Kita, I promise. I really promise."

Her tone had grown softer, almost pleading. She tried to look sincere. Maybe in her heart she even meant it. "Please?" she repeated. "I need this. I'll be back, *promise!*"

When Mama made promises, it always scared me.

(**20**)

MAMA KEPT HER PROMISE this time. She was home by the time me and the littles were walking out the door for school. She gave Lilli and Lamar quick kisses on the head but only gave me a sidelong look.

"I'll be home late. I have a game tonight," I told her.

She only waved a hand in response.

Despite the day's start, Friday night's game went great. None of us dropped the baton—at least, not the middle school girls. After our performance, we ate hot dogs and hamburgers in the stands. Quintin and a few of his friends hung out with us, too.

"The gold sparkles make your cheeks shimmer," Niecy said, leaning into me. I made a face and we laughed.

Later, we all walked home together. Chasity managed to be somewhat low-key when she blew kisses at me, Quintin swaying close to my side. It was the perfect night.

Until I got home.

"Kita?" Chasity frowned. She was staying over at Niecy's (after the last time I brought up a sleepover to Mama, I knew it was best not to ask again) so they walked me home first. "Is your mom having a party? She didn't even invite us!"

I thought Chasity was playing. But then I saw the cars filling our driveway and lined up in front of the town house.

"Mama didn't say anything to me about a party. Maybe she let one of the neighbors borrow our parking spaces?"

Even Chasity didn't believe that lie. Neither did I.

The girls waved goodbye, wary looks on their faces, and we promised to get together the next day. I sucked in some air, trying to ready myself for whatever was going on at home.

"Kita!" A chorus of voices shouted my name like a cheer.

My mouth fell open. I shut it quickly, afraid a scream might escape.

"Mama! What is going on?" My eyes bugged and my wide-eyed expression morphed into an epic scowl of confusion.

I recognized the two women on the sofa. Robyn and Tiarra. Two of Mama's old running buddies. I'd never liked either one of them. Each held an open can of something with alcohol in it. A woman sitting on the floor was peeking around their legs and also held a can, too. I didn't recognize her.

Mama tossed her head back and let out a howling laugh. She was holding the same kind of can as the rest of them. "I told y'all. She think she's my mama." Turning to me, fake smile in place, she said, "You don't have to be so serious all the time. You don't want me going out so I'm having some friends over. Is that okay with you, *Mom?*!" She said "Mom" in this exaggerated way that made all of them burst out laughing again.

I bit down on my lips and moved as fast as I could with my book bag and gym bag and headed up the stairs.

The woman sitting on the floor called out to me. "You look beautiful in your twirl costume," she said. She pushed to her feet and moved toward me. Her eyes held a look different from the others' glassy-eyed mean girl expressions. Her eyes weren't quite sad, but maybe understanding. "I'm Hillary, by the way."

"Hi," I said. "And thank you."

She looked like she wanted to take another step closer, to say something. I didn't give her time. I disappeared up the stairs leaving another flood of laughter chasing my heels.

Lamar snored like a baby bear inside his bedroom, curled on one side, bare feet sticking out from under the cover. Lilli, on the other hand, sat bone straight in her bed, arms crossed over her little body.

I was so startled to see her sitting like that, I took a step back. "Were you waiting for me?" I asked.

"Mama is mean!" she said. She didn't answer my question.

I shrugged my bag off my shoulder, then sat on the pullout sofa to take off my marching boots. Fresh air felt cool on my hot feet. Stalling. When I finally looked at her, I tried to make her smile.

"She's not mean, just goofy!" I stuck out my tongue, stretching my face like I wanted to lick my eyebrow. A truly silly face. Lilli didn't laugh. She didn't even smirk.

"She is mean," my little sister insisted. She leaned closer, as though spies had placed microphones in the hall. "Mama pinched Lamar tonight when he cried about something."

I pulled back like I'd been slapped. Mama was usually so good with Lamar, and he was good with her. Why would she pinch him?

But I didn't want Lilli to be worrying about all that. "Here, help me with these buttons, Lil. Be gentle." She stood on her bed and slowly undid the buttons and hooks on the back of my dance costume.

"She's going to go back to the way she was before. Just wait and see!" Lilli sounded like some old grandma. And with that sleep bonnet on her head, she looked like the granny in "Little Red Riding Hood." Did that make Mama the Big Bad Wolf?

I shrugged out of the shiny leotard and wrapped myself in my robe.

"Look, Lilli, ease up. Mama deserves to have her friends over. She deserves to have fun, too." Lilli's little lip began to wobble and she looked away.

Part of me believed what I was saying—Mama did have a right to have a good time. The problem was our mama didn't seem like she knew how to end the party. Could this time be different?

I sighed. "It's getting late. I'm going to take a shower. Why don't I tuck you in?"

"No!" Lilli yelled, pulling up the covers herself and burrowing underneath them until the silk of her bonnet disappeared.

I couldn't do anything but head toward the bathroom.

Lilli was asleep when I got out of the shower. Thank goodness for that, at least.

The sounds of Mama's laughter wafted up the stairs, making my stomach tighten.

I hope you're wrong, Lilli. I hope you're wrong!

(**21**)

MY FACE WAS LOCKED in a scream.

Fiery shades of orange and red, tinged with charcoal and blue, leapt from my scalp.

Nobody would listen. I was being ignored. I was tired of it.

The muscles in my neck were locked. My chin was thrust toward the sky. My anger was the fire I'd spent my whole life throwing water on, only now it was burning out of control.

It was my self-portrait. My art project. Mr. Sanders had assigned it earlier this week. I'd been working on something else, something safer, less angry, but today blew open something inside me. I'd grabbed my art supplies and just . . . let it out. Hours passed. Muscles and tendons wound tightly in my neck, shoulders. Not from tension. From overuse. Fingers and hands. Charcoal, marker, and paint bled from my fingertips to my elbows.

I looked sooty and bruised.

Lilli had been right all along. Mama hadn't been simply blowing off steam and having some friends over. She'd been gearing up to become more and more reckless.

As soon as I walked in from practice today, she told me she was going out with her "girls," and would probably spend the night at Robyn's.

"Mama! What about the kids?" I'd snapped, not even caring if she got mad or not.

"Look, Kita. I already cooked dinner. They've already eaten."

I looked in the kitchen—which was a wreck, by the way—and saw the leftovers of chicken nuggets and frozen french fries.

"Mama, what about a vegetable? They can't eat like this every day."

"Then you feed them! Cook a full seven-course meal if you like. I don't care. Now get out of my way. I'm going out with my friends!"

It was like I was the grown-up fighting with *my* teenage daughter. And I wasn't even a teenager myself yet! Dealing with her was exhausting.

Mama slammed the door behind her, leaving me, Lilli, and Lamar alone.

After all that, I figured we could use a way to take our minds off things. I took Lamar and Lilli to the little neighborhood park. At least I didn't have a show the next day. No football. An away week.

Still, I had other things on my mind—school projects coming due, a big performance next week, and then there was the trip to the aquarium tomorrow. All I'd wanted to do when I got home was eat, shower, and take a nap before doing some homework.

I hadn't planned to stay out long, but Lamar didn't want to leave. As usual.

I'd just about talked him into it when a couple of older kids walked up to my brother and started picking on him.

"What's up, fat man!" said one. The other dude was *ha-ha-ha*-ing it up.

The first dude asked, "Why his head so big!" Lilli stood her little-self up and said to those boys:

"Don't you have something better to do? Leave him alone!"

"Shut up, you little troll doll!" the taller boy said. I was on the swings, getting ready to put a stop to it, when my brother's face clouded over with storm clouds.

"Don't be mean," said Lamar. He had been sitting in a sand pile. I'd jumped off the swings knowing the first boy pushed his luck too far.

Lilli walked right up to him and slapped him dead in the face. She had a metal shovel. I had asked her not to bring that thing. She'd stashed it in the wagon I used to bring Lamar up the street, along with our other stuff.

It was time to go. Those idiot boys took off, one with a nose-bleed. *That's what he gets.*

But Lamar didn't handle change well. His school called it "transitioning," which was how they described going from one place or activity to the next.

Leaving was already going to be hard. Leaving after a fight was a disaster. He raged, whined, cried, stomped all the way to the town house. Even when I offered to pull him in the wagon, he was all out of sorts.

I'd left the AC blasting. The house was cool, and the air smelled clean like Pine-Sol and a little lemon-scented cleaner. My two favorite smells in a house.

"I can order pizza," I announced, feeling guilty. I was as bad as Mama, trying to soothe them with fast foods. But sometimes you had to work with what you had. "But you can't eat pizza with sand in your butts. It'll make you sick!"

Lamar started yelling.

"I DON'T WANT NO PIZZA! I DON'T WANT A BATH! I DON'T WANT YOU TO TALK TO ME 'CAUSE YOU'RE A STUPID HEAD!" A stupid head? Me and Lilli looked at each other. That was a new one. Then he shoved me—hard.

"Lamar!" I said, feeling the breath rush out of me. He never got physical like that with me. What happened back in June, when I'd hit my head on the counter, had been an accident. I'd tripped. This was intentional. And Lamar wasn't much smaller than me these days.

It took a little begging, but I finally got him to come upstairs for bath time. "Lilli goes first. Then it's your turn. Okay?"

His large head drooped, and he trudged up the steps behind us. He did okay, playing by himself in the hallway while Lilli bathed. That is, until he stretched out on the floor outside the bathroom door, kicking the walls and punching the air with his fists.

"Please, Lamar. You can have extra pepperoni and . . ." I leaned over him, about to tickle his tummy, which was peeking from under his shirt.

Lamar sat straight up, fast. His forehead crashed right into the bridge of my nose. Blood spurted across the wall like I'd been shot. Then I passed out.

~~

When I came to, I found Lilli slick with bathwater, holding her monkey robe closed with one little hand while laying her bath towel over my eyes with the other. My face throbbed. My nose didn't feel broken when I touched it, but my face was bleeding. I was a bloody mess.

"Kita, you all right?" my little sister said. I blinked several times. The scented bubble bath suds in the towel were beginning to sting my eyes. Lilli's eyes were huge and round. Tears rolled down her face.

Seeing me like that must've scared her to death. "I'm all right, Lilli, don't worry." I hugged her and she sobbed against my neck, tears mixing with the sweat still on my skin from the park. Hiccupping, she continued, "I didn't know what to do, Kita. I didn't know what to do."

"You did good, Lilli. You did good." That was when I noticed Lamar. He was having a different kind of spell. Much as I hated his rages and fits, this one terrified me even more. He had closed his eyes and was rocking back and forth like he was in a trance.

"I did bad. I did bad," he mumbled over and over. *I did bad. I did bad. I did bad. I did bad. I did bad.*

"No, Lamar, it's okay. See? I'm okay." He was not convinced and from the way I looked, I understood why. Probably the sight of me all bloody and Lilli shivering and sobbing didn't help.

"Lilli, why don't you get your jammies on?" She sniffled and walked herself to our bedroom.

Using a fresh towel, I cleaned my face with cool water. I walked back in the hallway to find Lamar still rocking and mumbling. "Hey," I said gently. I reached out my hand to rub his arm. "Mar-Mar, it's okay. Kita is okay. You're not bad." Tears stung my eyes and I took Lamar into my arms, holding him close. "Never let anyone tell you you're bad, okay? You're perfect just the way you are. I love you so, so much. Never forget that."

Lamar didn't answer, but he did calm down, and that felt like answer enough.

"I'm a shark!" His voice was shy, his eyes hopeful. "Swim-swim, swim-swim."

I let out a sigh. "Yes, baby, you're a shark. *Grr!*" I growled, showing my teeth. When he laughed it wasn't mean. He was happy again. I'd play shark all day to make that kid smile!

When Lilli came back out in her pj's, we led him to the bathroom. I helped him undress. Lilli kept her face turned away so she wouldn't see him naked.

I never wound up ordering the pizza. We were all so exhausted that by the time Lamar finished his bath, we were falling over with sleepiness.

It was after one in the morning when I woke and went to the bathroom. I looked at myself in the mirror. My nose was swollen; my eyes were puffy. And I hurt.

Before I even made it to my room, poor Lamar started screaming. His night terrors. Social services told Mama once his

141

insurance would pay for a part-time home health-care worker. She said no. Said *she* could handle him.

Really, Mama didn't want them here because she was scared they'd report her.

I rocked Lamar back and forth in the dark. My fists clenched as the sickening slurps of the shark grew stronger in my mind— not Lamar's playful shark, but the one that couldn't stop trying to destroy me.

One fun fact about sharks I'd learned in Mr. Gavin's class: Mama sharks didn't stick around to raise their young. They just popped them out and left them with their siblings to raise each other. Tired and angry as I felt, a bitter laugh bubbled up.

Maybe it wasn't me who was Shark Teeth, maybe it was Mama.

Sometimes I just hated her. It was awful feeling like that. Nobody wanted to be the kind of person who hated their mama. But sometimes I did. I really, truly hated her.

(**22**)

NIECY MET UP WITH me the next morning. Sean and Saint, the two boys on the dance team, came, too. "Girl, what happened to your eye?!" Niecy asked. Soon, all three of them were fussing over me. I waved them all off.

"It's fine, it's fine. I was roughhousing with my sibs last night and things got a little out of hand," I lied. Niecy didn't believe me, I could tell, but she didn't say anything.

Once we made it to school, Sean lightly applied a little concealer and powder to cover up my bruise. "Now you'll be looking fine in the glow of the aquarium!"

Ugh, the field trip. I'd almost forgotten with all the drama last night—not to mention the lack of sleep.

Buses sat huffing and puffing in the school's rear parking lot. I was about to drop my head, as though praying. Maybe I was praying. I felt a light tap on my sleeve. Quintin was smiling at me.

"Hey, I didn't know you had Mr. Gavin, too," he said.

"Oh, yeah, I have his fifth period."

"Dang, I wish we were in the same class. At least we still get to field-trip together. Do you, uh, want to sit together on the bus?" The stupid blushing seemed to touch every inch of skin I had. A warm, tingling feeling filled my belly.

"Okay," I said, not exactly looking at him.

"Oh man, just noticed your eye! Does it hurt?" he asked.

I shook my head. "Right now," I said, "I'm doing a lot better."

Buses and school kids swirled around the entrance to the aquarium like confetti. An explosion of color and noise. Lilli and Lamar would have had a ball here. The thought caused me to cringe.

I'd felt myself getting stiff during the bus ride. I really wasn't trying to be a part of a *Jaws* sequel.

"What's the matter?" Quintin asked me.

Dang! He'd noticed. I'd been so worried about a thousand things—would he look at my teeth again; would I do or say something that he'd think was weird; did my breath smell okay?

He didn't say anything. I sat next to the window, and he turned around in the aisle goofing with his boys.

Still, as soon as I spotted the banner Enter the Great White Habitat, I'd tensed up.

"Not crazy about sharks," I mumbled as we inched our way off the bus. He gave me an energetic shoulder bump. This time when I looked at him, he reminded me of a floppy-eared puppy. I laughed.

He laughed, too.

Somehow that pushed some of my tension away.

For the next hour or so, Mr. Gavin led us around, discussing the scientific stuff no one cared about. Instead, my fellow students

144

were racing to take selfies in front of certain statues or displays. Okay, Quintin and I did it, too.

Younger kids from elementary schools, probably, played in splash pools. A scream leapt into the air, causing me to jump. Quintin caught me, held me for a second. My heart swelled with . . . *something*. I was in that Netflix romantic comedy again. Smiling into the sunshine.

"As soon as we finish our lunch," Mr. Gavin announced, "we're heading for the most amazing aspect of our trip. Take notes. We're heading to see the sharks!"

I couldn't see my face, but based on how Quintin looked at me, I knew my already pale brown complexion had gone even paler. I balled my hands into fists. My lips felt numb.

He reached down and gathered my fingers into his hand and gave a little squeeze. When lunch ended, everyone migrated into a line behind Mr. Gavin and the aquarium guide. Quintin squeezed my fingers and smiled at me once more before following the group. After a big exhale, I followed.

We were engulfed in a belly of glass. Transparent walls held back the flow of tons of water.

And sharks.

The entire world was made of blue-and-silvery colors that painted every inch of the space. *Rainbow Fish* come to life. Everyone pushed to get closer and closer to the glass. I was helplessly squished too close to the tank.

"Kita!" Quintin called. When I looked up, a camera flashed. His phone. He waved me over.

"See why you don't have any reason to worry?" he said. He held out his phone and showed me the picture.

It was me, almost in complete shadow. Behind me was the biggest, meanest-looking shark, realer than anything I'd ever pictured in my nightmares.

At first, I wanted to scream, to cry, to run away. How had I wound up here, nearly in the mouth of the beast? But Quintin kept smiling, kept looking at the photo.

"See?" he said. "It's in there and you're out here and you're perfectly safe. You're okay."

He was right. I smiled at him, and he grinned at me, and I let out a big breath of air. When I looked at Mr. Gavin, he was like a little kid at his own birthday party. For the first time since I'd joined his class, I really listened when he explained about sharks.

My whole life, I'd only seen them as predators. Man-eaters. Big, bad fish.

However, he broke it down for us:

Sharks helped the ocean maintain a healthy ecosystem. If they didn't eat the animals beneath them in the food chain, the ocean would overpopulate with those animals. That would affect something called "biodiversity." Sharks made it possible for the coral reefs to stay healthy, too.

When he put it that way, sharks didn't seem as bad as I'd always believed. It was just nature, the circle of life, that made them the way they were. Maybe it was unfair to blame sharks for the weird, slimy, crushed feeling that took over me sometimes.

Maybe.

Still, when we stopped in the gift shop on the way out, I found the perfect thing for Lamar—a plastic toy shark. I stared at it, squelching the momentary fluttering heart. It's only a toy, I told myself. I wasn't afraid—well, I wasn't *as* afraid.

Was that improvement?

～〜

We made it back to school by the end of last period. Quintin and I sat together on the bus home, too.

When Niecy found me at my locker, she was grinning.

"What?" I asked.

"Your face is all blushy pink with love!" She made kissy sounds at me. I threw a rolled pair of socks at her.

"Shut up!"

She made me tell her all about the trip to the aquarium—and Quintin.

I was picking up my bag when a magazine fell out. Niecy snatched it up before I could grab it.

"A home design magazine?" She let out a bark of laughter. "Girl, you planning your love shack for you and Quintin?"

"Give it back!" I launched myself in Niecy's direction. For a girl with curvy hips, Niecy was light on her feet. We got to cutting up, laughing our heads off. I tried again to get my magazine back. I'd checked it out of our library—thought it might be fun to look through on the bus before Quintin asked to sit with me.

"Niecy, if you tear up my magazine . . . I'll tell!"

"Oooh! Please don't tell on me, I'm so scared," she sang out, not sounding scared at all.

I tried a few more times to grab the magazine. Chasity popped up the way she did sometimes.

"Hey, Chas! Catch!" Niecy yelled.

At that point, we were all laughing like total idiots. I tripped over my bag and went flying across the room.

The door opened just before I could crash into it.

Miss Kadejah caught me mid-skid. The magazine dropped, hitting her in the head.

"Oh boy!" I said.

She reached out to me, then pulled me to my feet. She touched the top of her head. The magazine lay on the floor between us. I bent to pick it up.

My legs were shaking. Hands too.

Chas and Niecy stood frozen. Ice sculptures. Miss Kadejah didn't say anything, only held out her hand for the magazine. I was turning purple with embarrassment. I handed it to her and felt myself cringe. My gaze drifted over to Niecy without moving my body much. Talk about feeling your heart in your throat.

When I finally got the nerve look at Miss Kadejah, I was shocked. She was thumbing through the home improvement magazine.

"I've got this copy," she said. "Are you into home design?"

"Um, yes. I mean, I do. Like watching decorating shows. I saw this magazine in the school library, so I checked it out." The words tumbled out in a fast flurry. What I didn't need was Niecy and Chas telling the assistant principal that I was fake decorating a nonexistent love shack for me and a boy. Even if the boy was Quintin and he was beautiful.

She smiled then, Miss Kadejah. Then she raised her head and looked the way people do when they get a sudden idea.

"Girls," she said, looking at all of us, "I'm thinking of going out for coffee and dessert. It's a Friday and I'm in the mood for a little treat. Who wants to join me?" Her laugh sounded like music.

All three of us shot our hands up. Then Chas lowered hers and frowned. "Uh-oh, I can't. I have to go home. I promised my mom I'd watch my little brother for a few hours."

I flinched. It took all my strength not to ask her if she was sure her mama was coming back. Instead, I chewed my top lip. Miss Kadejah said Niecy and I had to contact our parents and get permission.

"I need to either speak to them or see a text from them saying it's okay," she said. "Got it?"

We did.

I sent Mama a text saying I was going out after school. I did not put it in the form of a question. Her answer:

Ok

~~

I'd never been to the Beanie before. Mama didn't like coffee. And I'd never been any place outside of school with a teacher, let alone an AP.

We got our drinks—mine was a banana and strawberry smoothie.

Miss Kadejah got something called a cappuccino; Niecy got a white mocha with extra whipped cream on top. A table opened up by the window, overlooking the street.

"Let's sit there," Miss Kadejah said.

She took a sip from her cup. She looked out the window, too, for a while without saying anything. Me and Niecy did the same. I did a little shrug and tried to hold back a nervous giggle.

It felt so grown-up and different from my normal life. Downtown, sitting in a café drinking a smoothie. My insides felt fizzy and light. I wasn't used to that but I liked it.

"So. How are you girls doing?" Miss Kadejah asked.

Niecy jumped in first and I thanked goodness for my loud-mouthed friend.

"I'm good, Miss K. I love dancing and twirling. I'm learning so much and one day, when they're doing a biography on my life, my time as a twirler will make me look like I was always amazing!"

Both Miss Kadejah and I looked at each other, then burst out laughing. Niecy laughed, too.

"And how about you, Miss Kita? I noticed you had a bit of a bruise. You doing all right?" The way she asked, she tried to keep her voice light and soft, like she was asking if my smoothie was okay. Only, her eyes showed how serious she was.

"Yeah, I'm good. Just got a little too rough playing with my siblings." The lie sounds more convincing the second time.

"Ah, you're lucky. I was an only child. Didn't have any siblings to scuffle with," she said.

We all laughed at that.

Miss Kadejah pulled out the magazine and slapped it on the table. "Now I need to know what kind of taste you all are working with." The three of us flipped through the pages and started pointing to rooms we wished we had.

"I think this kitchen is amazing!" I said, flipping the page and showing a beautiful, white kitchen. Without thinking, I looked at my AP and asked, "What does your kitchen look like? I'll bet it's gorgeous!"

She smiled. "I do love my kitchen. Though it's never quite as neat and tidy as that one!"

We drank more of our drinks. Niecy pointed out the most ridiculously over-the-top rooms and me and Miss Kadejah laughed and laughed.

"Me and Niecy are going to live next door to each other—"

"Niecy and I," Miss Kadejah corrected.

"Right. Niecy and I plan to live next door to each other when we grow up," I said.

"If that's true," Niecy said, pooching her lips and giving us a little neck roll, "then me and Kita will be living in L.A. and doing it up big!"

"Kita and I," Miss Kadejah said again. She took another sip from her cup. "'Niecy and I.' I want you girls to practice using proper English. When the person speaking is doing the action, use 'I' when referring to yourself." She smiled again and made her eyebrows bounce.

Niecy immediately turned to me and said, dramatically, "Will

Sharkita and I join the drama club in the spring? Will we star in the spring production?"

Using my best TV announcer voice, I responded:

"Niecy and I will not be starring in the spring production because I will not be joining the drama club."

We were all laughing. I had feelings in my belly that I wasn't used to. Warm, happy. Being a twirler had begun giving me that feeling more and more. Being around Quintin, too. I felt joy, but a shadow hovered around me. Like a warning that this wouldn't last forever.

Mama.

Niecy and Miss Kadejah were chitchatting like girlfriends lunching at the beach. Miss Kadejah told us how she'd gotten the job here in Grove City so fast that she still had barely unpacked yet.

She laughed, tossing her head back. It made her look younger, prettier. More like a person and not someone who could crush you by being disappointed in you—or send you to detention. I found myself laughing, too.

"This feels nice," Miss Kadejah said. "Like we're three single ladies out for an afternoon. You girls make me feel young, connected. Thank you!"

Of course, Niecy couldn't help being Niecy.

"Hey, that first day when Chasity asked you why you had a white lady name, you said it was because you were married. But you just called yourself 'single.' Did you get divorced?"

Boundaries, Niecy. Please!

Miss Kadejah told us about her husband. Mr. Sapperstein had passed away three years earlier. "He had . . ." She cleared her throat. "An illness. I was finishing my PhD and he was starting his residency in medical school when he got sick."

She drew in a deep breath and blew it out. Niecy and I exchanged looks and Niecy's face said, *How was I supposed to know?*

Niecy said, "I'm so sorry, Miss Kadejah. I mean to . . ."

"No, no don't worry, sweetheart," she said. "Jason was funny and witty. He loved cartoons and watching football while lifting weights. He was the smartest person I knew. And I'm glad you asked. I like talking about him and I don't get to do it enough, so thank you."

She told us other stuff about herself and her life before and after her husband died.

I liked talking to her. Mama used to talk to me like that. Way, way back. Before Lamar was even born. We still lived with Granny back then. Mama would talk to me, tell me her problems. I always wanted to help. Always tried to help. Back then, she would tell me she didn't have a lot of girlfriends because they were all off at college. Being free because they didn't have babies or responsibilities.

The memory of Mama talking to me that way, how she left me feeling that if it wasn't for me being born, maybe she could have gone to college and been happy with her friends. A flicker of anger replaced the sadness that usually came with that memory.

Miss Kadejah gave me a look, then said, "We all deserve to be happy, girls. Remember that. Life has a way of telling us—women especially—that what we want can wait. You deserve to find happiness every day. But don't forget, you have the power to bring happiness, too."

Niecy's phone beeped. She looked at the screen, then looked up.

"Mama is going to pick me up from here. She has some errands to run tonight and doesn't want me home alone the whole time. Is it okay if I go wait for her outside?" she asked.

"Come on. We'll wait with you," Miss Kadejah said. She paid our bill and we thanked her for our drinks. Once Mrs. Hall rolled up and took Niecy away, Miss Kadejah said she'd take me home. A worry struck me in the forehead.

If she drove me home, she wouldn't want to go inside and meet Mama, would she?

It was after five o'clock. I hadn't realized it was so late. What if Mama wasn't there? What if the kids were alone?

I was holding my breath as we rode. The stereo was playing music I thought I knew but wasn't sure.

Happy to have anything to distract me, I asked, "Who's that?" pointing at the controls.

"That's Mary J. Blige. *My Life.* I've been listening to this album since I was your age."

Of course, I didn't mean to, but since I didn't have good sense, I instantly pulled a face and squinted like Niecy, saying, "Really? Since you were my age?"

She glanced over, then barked out a laugh.

"Even assistant principals were once twelve. Back then . . ." She let her words drop off. Her eyes clouded over for a second.

"Well, back then, life felt tough. When both your mom and dad are educators, expectations are high. Bullies don't like smarty pants. And I had my first heartbreak. Through it all, it was like Mary understood. She had that effect on women from twelve to thirty-five and up. Anyway, we can listen to something else if you'd like."

"No, I like it. I know who Mary J. Blige is. I just never heard that song," I said.

Talking to her made me feel good. I knew I'd never want to disappoint her. Even if most of what she knew of me was a lie. I didn't want her to ever know about the real me—the one with the horrible shark-swallowed crushing feeling in my chest.

I was saying goodbye and thank you, sliding out of the SUV, when I saw her looking past me. That was when I turned. And ended up face-to-face with Mama.

(**23**)

I WAS TOO SURPRISED to see Mama beside me to make a sound. Staring into her eyes, I wondered what she was going to do or say.

Dr. Sapperstein must not have picked up on the tension because she just said, "Hello! You must be Sharkita's mom! I'm the coach of her majorette squad, as well as the assistant principal, Dr. Kadejah Sapperstein."

She was out of her SUV and right there, talking with Mama before I could blink an eye. I felt the two of them seeing each other. From Mama's side, here's this woman, tall and curvy with skin color like a vanilla latte, glittery diamonds on her fingers, expensive-looking clothes.

And here Mama was, a petite, beautiful woman with wavy black hair pulled to one side in a ponytail holder. Could this really be happening? I wanted to shrink into the pavement. The bruised area of my face began to itch.

"Don't touch it too much," said Mama, pulling my hand away when I reached up to scratch. "You'll only irritate it."

Mama turned on her hundred-watt smile and faced Dr. Sapperstein, finally accepting her outstretched hand. "So nice to meet you, I'm Brittany." Mama was using her extra-fancy white lady voice. The same voice she used on the lady at Duke Energy when our bill was overdue, back before I took over paying the bills.

The two of them said their how-dos and torched the sky with the wattage of their beaming smiles. "Sharkita is a wonderful girl. She works so hard at school and is an excellent twirler," Dr. Sapperstein said.

"Oh yes," said Mama, rounding out her vowel sounds for extra fanciness, "she's a lovely girl. I don't know what I'd do without her."

Oh, so I'm lovely now?

It went on like that for a few more minutes. I was stuck in place in this alternate dimension lit only by white-hot smiles and unwanted praise.

Just when I thought I couldn't take it anymore, tapping the hood of her SUV twice, Miss Kadejah said, "Well, I'd better be going. Thanks for letting me take your daughter out for a little treat this afternoon, Ms. Lloyd. I love spending extra time with the twirlers." As soon as the words left her mouth, I knew Mama would correct her.

"Mrs. Ambrose," Mama said. When Dr. Sapperstein gave her a look, Mama went on, "I was married for a while. After Kita was born."

"Of course, Mrs. Ambrose. So nice to have met you," Dr. Sapperstein said.

"And you, as well," replied the creature inhabiting Mama's body.

Then Dr. Sapperstein turned to me and added, "Sharkita, I'm always here to talk. Be careful from now on with your little brother and take care of that eye! Our team needs you. Ciao!"

She climbed back into the gleaming black SUV and rolled away. Mama and I walked inside, silently. But she played with the tiny braids dangling past my neck that Chas's sister had done the previous week.

"The only thing to do about that eye is to keep a little K cream on it; and maybe massage it," Mama said absently.

I blinked. When she saw my surprise, she shrugged. "I was a majorette, too. When you're learning those tosses, you get hit in the face sometimes."

She walked ahead, up the steps, but I stood still on the bottom step. I said, "Mama, you know I didn't get hit by a baton, don't you? Lamar did this. He didn't do it on purpose, but he had a really tough time this weekend with you gone."

Mama turned back, looked at me over her shoulder, then gave me this stupid, condescending smile, like she wanted to say, "No big deal."

Instead, she said, "If it's causing you pain, I'll make you an ice bag to take to your room. Keep it on your face while you study. Dinner will be ready shortly."

There was a heavy pounding in my chest. Really, really, really couldn't take more of her attitude. Was she kidding me? I sucked in air, felt myself wobble, then climbed the steps, eager to go upstairs and leave her to manage *her* children for the rest of the evening.

Mama fried the chicken that night and I did the laundry. She took care of Lamar and I finally climbed out of my funk long enough to help Lilli.

My little sister asked, "So, how much longer?" I knew exactly what she meant.

"*Shh!* Lil, be quiet, she'll hear you," I said. My head had begun to throb again. Pressure filled my skull from ear to ear. What I didn't need was pressure from a five-year-old who acted like she was thirty-five. "It's like you want her to fail!"

I cringed. Had I just said that? It was like I was using my mouth but Mama's voice was coming out.

My tone felt particularly harsh inside the hushed tones of the soft, pink room.

Lilli didn't back down. She'd sharpened her own razor blades. "I don't care if she hears me." Defiance painted her beautiful little face—looking so much like Mama.

"She is trying, Lil," I said, my tone pleading.

With her arms crossed over her tiny body and jaw clenched, baby girl wasn't having it.

"I don't like this, Kita. I wish we had a full-time mama. A mama who wants to be a mama every day, not just sometimes."

I let out a sigh, but she wasn't finished. Her little bow-shaped lips were pulled tight like drawstrings. Her penetrating glare was more than I could take. I honestly couldn't stand how easily I let Mama whisk me away on her magic carpet, again and again.

I wished to God I'd been as strong, as smart as Lilli when I was her age. I pulled her into a hug and held on.

What I whispered in her ear was supposed to sound like encouragement, but to me it was more of a prayer:

Please, please, please give Mama a chance to show she can take care of us. That she wants to. Please!

24

NEW MAMA RETURNED FOR a while. She stayed on the right track for a week. We fell into our groove again. I came home from practice, checked the bank account, paid bills, daydreamed about Quintin—that part was new. It was like drinking a magic potion.

On Friday, Mama even brought Lilli and Lamar to the football game. I was so nervous. It meant so much for me to have them there.

We marched in formation, silvery uniforms catching the fading sunlight, us shining like mini stars twinkling into the dusky hours. Me. Twirling my baton, the one Mama gave me, and feeling such a lightness in my heart as I tossed that *thang*, caught it, and did a twirl. Dancing. Catching the beat and working it hard, in rhythm with the rest of the team. We were perfect, like a sunset bleeding into the night.

I wanted that feeling to last forever.

Later, I saw Quintin—I'd been seeing a lot of him lately, talking to him more and more. Even when I didn't tell the whole truth, it felt good to have somebody other than Niecy or Dr. Charles to talk to. Maybe I didn't need professional help. Maybe what I needed was more friends.

Texting with a boy made you feel different. I wasn't getting all goofy-headed about it. I'd seen how Mama acted with men, and I wasn't about that life. But I knew Quintin was different.

And I was different, too.

One night he texted:

Why Ur eyes so sad sometimes

How do you answer something like that? My eyes were sad? Really? I'd never noticed. Or maybe I had, but just thought that was how they were supposed to look.

Being seen like that felt exciting and terrifying. I rolled myself into a ball and listened for the sneaky sound of wine bottles being placed in the bottom of the recycle bin. I pictured Quintin's face, his smile, and his eyes that were not at all sad. But I did not answer his question. I fell asleep holding the phone, thinking, *I deserve to be happy, too!*

But that's the thing about happiness. It doesn't stick around long, at least when Mama is in control of it. Mama took off again the next day after the game. It was Tuesday before we saw her again, breezing in like she'd only been gone a minute. I was mad enough to fight her. Lilli looked at me like, "Told you she don't want to be here."

I'd had enough. I wanted to do something—anything to get Mama into trouble, make her be better.

And I almost had my chance.

That week, Mr. Sanders handed us back our self-portraits. A big "A+! See me after class" was written on the grading sheet attached to mine.

"Dang, Kita!" Chasity said, looking over to see my work. "I knew you were good, but that's like REAL GOOD."

I couldn't even thank her—all I could think about was the "see me after class" Mr. Sanders had written. What had I done wrong? My stomach was in knots the whole rest of the class. I was practically shaking by the time the bell rang.

Chasity waved goodbye to me as I made my way up to Mr. Sanders.

"Ah, Miss Lloyd," he said. "Thanks for coming to see me."

"Is everything okay?"

"Oh, yes, yes, yes," he said. "Miss Lloyd, your collage—the self-portrait—it was breathtaking. So much passion, so much emotion. I asked for a picture of the real you, and you did that!"

That wasn't what I'd expected. "Oh, uh, thank you. I—I . . . uh, I'm really happy with how it turned out."

The truth was, when I was doing it, my insides were churning, fighting for the chance for me to show a piece of myself. Show that I was more than long legs and bad teeth. With everything else going on, I hadn't really thought about it that much—how other people might react to it. It was like once I got that feeling out, I felt better. I was good. I'd thought that was all, but apparently it wasn't.

"I showed your piece to Dr. Sapperstein. She was impressed,

as well," Mr. Sanders said. Then he cleared his throat. "She'd like to see you in her office. Nothing's wrong . . ." he rushed to say, then let his words drip away.

"Oh, uh, okay. Should I go now?" I asked, voice squeaking.

"I think now is best," he said. "I'm sure you won't be long. She'll write you a late slip for your next class, if you need."

"Okay," I said. My legs felt cramped together, like I was trying not to pee. I silently walked out of the room.

What could Kadejah—I mean, Dr. Sapperstein—want to say to me about my self-portrait?

It took less than two minutes to reach the front offices but it felt like the longest walk of my life. That creeping, tightening sensation crawled up my body, slithering around my abdomen. Squeezing. I knew something bad was coming.

"Come in," called a familiar voice when I finally knocked on the assistant principal's door. My feet felt stuck, but I pushed open the door. Dr. Sapperstein looked up and I met her gaze. You know how you see someone and instantly you know they're making a decision about you? A decision that shows in their eyes? That's how it felt. I could see her seeing me and thinking something—but I had no idea what that something was.

"Sharkita, come in!" she said, sounding light and full of joy, though her eyes looked serious.

I inched my way toward her desk and felt myself sink into a chair facing her.

When she sat, she surprised me by taking the chair next to mine.

"First, Sharkita, let me say, your self-portrait is really strong.

Exceptional, really. Who knew you were so multitalented! Tell me, what made you use that imagery to tell Mr. Sanders about yourself?"

"Um . . ."

I felt like I was in a washing machine and it was on the spin cycle. My thoughts and feelings were moving around me like a tornado. The best answer I had was a weak shrug and, "I dunno." Then I sat mute while heat rushed into my pale brown cheeks, igniting them. I ducked my head even lower.

Dr. Sapperstein was quiet for a moment, then she cleared her throat.

"I just wanted to check in with you, Kita. Those were some pretty powerful emotions you were creating with." The concern on her face was filled with warmth. Almost motherly. A real kind of mother, not like mine. I almost couldn't stand her looking so concerned. I was fine. I was okay. I'd be okay.

"No, ma'am, nothing's wrong. I'm fine," I said, my voice dusty and dry, my head down, my eyes studying the carpet.

She reached over, touched my wrist, held on to it. "Sharkita, do you know why you're here? In my office?"

I shook my head.

"I'm concerned, Kita. I noticed lately you've been more tired, more distracted. Like you have something heavy weighing on your shoulders."

She noticed a lot of things, things I thought I wanted people to notice.

Now, someone was paying attention and I didn't like it.

"I'm okay, really," I said, doing my best impression of Mama when she's at her best. "Just stressed about my classes. Dr. Charles gave me some tips the other day when you set up that appointment for me. I'll try to use them more."

Miss Kadejah looked at me for a second in that way that she did, like she's seeing right through me. "Well, I'm glad you're finding the counseling sessions helpful. Dr. Charles is there to talk about anything that may be on your mind. And I hope you know I'm here for you, too."

I gave her what I hoped was a convincing smile, but I left her office that day feeling more unsure than ever. Should I have said something about Mama? Told her she'd been leaving us alone again for days at a time?

But then I thought of Lilli and Lamar, of us being separated again. And I knew I could never.

(25)

THE THING IS, THOUGH, a lot of my life was out of my control.

Even though I hadn't said anything about Mama to Miss Kadejah, there was a knock at the door the next morning.

"Orange County Sheriff's Department," came a strong female voice. Fear like nothing I'd ever known climbed on top of me and nearly rode me into the ground. It was like the good Lord heard inside my head and said, *Okay, you thinking about causing trouble? Here you go!*

Seeing them on the doorstep brought the squeezing feeling back instantly. My mouth went dry. My throat felt tight. Goopy antibiotic cream covered my fingers. I'd been applying cream to Lilli's eczema patches. I felt like an idiot standing there with my finger coated in sticky skin cream.

I looked over my shoulder at Mama. She'd staggered into the kitchen and was leaning one-sided against the sink. Lamar didn't even stop watching his program, but Lilli looked at me and I could see the dare in her eyes, challenging me. Her big, almond-shaped eyes saying, *Tell them! Tell them the truth!*

The police officer was a Black woman with her hair cut short. She was cocoa brown with eyebrows thin as razor blades.

"Miss, we got a report that there were three minors here alone. Is there an adult in the house?"

"Uh-um," I stammered, "Mama is in the kitchen, but she's not feeling . . ."

Mama came up behind me, grabbing the side of the door for support, cinching her robe around her waist. She looked almost as small and helpless as Lilli standing in front of the tall deputy lady. At least the robe was clean. I'd just washed it.

She said, "Yes, can I help you?"

"I'm Deputy Burton, Orange County Sheriff's Department," said the woman police officer. "We received a complaint, an anonymous call, that the children were home alone. May I have your name, please?"

Mama did the best she could to pull herself up tall. I could smell the minty mouthwash pouring off her breath from where I stood. She must've hit that Listerine bottle hard before she came out here.

"I'm Brittany Ambrose and I'm running late for work. I don't know who called you, but as you can see, my kids are just fine." Mama tried to step back and push the door closed, but Deputy Burton wasn't having it.

"Yes, ma'am. Would you mind if myself and Mrs. Dorothy Grieves from social services enter the premises? We just want to see the children and make sure they're all right."

Mama gave me a quick look. As hung over as I figured she was, her red eyes had all kinds of meaning in them. She swallowed hard and let the deputy and the social worker in.

"Hi, young lady, you sure are a cutie pie," the deputy said to Lilli. I rushed over and grabbed my sister before she could tell on Mama and get us in trouble. "Do you have some kind of injury there?" The deputy noted the area of my sister's back that was exposed because I'd pushed her shirt up.

"Lil, say hi to the nice police lady," I said. I grabbed her hand and she snatched it away. I gave the woman a weak smile. "She's got eczema. We're just putting cream on it for the itching. I'm helping out. Getting them . . . her ready for school."

So, we learned that lying on command was not my specialty.

The deputy flicked her eyes back and forth between us like she was trying to figure out if there was a problem, then Lamar popped up and started shooting at the people with an empty toilet paper roll from the bathroom.

"You have beautiful children, Mrs. Ambrose," said Deputy Burton. "May I speak with you over here, please? Mrs. Grieves is going to talk with the children."

She led Mama into our small kitchen, which really wasn't private since it looked right into the living room. I was staring at them, trying to figure out how to feel, when Mrs. Grieves said to me, "Sharkita, you have really grown up. You're still cute as a bug!"

I frowned. Lilli and I exchanged looks. Mrs. Grieves, balancing a folder in her lap, sat perched on the arm of a chair across from me.

"I don't know you . . . *do I?*" my voice cracked. Memories as silent and scary as sharks underwater began to surface.

Granny.

That day she'd called the cops on Mama.

A social worker came with the police.

She looked like a giant back then.

Mrs. Grieves.

Now the woman smiled, her blue-gray eyes flashing with whatever memory she was calling up at the same time. "Way back. That was long before I became a supervisor. You had to be about three years old."

Couldn't help it. I turned my face away, unable to stand it. Lilli pulled my hand and asked, "Kita? You remember her?"

I snatched my hand away. My face felt hot, my eyes close to tears.

"Not now, Lil!" I snapped, then tried to smile, to cover up. But there it was. Mrs. Grieves looked like she'd heard a million lies, and here I was about to add one more.

"I'm sorry, uh, I don't know who could've called you guys," I said.

Lilli looked at me and smirked. I was using my white girl, private school grammar.

Mrs. Grieves said, "So, there're no issues in the home?"

"Kita! Ju-ju! Ju-ju! Ju-ju!" demanded Lamar. Thank you, sweet Jesus!

"I need to get my brother some juice. I'll be right back." I sprang off the sofa and ran into the kitchen. The deputy was still talking to Mama. When I opened the fridge, I felt such a surge of relief to be away from Mrs. Grieves's knowing eyes that I almost threw up.

Boiling acid churned in my belly. I grabbed Lamar's juice and was leaving the kitchen when the officer said, "Baby girl, are you all right?"

Mama slowly turned her neck in my direction. She was a little bit behind the deputy but heat from her gaze practically set Lamar's apple juice to bubbling.

"Huh?"

The deputy said I'd made a noise, like a groan. I told her I was fine. "Really! Everything's fine!" I said, before rushing back to the living room. Mrs. Grieves had moved from the arm of the chair to where I'd been sitting beside Lilli on the sofa.

Now another wave of panic washed over me. What on earth was Lilli saying to her? I charged back in there, holding the juice out like it was radioactive.

"Here, Lamar!" My voice was too loud. Even Lamar gave me a funny look. But soon as he took his juice, his mind was off to conquer other battles.

"Are you okay, Sharkita? Lilli is telling me what good care you take of her and your brother. Are you being taken care of, sweetheart?" She sounded so sincere it was almost enough to send me into a crying fit right there. But I was working hard to hold myself together.

"Oh, everything's fine," I said, my voice too high, sounding like some kind of clown.

"Well, I—"

"Mrs. Grieves," called the deputy. She was moving away from the kitchen and back toward the front door. "I can't see any problems right now. I've spoken with Mrs. Ambrose. For now, unless you say otherwise, I can't see any reason to go further."

Mrs. Grieves stood up and nodded. She heaved a sigh that I didn't like at all. The kind of sigh that said, *Oh, don't worry. We'll be back.*

Within sixty seconds, they were back in the deputy's ride and pulling away.

Soon as they left, Mama stomped up the steps. The stomping upset Lamar, so he started snuffling. An ache climbed into my body and went straight through to my soul. Lilli pasted me with a filthy look.

"Why're you looking at me like that?" I asked, dreading the answer.

"You telling stories, Kita. You shoulda told them peoples the truth!"

If I'd known what was coming, I might have.

(26)

MAMA NEVER DID FIND out who called the county on her. Guess it didn't matter. But it scared her. Scared me, too. The next few days she was back to her New Mama routine, but even Lamar wasn't buying it anymore.

She took us shopping. Bought Lamar jeans and T-shirts, but the only clothing he'd been happy about was his new Miami Dolphins sweatshirt. She bought him a couple of games, too.

Lilli got new leggings, four dresses, a bracelet, and earrings, because her ears were pierced.

I told Mama I didn't really need anything. She bought me new shoes, anyway. A pair of white Nikes with a pretty pink swoosh. I couldn't believe it. They cost one hundred dollars. It felt weird knowing I was walking on so much money—money that could have gone toward food, bills. But man, they looked awesome on my feet. I wore them out of the store and everything.

Even though I hadn't been able to think up anything for myself and the shoes had been Mama's idea, I did ask for some cash so I could get something for someone else.

Mama gave me a couple bills and I darted into a nearby shop. A few minutes later, I returned with a shopping bag and a huge grin.

"What's that?" Lilli asked.

"It's for Niecy!" I said. Mama glanced at me and I braced myself for her to say something negative. She only smiled and gave me a little shrug.

I kept on thanking Mama all the way home, couldn't help it. She patted me on the knee and said, "Of course, honey. Can't nobody say my babies aren't taken care of now."

After she said that, when I looked down at my new shoes, it was like I was looking at somebody else's feet. Because Mama didn't actually buy these shoes for me—she bought them for everybody else to see.

I wasn't about to complain, though. The plastic bag crinkled in my grip. New Mama stuck around long enough for me to catch up on my homework and do my assignments.

Mrs. Bailey had assigned a one-page, typewritten essay or verse poem. I chose the poem—it was the kind that didn't have to rhyme. She told us to choose one of the following words as our theme:

a. Joy
b. Happy
c. Green

d. Screaming

e. Sunshine

It was a strange list of words and almost everybody in the class started complaining about it. I chose "sunshine." It was due Friday, and that morning I had set my poem on the kitchen table while I helped Lilli look for her new bracelet to wear to school.

When we went back into the kitchen, Mama was standing there, lips moving with no sound coming out. She was reading my poem.

When she looked at me, I saw something in her eyes I had never seen before—pride.

"You wrote this?" she asked.

I nodded.

Then she nodded, too.

"Kita, you're a lot smarter than you give yourself credit for. A lot smarter than I give you credit for." You could have pushed me over with a feather right then, but Mama kept talking, "No matter what nobody else say, this is good. You are good." She didn't say it with a smile or playfully—her voice was full of intensity and meaning. Like what she was saying was the most important thing ever.

She didn't try to tell me about a time when she did it better. Or try to put it down on the sly. She said it because she meant it.

"Thank you, Mama," was all I managed, but I was smiling as I moved Lilli and Lamar toward the front door to leave.

"Oh, and Kita," Mama called to me again. I turned, that stupid smile still on my face. "Come home right after your game tonight. I'm gonna need you to watch the kids."

~⁓

My mood had turned fully sour by the time I got to school. I'd been all excited about giving Niecy her gift, too. Ever since the first day of school, I'd felt guilty that she'd given me such a great gift and I'd lost track of the one I'd had for her back in the summer. (It was three of Niecy's favorite candies, including a lollipop called "Pop Star!")

Still, soon as I saw Niecy on the way to school, I thrust the bag at her and she instantly started cooing and prancing.

"Oooh! For me?" She tore into the bag and removed the item. It was one of those clapperboards movie people use before shouting, "Take One! Action!"

I tucked my lips inside, dying to know what she thought. The look on her face was everything!

"It's *The Niecy Show*, starring y'girl, Shaniece, take one!" She snapped it open and shut, open and shut.

Then she hugged me. "Thank you so much," she said. "I love it. Thank you."

We fell into step beside one another.

"Mama saw my poem this morning," I said after a few steps. My new shoes were packed in my gym bag. Didn't want to get them dirty before our game. I was going to wear them afterward while we hung out in the stands with Quintin and everybody,

"Ol' Britt has taken up reading, huh?" she said. I looked over at her and saw her grinning at me. I pushed her a little.

"Mhmm. Then she had the nerve to tell me to come right home tonight 'cause she's got somewhere to be."

I couldn't believe Mama—but then again, I could. Did she even really like my poem? Or was she just saying that to butter me up?

"Don't let her get in your head, Kita. Maybe it's time for you to push back."

Now that was a thought.

The day dragged on. A blanket of dread was draped over me. More and more, I was thinking Niecy was right. Mama had to learn that I wasn't her personal slave. Some kids had to rush home and do stuff because their parents were sick or disabled. That was one thing.

But getting treated like a puppet because your mama couldn't leave the party, that was something else.

I was ready to write the whole day off until game time. Walking into the locker room to get ready with all my teammates had a way of lifting my mood. Especially when Niecy got up to her theatrics—that spring musical couldn't come soon enough! My girl needed to *perform*! I had never really understood that part of my best friend, but after so many games, I got it now.

Once I shoved the Mama-thoughts out of my brain, everything about that evening felt like a dream. The sunset painted watery purples and grays along the horizon. Deep bass voices from men talking football undercoated the high-pitched squeals of little kids and the "hey, man, whatsups" of teens.

We stood in formation. Drum Major Paul gave his whistle eight toots, and we were on the move. Each time we performed a field show—that was what they called performing at football games—I came alive. No matter what else was going on, the energy, the lights, the sparkle, the drumbeat, all of it gave me life.

And hope.

I pointed that baton toward heaven and felt like that Poseidon dude with his giant fork. A trident, I think it was called. Instead of the hammering, fearful heart that nearly overtook me the first time, my heart now followed the eight count of the band. I had used Dr. Charles's idea of thinking about Niecy and Chasity and the others instead of focusing on myself. It helped me stay calm.

For music we went old-school this week. Something from the early two thousands—"Glamorous" by Fergie featuring Ludacris. I liked the song. Liked the way it let me sway my hips. I glanced at Niecy. She was getting it done with her solo.

I grinned at her and she grinned back.

Chasity strutted her little self up front next. She did a hip roll that brought everybody to their feet. Then the song broke down. The tubas got nasty with rhythm. The drums were pumping fire.

My solo.

Baton raised to the stars, I dropped into a pose the way Drum Major Paul had showed me. *Oo*s and "get it girls" rustled the wind. "G-L-A-M . . ." the song blared, notes turning into words. The baton, the one Mama gave me when I thought she was giving me her blessings, gleamed in the lights on the field. "O-R . . ." Bass and horn twirled my fingers and the baton sailed into the night sky, returning magnetically to my fingers . . ."O-U-S!"

The crowd exploded. And a starburst blasted inside me. I was feeling myself and it felt good. It felt great!

Then when we got off the field, I saw Quintin coming over with his crew, and I was feeling even better.

"You killed it out there, girl!" he said, that smile of his lighting me up like the ones on the field.

"Oh, thanks," I said, cheesing, too.

"Some of us are going to the Spoon after this," he said, referring to a nearby fast-food place. "Do you want to come?"

"I'm sorry I—" I automatically started to answer no, remembering Mama's final words that morning. Then I stopped. Mama was always complaining about how because she had me, she missed out on all the fun of being young—but why did that mean I had to miss out on my time? She didn't even ask me if I could watch the kids tonight. She just told me to do it. Well, I was done with her. "You know what? Yeah, I'm coming."

That got a big, loud, "YEAH, GIRL!" out of Niecy, and Quintin smiled super big.

"I'm glad you're coming," Quintin said, before pecking me on the cheek. *Oh man!* I turned a thousand shades of red. All at once, every love song in the world made sense to me. It was just a quick little brush of his lips against my skin, but it was pure magic. Niecy grabbed my arm and shot me the silliest looking OMG face. We started giggling like first graders.

All the while, I couldn't help thinking:

This is what Mama was making me miss out on. Fun. Friends. A maybe-almost boyfriend. I wasn't gonna let her take this away from me again.

But just as the thought entered my brain, my phone vibrated. Since my twirl uniform didn't have pockets, I kept my phone tucked in the top of my bra until after we were done performing. I pulled it out.

Don't forget to come right home when you're done. I'm going out.

I didn't bother responding.

A couple minutes later after finding spots in the stands to watch the game, my phone buzzed again. Wasn't worth taking it out. I knew it was Mama.

My phone went off two more times, and the buzzing somehow felt angrier each time. Finally, I told Niecy I'd be right back and went behind the bleachers.

The scent of roasted hot dogs, grilled burgers, and fried catfish curled softly in the air. That was how we did things in the grove. If Big Luther was here, there'd be a line to the parking lot for his barbecue ribs and chicken.

A sigh puffed from my chest. Multiple texts and voice mails waited for me, all from Mama. I let out another sigh and called her.

"Kita, where the hell are you?! I told you I needed you home right after your show!" It wasn't the warm Mama who complimented my poem this morning who picked up. I could almost smell this Mama's wine breath through the phone.

I hoped Lilli and Lamar were okay.

The courage I'd been working up almost left me. I automatically began biting my lip. However, when I felt Niecy on one side and Chasity on the other, I knew what I had to do.

"Mama, some friends and I are going to the Spoon after the game, okay? I still have money left over, so I'm straight." I laid it out there, just like that. No question. No asking. Just like she did to me this morning.

Silence. Then a quiet, angry voice.

"I have somewhere to go tonight, Kita. I already told you. You need to come on home," she said. Firm. Direct. I drew a breath. Not tonight, Mama. This one time, I'm going to be strong, too.

"Mama," I said, feeling the pressure building in my chest, filling my rib cage, "I want to hang out with my friends."

"Some! Some! Some!" Lamar was chanting in the background.

Lilli was singing "Over the Rainbow." It would have been funny if Mama wasn't ready to come through the phone and beat me.

"Kita! These kids are going crazy. I need to get out of here. Robyn says if I wait till after nine I'll miss happy hour." And there it is. The only reason she had to go now instead of letting me have my fun for a couple hours. Unbelievable.

"No, Mama. It's my turn," I told her. "I promise I'll be home by nine. You'll still have plenty of time to go out."

Now her voice forced razors into her words, her tone hard with sharp edges. "You listen to me, Sharkita. I can't handle all their yelling and banging around right now. Get home or I will leave them!"

Chasity squinted at me, seeing my body flinch.

"What's she saying? What's she saying?" said Niecy, her whisper coarse like sand.

My body felt like it was on fire. People my age were always

doing stuff together. It was called being young. Mama had been young once. She liked it so much she couldn't seem to let it go. But like I said to her already: it was my turn.

"Um, look, Mama, I can't do this right now. Please. Let me do this one thing. I'll be home by nine."

"Mama! Mama! Mama! Ju-ju! Ju-ju! Ju-ju!" Lamar chanted in the background.

"Kita, I swear to God—"

"Goodbye, Mama." And with that, I hung up on her.

~⁓

On the two-and-a-half block long walk to the Spoon, Quintin held my hand. I was cheesing so big that Niecy had to say, "Dang, girl! Stop smiling so hard before your jaw locks up!" I blushed, but everybody laughed. It was all good.

At least, I wanted it to be all good.

I couldn't stop thinking about Mama. Would she risk everything for happy hour? Even with the police department showing up on our doorstep? I pushed those thoughts out of my head. She was always saying I worried too much, after all, and making problems out of nothing.

Me and Quintin didn't say much as we walked along, just looked at each other, then away again. It was a good feeling.

But my phone kept *buzz-buzz-buzz*ing with reminders of Mama. Eventually, I turned it off.

Niecy kept her eyes on me. She whispered, "It's okay. Don't worry about it. You have your fun, girl."

Easier said than done.

We found a table with a sticky red vinyl tablecloth, which was soon filled with wings, hot sauce, barbecue sauce, frozen red slushies, fat homestyle french fries, and glasses of soda and water and juice. And people ranking on each other.

"Awwww, man," said Mario Houser, a drummer in the band, "Niko, you can't talk about nobody. Yo' grades in science so low, Mr. Garvin gonna' have to use a microscope to find your GPA!"

Everybody laughed. Roared. Niko snapped back. "Man, I know you ain't calling nobody dumb. Yo' daddy so dumb, he tried to study for a DNA test."

Silence.

Seconds passed.

Nothing?

Then everybody roared again and Niko, who had started to sweat, thinking his clapback had failed, grinned.

I automatically tucked my lips tightly over my teeth, not wanting my night to be ruined by someone choosing to make cracks about my shark teeth next.

Quintin leaned into me again, whispering, "Are you getting cold? I can give you my jacket."

"Thanks, but I'm good," I said.

He had no idea how good sitting so close to him, smelling him, and watching him made me feel. The vibration of his words bumped into me as they rumbled up through his chest, spilling off his lips. Just everything about him. I wished that feeling could last forever and all my life.

Eventually, though, we all had to go home and that rosy feeling started fading away.

"I'll walk you," Quintin said to me. Okay, maybe I could hold on to it for a little longer. "Trent, man, you live by Kita, right? Want to walk with us? Me, you, Kita, Niecy. Come on." Trent was a short kid with a big forehead and glasses. He got called "fivehead" a lot. But what I always liked about Trent was he seemed happy no matter what people said about him.

"I'm down wit' it, Big Q," he said. I looked at Quintin.

"Big Q?"

Now he looked embarrassed, which was good because, *really*? Big Q?

"Nobody calls me that but Trent, and he don't count!" Quintin said.

"Show a brother some love, Big Q!" Trent said, bouncing around like he was dribbling a basketball, head-fake, then a layup.

We walked along, talking about nothing. Niecy saying, "I can't wait till I'm famous and can come back here in my limo. I'm going to be a superstar!" Then she started some song from the Black version of *The Wizard of Oz* called *The Wiz*. That made me think of Lilli. Was she home alone singing "Over the Rainbow"?

"Ease on down, ease on down the ro-ooad," Niecy sang. She loved that song, which was the only reason I even recognized it.

Then Trent got to talking to Quintin about college football. Trent knew everything about football, even though he was too small to play. He talked fast, used his hands a lot. While Niecy was "acting" all the time, Trent made whatever he was talking about come alive.

184

Their voices were like background music. A few night birds called out, cars passed on the highway above our heads, and echoed beneath the overpass. But my heart was beginning to beat faster and faster. The fear started coursing through me like liquid heat.

Couldn't be sure whether I was hoping Mama was at home, or that she wasn't. I crossed my arms over my body as I walked. Mentally, I began stiffening my spine, getting myself ready.

I thought about how paralyzed and awful I felt when that shark feeling took over. I couldn't even imagine any of my friends knowing about that, let alone seeing it firsthand. I pushed the thought out of my mind.

Up ahead was the entrance to our little development. A shadow moved and something about it felt familiar. I concentrated on the inky shape. It seemed to be vibrating side to side, side to side.

Lamar.

Outside. In the dark. Looking like he just fell out of a spaceship and didn't even know what planet he was on.

"That little dude look like he has some problems, man," said Trent, cackling one of his laughs. "That's definitely a short bus situation right there!"

"Shut up, man!" Quintin said, pushing Trent in the chest.

My little brother was outside. All alone.

I didn't know or care what anybody thought, I just sprinted, throwing down my bag, baton, everything.

"Lamar! Why are you out here, baby? Where's Mama?" I was panting, kneeling in front of him, holding his face in my hands.

That was when I noticed the dark smears on his face and hands. The tracks from tears that had streaked down his cheeks.

The smell of smoke in his hair.

First look at the town house, everything appeared normal. But the smell of burning wood was unmistakable. Somewhere inside, the house was on fire.

(27)

I GRABBED LAMAR'S SHOULDERS, kneeling down so we were eye to eye. If I startled him or looked angry, he would shut down. Panic gripped my body and words came out in broken bits.

"Lamar, sweetie, where is Lilli? Is Lilli inside?" I heard Quintin say he was calling 9-1-1. I kept all my focus on my little brother.

His tiny eyes were round as marbles. Fear crawled all over me. But he was afraid, too. His body was shaking. He kept shifting side to side.

"Lilli, gone. Can't find Lilli," he mumbled, like he was far, far away.

"Where's Mama?" I said, standing again, and looking wildly around the streets, like maybe Mama was hiding in the bushes.

But Lamar kept repeating the same thing: "Lilli gone. Mama gone. Kita gone. By myself."

Trent said, "Dang! Sorry, Kita. I didn't know that was your

brother, I have a cousin like . . ." but I wasn't listening to him. The blood rushing into my ears roared. I couldn't hear anything except the terrible, frantic pace of my heartbeat. A crushing weight inside me threatened to break me in half.

Mama, how could you do this?

"Can y'all help me with him? My sister is missing. I need someone to stay with Lamar while I look for Lilli," I said.

"But," Quintin looked confused, "where's your mom? She should be around here, right? She wouldn't just leave two little kids at home. Shouldn't we call the police? She could be hurt or missing or something?"

His eyes were about as big as Lamar's. He had taken a few steps back, like he didn't want any of this unfolding tragedy to get stuck to his Jordans. His question reminded me that in other worlds, with other families, the idea of leaving small children alone was unreal—a holiday movie with wacky burglars and a crafty kid.

He thought my mom had to be hurt or lost somewhere for this to happen.

No time for explanations.

All I kept thinking was, *What if Lamar is wrong? What if Lilli's inside?*

When I looked up, I saw black clouds of smoke puffing out of a side kitchen window. I ran to the front door. Ripped it open. Was greeted by a belch of black smoke in my face. All I saw was smoke. No flames. But it was hard to see. It smelled tarry and awful.

Lamar wailed and I turned. Anguish mashed his features. "Lilli gone. She go find you," he said.

I had to go. *Think, think, think!* Where would she go looking for me?

"Trent'll stay," Quintin said, waving me over, "I'll come with you."

Trent agreed.

"Let me go in the other direction and look," called Niecy, waving her cell.

The night air smelled of smoke and fear. "Let's go the same route I take to school," I said, trying to find any logical thought in my brain as panic overtook my entire body. We took off.

Running, running, running.

Heart rate, fast. Fists in knots. Shoulders aching from carrying this load.

My phone chirped. I grabbed it. Fingers slick with perspiration. It tumbled to the ground. I tried again.

"Hey," came Niecy's voice. "I'm over here on Reynolds and I went all the way around the block. She's not over this way. At least, not that I can see."

Desperation. It burned inside me. "Thanks, Niecy," I muttered, hanging up before she could say more.

Nothing more to say. *Lilli is gone, gone, gone!*

"Lillieana! Lillieana!" I yelled. I sounded hysterical, but I couldn't control it.

"Kita, calm down, it'll be okay," Quintin said. I tried to shake him off, but I was flinging tears.

"Lillieana! Lilli! Lilli! Lilli!" I yelled and yelled.

I began to shake. Uncontrollably. Knees knocking. Teeth chattering. I felt a coldness seeping through my body. It felt like death. Quintin encircled me in his arms. An hour ago, I would have thought this was the most romantic thing in the world. Like starring in my own romantic comedy.

But the colder I got, the less I could feel anything.

"Kita, you can't find her if you can't walk." He gave me a gentle shake. Got my attention. He said, "You have to take a breath. We'll find her." It took a moment, but I managed to settle myself down—some.

"Should we check the park, too?" Quintin asked. "It's on the way." When I answered yes, he grabbed my hand, tugged me and I followed.

My ring tone sang out again. Niecy. "What can I do, Kita?"

"Can you check that field over on Clifton Avenue?" I asked. "Text me if you see anything?"

"Okay, baby girl. And you text me, too!"

Shifting shadows engulfed us. Headlights from the highway and cars on the overpass lit the park's corners and made the twilight dance. It would have been beautiful except for the squeal of sirens in the distance. Getting closer. Fire engines.

No sign of Lilli. The sandpit, the pirate ship, the swings—all empty.

Think! I told myself. *Think!*

We had to keep going toward Grove Middle. She had to be somewhere along the way. We took off again heading up the street.

Every black patch of grass made my heart drop. I'd seen too much TV. Too much news. I knew what could happen to little girls alone in the dark.

The thought made me shiver and I tasted fear in the air around me. We cut down Asher Street and were close to Grove Middle when I heard a noise. Sniffling.

"Lillieana?" I said into the dark cluster of bushes. The leaves rustled and the shadows moved. A tiny hand stuck out, reflected in the glow of the rising moon.

I pulled her up off the ground and into my arms. I hugged her and squeezed her and cried like she'd been gone for a hundred years.

"Mama left us," she said in a small voice. "I was trying to find you, Kita. Lamar turned the stove on again."

"I know, baby," I said. "I know!"

I heard Quintin talking to Niecy on the phone, letting her know we found Lilli. After a second, he put his hand on my shoulder. "Kita, we gotta head back." I nodded.

The closer we got, the more the streets filled with cars and people. We tried to get back to our town house but were led away. I dropped onto a curb where neighbors had gathered.

I pulled Lilli onto my lap and someone pressed icy-cold bottles of water into our hands. I'd downed two bottles before I felt like I could breathe. Lilli was draped over me, crying softly into my hair.

"Kita! Kita! I'm so sorry!" Niecy was standing there, tears in her eyes. "I'm so, so, sorry! I shouldn't have pushed you to go out with us. We should've all gone home!"

It was like I was outside of myself looking down. Like this wasn't really happening to me. It was some other family. Someone else's tragedy.

The whole scene was a disaster. Cops, firemen, neighbors filled the street in front of our home. Lamar stood in front of me. Eyes glazed and body still.

Mama, how could you let this happen?

How could I let this happen?

Guilt heavy enough to bend my spine weighed on me.

It wasn't Niecy's fault. I'm the one who should have known. Should have known Mama would leave them. I knew we couldn't depend on her. I knew she was unreliable.

It was all my fault!

My head dropped into my lap and exhaustion took over. Much as I wanted to stay strong for the little ones, I felt myself falling apart. Not enough strength to hold myself up. Not enough duct tape in the world.

Niecy came over and pulled me into her arms, hugging me, telling me it would be all right. She was still trying to make me feel better when Mrs. Grieves, the social worker, showed up.

"Sharkita! Honey, we need to get you kids to safety. Where is your mother?"

"I'm sorry," I mumbled. "I shouldn't have gone out with my friends. Mama was home. But she wanted me to come back. She wanted me to come back so she could go out with . . ." My voice drifted off, gone like smoke through an open window.

"Sharkita," Mrs. Grieves said, standing and looking back and forth from the town house to us. "Where is your mother?"

I swallowed a hard lump lodged in my throat, looking at the ground. My new sneakers were streaked with soot and sand and dirt.

"Sharkita!" Mrs. Grieves had one arm wrapped around my shoulders, pulling me to my feet. "Where is Mama?"

Where is Mama? Who knows?

Maybe this time she was gone for good.

(28)

NOW HERE WE ARE. The moment I've known was coming since that day back in August when Mama came back to us eighty-six days ago.

We are in a drab building where the wall color and the floor leak into one another.

A group of social services people come talk to us. Someone brings in cots.

Lilli has passed out asleep, exhausted. Lamar is counting things, never going past four.

"One, two, three, four . . . One, two, three, four . . . One, two, three, four . . ."

That left me, tired and grainy-eyed, trying to answer all their questions.

The social services building looks like something out of the olden days with big metal desks, wall calendars, and carpet so old and stale all that's missing is the taped outline of a dead body.

Questions. They fire them at us.

Do you know when the fire occurred?

Where was your mother?

Where were you?

How did your siblings wind up alone?

Mostly, I sit in silence. My head hurts. All I want is sleep. Then one of them mentions "placements."

"Placements?" I ask.

"Homes. We have found really good temporary homes," Mrs. Grieves says.

My brain struggles to comprehend.

"What homes?" I say. Dread fills my belly. Mrs. Grieves gives me a sympathetic look.

"Sharkita, your home isn't safe right now," she says. And I know she's not just talking about the fire.

"Will we at least be in the same place?" I ask, hoping it won't be the same as this summer.

But Mrs. Grieves shakes her head. "I'm afraid not many places are equipped to take in all three of you at once. And because of Lamar's disability, we've found a therapeutic foster home for him. He'll be getting the support he needs, Sharkita."

"I can give him what he needs!" I shout, feeling at the edge of a cliff. I am disintegrating. Coming apart from the inside out. All the little bits of me flying in all directions.

I failed.

I failed.

I failed.

The only goal that ever mattered and I failed.

Would I ever get them back? My siblings or the little pieces of my soul?

"You have done the very best you could," Mrs. Grieves says, grabbing hold of my hands. Her fingers are ice-cold. "But you are twelve, sweetheart. You deserve to have someone to take care of you, too. You can't do this on your own anymore."

"No." I begin shaking my head. "I don't need anyone taking care of me. I'm okay! I'm okay!" No matter how loud I get, even I don't believe me, but I can't seem to stop yelling.

More parts of my DNA chip away and swirl beyond my grasp.

Mouth dry. Heart racing. Muscles tightening. Skin crawling. Stomach on fire.

It's too much. *Too much. Too much. Too much. Too much. Too much.*

"Sharkita? Are you all right?" Mrs. Grieves's voice feels miles away.

The shark returns. Large and menacing. Not one. Hundreds.

Scary, mouth open, belly like a swamp, pulling me on a tide into dangerous depths.

I start to shake. I'm slightly aware of my body crumpling, falling to the floor. I am sinking underwater. Voices bob on waves.

"Call 9-1-1!" The voice far away wobbles from a distant shore. I'm drowning. I can't breathe. Can't move.

I fall into darkness.

～〜

I wake up in a hospital bed with a doctor the size of Bigfoot standing beside my bed.

"Lilli? Lamar?" my first thought as I come to. "Lilli! Lamar!" I try to yell over and over despite my chalky mouth and dusty lungs.

Mrs. Grieves shows up right then, tells me not to worry about Lilli or Lamar because they are "safe and sound in good homes."

I want to scream, yell until they bring them to me. But my body won't let me. It's like my energy is melting down, down, down, leaking out my toes. My shoulders slump and I lean back on the bed again.

Mrs. Grieves continues to tell me something about how well they're both doing or whatever. I don't even care. I shut my eyes and pray for sleep or a coma or something. Maybe, if I'm lucky, they'll find one of those diseases like on *Grey's Anatomy*. Something to explain why I'm so messed up, why I keep messing up.

Nothing matters now. I failed. Failed to keep us together and now we'll probably never be family again.

"Kita? Sharkita, can you hear me?" she asks. I feel Mrs. Grieves and Bigfoot get closer to the bed even though their voices seem farther away.

I roll over and turn away. "Can you leave me alone? Please? I . . . I'm tired."

Mercifully, I hear their feet shuffle across the tile floor. They leave the door open. Gotta keep a close eye on the screaming insane girl. Just like Mama said I was.

Whatever.

I just want to sleep for a thousand years.

When I wake again, I'm shocked to see Miss Kadejah. She's sitting in a corner chair with a bunch of yarn draped over her hand and lap.

Knitting.

Her bright blue yarn reminds me of the sky. I squint at her, trying to make sure she's real.

"Wh-aaat," the word hangs in my throat. I try again. "Um, Miss Kadejah? What are you . . . ?" By now I'm on my elbow, squinting harder, still trying to make the vision clearer.

She sets aside the yarn and needles and comes closer to the bed.

"Well, hello!" she says in her bright 'I have a dream!' voice. "I was beginning to think I was going to have to bring Drum Major Paul in here with his whistle, along with his brass and percussion sections!"

Her smile is so warm and inviting. Beaming. Still, painful questions hang behind her eyes. Along with sadness.

"Sharkita . . ."

I start shaking my head before she can continue. I turn away from her, head down, biting my lip. The tears forming in the corners of her big, bright eyes wash over me, pulling me down. An undertow of emotions.

She can't help herself. She reaches out and touches my shoulder. Even when I flinch and try to shake her off, she holds tighter. I try to pull my body into a tight ball. I'm at the bottom of the ocean. Hiding from predators.

The squeezing makes me gasp. Tears trickle down my cheeks.

Miss Kadejah has wrapped her arms around me, holding tight. She's sitting on the side of the bed, rocking me back and forth.

"Shush, child, shush. You're going to get through this. You are going to get through this. You are . . ." She repeats it over and over until my breathing slows and the tears dry up. When I've calmed, she gently turns me to face her. I draw a deep shuddering breath and sit up in the bed.

"It's all my fault, Miss Kadejah. All my fault!"

Something hard and sharp sparks behind her eyes.

"Nonsense!" Her word crackle like fireworks. "Sharkita Lashay Lloyd, you are a child. You are not responsible for what happened. This is NOT on you."

A lump forms in my throat. She means Mama. It's her turn to draw a deep breath and search for words from air too full of emotions.

"That was your mother's job, Sharkita, not yours." Her voice is softer. I know she wants me to smile and say I'm not drowning in guilt anymore. That I'm not to blame. That I'm not sick in the head, like Mama always told me I was.

But I don't have the energy to lie.

"Mama told me she would leave them. I didn't want to believe her. Not after everything that has happened. But I knew. Deep down, I knew she'd wander off. I knew it, and I decided to go out and have *fun*."

Miss Kadejah took my hand and gave it a squeeze. "Kita, look at me." It was a struggle lifting my eyes to meet hers, but I did it. She stared at me so intensely it was hard not to look away again.

"You are not responsible for your mother's actions. Do you hear me? There is nothing wrong with being twelve and wanting to have fun. But there *is* something wrong with being twelve and having to take care of your whole family even though mom is healthy and capable. You have to understand that."

Just then a nurse enters, saving me from responding. "Well, look who's awake!" he says in a kind voice. He goes on to tell me I am going to be evaluated to determine if I can leave. He almost says, "go home," but must realize I don't have one anymore.

"Did I get hurt somewhere?" I ask, rising to my elbows again.

The male nurse exchanges looks with Miss Kadejah.

"No, you're not injured," Miss Kadejah says, brushing my arm with her fingertips. "No sweetie, you're fine."

The nurse, whose name tag reads Javier, says, "You've been through a big shock, and we just want to make sure you have the tools you need to cope with how much your world is changing. We've brought in someone special for you." He hits me with his own megawatt smile and for just a moment I picture Chasity falling in love with him.

When the door opens again, I don't know what to think or feel.

At least, one thing is for sure, I can't say I am surprised.

Surprise takes too much energy.

"Hey, Dr. Charles."

(**29**)

DR. CHARLES WEARS ANOTHER BASEBALL cap—the Kansas City Royals. Was there a sports team this guy *didn't* like? His hands are shoved down in his jeans' pockets. His white polo is plain, clean. Unlike Kadejah, fancy in her sundress and expensive purse, he looks like a teacher on Saturday morning, not an Insta moment.

Behind him is the Bigfoot-sized doctor from earlier with Mrs. Grieves.

"I'm Dr. Bigelow," Dr. Bigfoot introduces himself. "You've been dozing off the other times I've popped in so we haven't had a chance to properly be introduced."

I offer him a weak smile. Turning back to Dr. Charles I ask, "Why are you here?"

He gives me one of his shrugs and a shy smile. "Kadejah thought you might benefit from seeing another friendly face."

Unexpectedly, hot anger awakes inside me. I snap:

"No offense, but I don't need friends. I need my brother and sister. I . . ." Hard as I try, I can't keep the stupid tears from my voice or eyes. "I want to go home!"

Then I start bawling like a baby. I feel totally out of control of my own body. My emotions are on full display. Dr. Charles instructs me to take a few deep breaths. Miss Kadejah rubs my back as he guides me through them.

"If you wouldn't mind, Miss Lloyd, Dr. Charles and I would like to speak with you," Dr. Bigfoot says once I've calmed down. He turns to Javier the nurse and Miss Kadejah, signaling for them to leave.

Kadejah gives me a squeeze before she heads out, and I'm almost scared to see her go. "Be strong, baby girl," she whispers in my ear. "I'll see you at later." I swear I hear her sniffle but she's out the door before I can confirm it.

Once it's just the three of us, Dr. Bigfoot pulls up a chair. I start to roll over, turn away from him, but Dr. Charles catches my eye. He gives a single shake of his head, and it freezes me.

The anger bomb that has been waiting to explode turns to dust. What did this guy want, anyway?

Dr. Bigfoot clears his throat. "How are you feeling?" the large doctor asks.

I laugh. A loud, terrible sound. Incredible! My house has burned down, my brother and sister are in foster homes, and Mama might wind up in jail. How did he think I felt?

Dr. Charles steps forward, touches my foot through the thin hospital blanket.

"Listen to him, please. Everyone here only wants to help you.

I want to help you. Dr. Bigelow. Dr. Sapperstein. Mrs. Grieves. So, listen and, you know, just help us to help you."

When Dr. Charles gets serious, not making dad jokes, you know the situation is hopeless. I blow out a sigh and cross my arms over my chest. Hold on tightly. I give them a shrug that I hope says, "I don't care anymore," because I don't.

Dr. Bigfoot says, "We need to talk about your anxiety." I puff out a laugh that is not fun or happy. I roll my eyes. I am Niecy, playing a role straight from the Netflix-for-teen-drama hand-book. I realize it's an advanced category.

This is it.

This is where they crack open my brain, see the same sickness Mama told me was there my whole life, and tell me I've got problems.

"What if I don't want to talk about anxiety," I say, arms still crossed, fighting back tears.

"Why?" Dr. Bigfoot asks.

"Huh?"

"Why wouldn't you want to talk about anxiety?"

The tightness in my chest grips me. I snatch my knees up to my chest. My left foot is uncovered. My body feels thin and shaky.

I swallow hard. Bite my lip. Squeeze shut my eyes.

He can't make me.

He can't make me.

He can't make me.

"I asked you a question," he goes on, voice gentle but prodding.

I don't look at him. Maybe if I keep my eyes shut tight, he can't see me.

Inhaling deep, I blow out a long breath, turn to him, and try on my toughest personality. I say, "You can't make me talk about something I don't want to."

I knew my face. Knew the muscles were straining in an ugly snarl. Lilli and me used to practice mean faces in the mirror. It made her laugh. Made both of us laugh. Only I was being the toughest *Where the Wild Things Are* monster I knew how to be in real life.

Grrrrrowl!

Dr. Bigfoot is unimpressed. Not surprised. It's hard to scare an urban legend, I guess. He sits back, writes something on his pad, then looks at me. Really looks at me. Then leans closer. Instincts tell me to pull back a little, but I don't.

"Miss Lloyd, let me be clear. You had an episode in the social services building that was potentially dangerous for you. You exhibited an extreme reaction that could be categorized as a panic attack. But I can't know that until we talk, and I get some information. To do that, I have to ask questions and you need to answer them." He says all this in clear tones that are neither angry nor mad.

Then he leans even closer and stares right into my eyes.

"If I can't get the answers from you that I need, I can't clear you to leave. They will be forced to keep you in the hospital."

My gaze flicks around the room. It was bright, like a kid decorated it. The sofa was purple, the clock on the wall was shaped like a grandfather's clock and painted in bold primary colors. A LEGO set was put together, sitting on top of a shelf.

Not a regular hospital room, at least, not anything I'd ever seen on television. A special room. For certain patients.

"Is this a crazy room?" I blurt. A fist is inside my chest. Squeezing, squeezing, squeezing. Can't breathe. I'm gulping for air. Gulping. Oh, God! This really is a heart attack. They have me in a crazy room for crazy people, just like Mama said they would.

My foot starts to shake, the left one that's sticking out from under the sheet.

A twitch blinks my eye repeatedly.

I pull myself tighter and tighter into a ball.

I'm going under . . . going under . . .

"My chest," I squeeze out, despite my throat muscles strangling. "I'm . . . it feels like my heart is exploding. What's wrong with my heart?"

I am rocking back and forth. Faster and faster. Squeezing myself in my own arms, holding on tightly. The pain feels like a knife blade cutting directly into my chest. Shark teeth ripping through my insides.

"Miss Lloyd," the voice of Dr. Bigfoot sounds muffled. Yet, he's close enough that I feel his breath on my face.

"Sharkita, try to relax," Dr. Bigfoot says. "You have a healthy heart. You are safe. You are not having a heart attack. Try to slow your breathing. That's good. Good, kid. You're doing great. Lie back. Yes, just like that. Lie back and concentrate on relaxing each muscle."

His voice is like a wave on the ocean. Serene. Floating over me again and again. He takes me through all the muscles that normally seize up when I'm having one of these terrible episodes.

He tells me to relax the muscles in my jaw. In my neck. Slowly, I feel the muscles he names release their grip, one by one. When he is done, I lie there, panting with tiredness. These episodes always drain me.

"Better?" he asks when I open my eyes. I nod. Now my eyes cloud up with tears again.

"Dr. Bigelow, if there's really nothing wrong with my heart, am I mentally ill? Is that what anxiety means? Why does it feel so much like a heart attack?"

He smiles for the first time, then slowly, deliberately, lowers himself back into the chair. He says, "Have you ever heard of a panic attack?"

I shrug. "I guess," I say. "I mean, I think it's like when somebody freaks out over something that isn't really a big deal. Right?"

He shakes his head. He says, "I'm going to run through a list of feelings or reactions. I want you to answer honestly as it pertains to you. Think you can do that?"

I nod, sliding my body until I'm sitting propped against the pillow. He mechanically adjusts the bed and asks if I'm comfortable.

"There are no right or wrong answers," he says. "Don't think long about it. Simply answer as honestly, as quickly as possible."

He asks me to say yes or no to the following:

- Feeling sweaty or having chills
- Chest pains
- Sudden fear

- Racing heartbeat
- Fear of losing control or going crazy
- Breathing difficulties, feeling smothered, or choking for air
- Feeling faint, nauseated, or dizzy
- Fear of dying

When I look at him, I feel color draining from my face. "My answer is yes to all of them. What does that mean?"

I want to reach out and grab his coat. Shake him. Make him tell me the truth.

"It's classic panic attack symptoms, possibly a panic disorder. Take a breath and we'll"—he points to Dr. Charles—"help you understand what's been happening to you. And how to handle it."

Dr. Charles takes over then. "Can you describe how the panic attacks start and how they feel once they've started?"

I clear my throat, and he stands and picks up a water pitcher with ice. He fills my cup and replaces the lid with the straw. He hands it to me and I gulp down what feels like buckets of water. It feels like liquid oxygen in my body. A memory. Mr. Gavin's class and a discussion about water molecules. H_2O = hydrogen and oxygen. So, water is liquid oxygen, I guess.

I know my brain is stalling. This has been my secret—mine—for so long that I don't know how to talk about it. Dr. Charles is patient. Dr. Bigfoot, too.

"It's just like the questions he asked me," I say, looking across the bed at the other doctor. "Except the biggest thing for me has always been this tingling sensation that comes after I feel like I've been squeezed."

"Anything else? Physical, I mean?" Dr. Charles says.

I tell him about the worst thing—worst of all.

"It feels like I'm being squeezed to death," I say. "Swallowed whole." I tell him how I wake up and can't move or speak or yell for help. How my scalp tingles and my face feels like it's being pulled in opposite directions.

"Sleep paralysis," Dr. Charles says easily.

When he looks at me, he sees that I've begun shaking again. I have so much fear, terror bubbling inside. I don't want to be locked away. So much sadness and pain fills me.

Dr. Bigfoot gets up and moves around to the other side of the bed. "Forgive me, Dr. Charles, for interrupting," he says, "but I am curious, Sharkita. Why didn't you seek help for this before?"

I think about that for a minute, even though I know the answer. For so long, Mama pounded it into me:

Don't put your business on the street! Her way of saying what happens at home is nobody else's business. I've been keeping secrets my whole life. It's like so much of my life is hidden behind this thick door.

And in that moment, something inside me decides to open it.

"Mama," I say.

My whole body braces. I've never told anyone about Mama or how she treats me and the things she says—not even Niecy, not all of it, anyway.

Now a new feeling flutters into my chest. I don't recognize it at first. Then it hits me—it's relief.

"Mama, she told me that people would think I had a mental problem if I went around advertising the fact that these weird things were happening to me. So I thought I needed to keep it to myself. She told me I'd get locked up if I ever said anything."

Dr. Charles nodded his head. "A lot of people used to feel that way—a lot of people still do. But those people are wrong," he says. I'm shocked at the intense way he says it. Like he really wants me to believe it.

He clears his throat and sits up, and his gaze is more comforting, less urgent. "The most important thing to remember is that it is normal. It happens to a lot of people and it's nothing to be ashamed of. I'd like to help you work through the sleep paralysis, panic attacks, and other issues that may be bothering you. We can meet in my office here in the hospital instead of school."

He tells me if I have any more attacks, I should remember what we did today—try to relax, remember that I'm not having a heart attack, take deep breaths.

I couldn't describe out loud how it felt to know I am not going to die.

Dr. Bigfoot tells me as long as I agree to meet with Dr. Charles twice a week for the next month, then once a week after that, he'll agree to discharge me.

As soon as the words are out of his mouth, my heart begins to gallop. Not as frenzied as sometimes, but faster than normal.

My first thought: I'm getting out.

Then: But where am I going?

(30)

MRS. GRIEVES COMES BACK LATER to check me out of the hospital and take me to my temporary home. My new foster home.

"Please, Mrs. Grieves, can you take me to see Lilli and Lamar first? I just need to know they're okay." I hate myself for sounding so pitiful.

She shakes her head and tells me my brother and sister are doing well, and I need to focus on taking care of myself. Then, she hands me something I didn't even realize was gone: my phone.

"I know you have personal information and photos on here, so I'm giving this back. But you are not to contact your mother. And if she contacts you, do not answer. Understood?" she says.

Mrs. Grieves has nothing to worry about. There is no one in the world I want to talk to less than Mama.

After completing some paperwork, she drives me to my new home.

Jackie Harris and her husband, Roger Harris, are the foster

parents. They are African American with two kids of their own—Kyra and Michael—plus two other foster children. Their house is super big but not very . . . uh, organized. Mrs. Grieves is acting like she can't see all the junk piled up on the stairs and shoved into corners. My skin crawls from all the clutter.

They lead me to a tiny room in the back of the house. Mrs. Harris says, "Kyra has a room upstairs that she shares with Sarah, and the boys—our son, Michael, plus Jarien, share a room, too."

I can tell Mrs. Harris wants me to be happy about it—my own room. But it has a musty smell. A half inch of dust stands on the furniture, and boxes wedged into corners bulge with goodness knows what. I start sneezing almost immediately.

"I—we thought it might be good for you to have a room to yourself for a while," Mrs. Harris says. She's trying to be nice, but her smile is pitying.

"Yes, ma'am," I mumble. "Thank you." She reaches out and takes my hand, squeezing my fingers. I fight down the panic pushing to the surface.

Soon as she touches me, soon as I feel her warm fingers on mine, the whole thing becomes real.

This is really happening.

My house burned down.

Mama is gone.

Lilli and Lamar are gone.

And I am here. In this tiny back bedroom with the dust balls.

"Mrs. Harris," Mrs. Grieves says. "I have a couple more

things to talk to Sharkita about, if you wouldn't mind giving us a moment."

"Of course. I'll leave you to it, and Sharkita, welcome," Mrs. Harris says before disappearing out of the room. I chew the inside of my lip, trying to bite back the panic I feel pushing into my throat.

"What happens now?" I ask.

Mrs. Grieves lets out a huge sigh. When she looks at me, I see thin lines etched against the white skin. Her brown hair has silvery threads of gray.

For a moment, I have the urge to sketch her profile. Then her voice cuts into my thoughts.

"I won't lie to you, Kita," she says. "Your mother is in big trouble. She knew this was her last chance."

"I know, I know, I know . . ." I say, sounding waxy and strained.

I drop onto the bed and tuck my legs up, sitting with my chin on my knees. "Where is she now?" My voice sounds like I'm in a hole, deep and dark.

Something sparks behind Mrs. Grieves's eyes. Anger? Sadness? Both?

"We're not sure right now. But Sharkita, your mom, once the police locate her, she'll be charged with three counts of child endangerment and neglect. Even if something miraculous does happen, I can't see us restoring her parental rights."

I was aware that Mrs. Grieves was still talking. But I didn't know what she was saying. Every time I thought this situation couldn't get any more real—it just kept getting realer and realer.

"What . . . what do I do?" I ask. My voice clogs with mucous and tears like confetti in the rain.

"Do your best here, Kita, that's all I'm asking. You've been a strong girl. You've had to be. So be strong a little while longer," she says, before reaching over and touching my hand. "I put my number into your phone so you can always reach me, okay?"

Then she is gone and I lie back against the wall, trying not to inhale the dust.

Home sweet home.

(31)

THE NEXT DAY, SUNDAY, the other foster girl in the house leaves.

She's going home-home. To her parents. Her mama. It feels like being punched in the gut watching her through the grimy window. I've only been here ten hours and already it feels like a lifetime.

Cleaning, organizing, doing laundry—all of it helps me cope. Mrs. Harris looked at me like I had two heads and a tail when I asked if I could help around the house.

"Child, you feel free to clean, wash, launder, or otherwise improve anything your heart desires!" she'd said.

Cleaning calms me down and helps me to think. I'll never get some rest if I don't do something with all the mess in "my" room.

Later, Mrs. Harris calls us all together for lunch. The Harrises are very big on eating meals together, according to Mr. Harris. Cabinets in a warm maple wood, like they describe it on home improvement shows, are scarred from years of use. Curtains faded from the sunlight cast a buttery glow around the room. Scents of cinnamon and tomato sauce mingle. It feels like a space for a family.

Not my family, though.

The boys—Jarien and Michael—are about eight or nine. They seem funny and I like them. It's hard to look at the little sister—Kyra. She's so much like Lilli. Even her hair.

"Do you like My Little Pony?" she asks, trotting her white pony with rainbow hair past me. I choke up, hot fresh tears I didn't know I had left, rushing up from a well of pain.

"Excuse me!" I say, sprinting from the table like a lunatic. Lying on the lumpy bed in the less dusty room, I curl into a ball.

I miss Lilli and Lamar so much it hurts. I failed them. If it weren't for me, we'd all be home. Together. A family.

Then an idea comes to me.

Yanking my phone off the charger, I hit a preset number and wait for the ring.

"Hello?" the scratchy voice answers after three rings.

"Granny! It's me, Kita!" My heart stops in the silence. Her hesitation is a living thing.

"Kita, what's going on? Where're you at?"

Furnace-hot heat burns my face. I feel so ashamed to tell Granny where I am, but hearing her voice brings tears to my eyes. Maybe this time . . .

"I'm in a foster care home. So is Lamar. So is Lilli. We're all in different places and don't nobody know where Mama is."

Hissing-like static comes through the line, but I know it's the

215

sound of Granny sucking on a cigarette. She exhales a wash of smoke before finding her voice.

"The cops and some social service people done already been around here asking questions. That was yesterday. I told 'em I don't know where Brittany done got off to."

"Granny . . ." I begin, my voice wobbly. She doesn't let me finish.

"Now, baby, I know what you're gonna say but I can't do it. I've raised my child. I'm too old to do it again. It's your mama's turn to be raising babies. She's gotta figure this out herself."

"But Granny, this time they're not going to let us come back home. Mama won't get custody. We won't . . ." The tears begin falling harder and harder. "We won't be able to live together anymore."

Crumpling to the floor makes it easier to bury the sound of my sobs into my own sweatshirt. Granny lets me carry on like that for a minute before she breaks in with a mean snort.

"Truth be told, you're probably better off without Brittany." When my whole body went perfectly still and silent, Granny opened up a locked drawer of family secrets I hadn't known existed. "Kita, I told you once before that after your granddaddy died, Brittany totally checked out. Sure did. Things got so bad I finally had to have her . . ." Granny's voice drops to a whisper, "*hospitalized.*"

What?

"What do you mean, 'hospitalized'?" I sit up, dragging my sleeve over my wet eyes and snotty nose to dry them.

After another drag on her cancer stick—what Mama called Granny's ciggies—she clears her throat.

"I mean she had to be placed in what they called a 'therapeutic unit' so she could have mental treatment. And after me spending almost every dime of her daddy's life insurance on trying to get her well, that ungrateful little hussy turned right around and got pregnant. Brittany ain't never cared for but one person in her life—her precious father. And once he was gone, she didn't give a damn about nobody else. Not even you kids."

All those times Mama had warned me about not telling people about my worries and that shark-bite feeling, warned me about being sent away, I thought she was . . . I don't know, just coming up with stuff to keep me in check. I didn't know it was real. I didn't know she knew from personal experience what it was like.

"Granny, I gotta go," I say. Even as she's stuttering out a final message, I shut off my phone. I can't. I just can't think about any of it anymore right now.

I climb onto the bare mattress and fall asleep. The linens are in the wash where I put them before lunch.

I wake up to a knocking on the door. I tell the person on the other side to come in. Mrs. Grieves—wasn't expecting to see her so soon.

"I wanted you to hear it from me," she says, looking like she'd rather not give this news at all. "Your mother finally reappeared. She has been arrested and is currently in jail awaiting bail."

Mama in jail.

The dark, evil part of my brain shouts, *Hallelujah!*

The pathetic daughter in me wonders, *Is she doing okay?*

Did Granny know yet? Probably not. Mrs. Grieves tells me in light of this news she's scheduled my next visit with Dr. Charles for tomorrow.

"The school van will take you and the new girl to school. It will pick you up fifteen minutes early at the end of the day and drop you off at the hospital. Dr. Charles's assistant, Donna, will meet you in the lobby."

"What new girl?" I ask.

She blinks at me like she doesn't understand, then she says, "Sorry, it's been a busy day. The Harrises have taken in another foster daughter. Come. I'll introduce you to LaWanda." Her voice drops. "She comes across a little rough around the edges, but it might be nice for you to have someone closer to your age here, until . . ."

I frown at her. *Until what?*

LaWanda is in the living room scowling. Mean-faced. Wide built. Tough looking. Michael and Jarien come in, take one look at her, and run away squealing. I don't mean to, but I can't hold back a puff of laughter.

"What's so funny?" asks LaWanda, mean-mugging me like a cartoon villain.

"LaWanda," Mrs. Grieves steps between us, "this is Sharkita. She's going to be staying here a few weeks, too. I think you girls go to school together."

Even though Mrs. Grieves had that hopeful smile going on, I know this girl is not buying none of her sunshine.

"What's wrong with her teeth?" LaWanda asks smugly, looking from me to Mrs. Grieves. I want to ask what's wrong with her whole face, but I just give her a side eye, then make a *pwff* noise with my lips, spin on my heel, and head back to my room. I don't have time for that.

Maybe that will be my new catch phrase—"I ain't got time for that!" More and more, that is how I feel.

Later on, sleeping on my freshly washed sheets that smell like sweet flowers instead of bitter oranges and lemon, I dream I am running hard. Something is after me. I can't see what it is. I don't know where I am or how to get there. All I know is that I am in trouble. So, I keep running, running, running.

～⌒

The ride to school on Monday in the little purple van is quiet. I catch LaWanda throwing looks my way several times, but . . . well, you know my new catch phrase, right?

I'd been dreading school, dreading what everyone would be saying. Even rolling up to the school in this grape jelly bean feels so embarrassing.

If I expected it to be bad, I would have been wrong—it ends up being so much worse than that.

The students' gazes touch my skin like spiders' legs. Their whispers rub against me, burning me all over. Not just the other students. Some teachers, too.

"Kita! I'm so glad you're back!" Chasity appears out of nowhere, arms out, heart open. The last thing I feel like is a hug, but once she grabs me, I think maybe she knows best. She walks me to my first class, and I'm even more grateful for that.

All day I hear them. Whispers. *Whisper. Whisper. Shh! Shh! Shh! Here she comes. Shh! Shh! Shh!*

My head throbs.

Thinking of u

The text from Quintin comes while I'm in Mrs. Bailey's class. I don't reply. What would I say? All I can think about is how I have no home, no little brother and sister, no Mama. Not even a grandma.

It is lunchtime when I finally see Niecy. She comes over to me in the hallway, but she doesn't say anything. She takes my hand in hers. Neither of us says anything. Neither of us has to.

Then Dumb One and Two show up.

Either they hadn't heard what's been going on with me or don't care. "It's *Jaws*!" One of them shouts the old insult, doubling over to laugh. "Since you been wearing your hair with those two twisty things on top, you look like Mickey Mouse."

"Yeah," begins the other one, "if Mickey Mouse had teeth like a shark!" He opens his mouth wide to yuck-yuck-yuck but his face disappears.

Quintin comes out of nowhere and punches that boy dead in the mouth. And then Niecy is going in on the other one. She winds up to deliver a follow-up shot, in case ol' yuck-yuck didn't get the message, but before she can land a blow, Miss Kadejah steps in.

"Quintin! Shaniece! Stop!"

The world freezes. Even the kids already in the cafeteria go silent for a few seconds.

Niecy gets a wild look, like she might swing on Miss Kadejah. Numbness grips my body. Even my lips. We're all herded down the hall and into the AP's office. I squeeze Niecy's fingers tighter and whisper, "Sorry."

Quintin's jaw is set in stone. He's not looking at any of us.

In the end, Miss Kadejah sends Dumb Two—Chester Dunbar—to the nurse's office to get an ice pack for his split lip. She tells him to stop instigating conflicts.

"As for you two," she says to Niecy and Quintin, "I appreciate that you were sticking up for your friend, and I can't say I don't commend you for that. But you must refrain from getting physical. I'd hate to suspend either of you."

Technically, we all know she is supposed to suspend them now, but she is letting it slide this time. Niecy gives me a look, then glances at Dr. Sapperstein's cool, pretty dress. Only I'm not in the mood to care, so instead of sharing that piece of normalness, I look away.

Dr. Sapperstein sends Niecy and Quintin back to lunch, but places a hand on my shoulder to keep me back. "Are you okay?" she asks. Her expression tells me she's asking more than I can answer.

The bell rings.

"I'd better get to class," I say, backing toward her door. "Mr. Gavin doesn't like it if we're late."

(32)

THAT AFTERNOON, DR. CHARLES GREETS me in his office.

We stand there looking at each other for a few silent seconds, then he says, "Let's take a walk."

I kinda don't want to. All I want to do is sit down and maybe fall asleep. I'm tired. And I don't want to be here. But I don't want to be anywhere else, so, whatever.

I follow him out of the office. He tells his assistant, "Kita and I are going to take a walk around the lake. It's much too pretty outside to stay cooped up in here."

Was it a pretty day? I hadn't noticed. I think about how I would take Lamar and Lilli to the park on nice days. I don't choke up when I think it, though. The numbness is creeping up from my toes. We ride the elevator in silence. I'm feeling more and more of nothing. By the time he pulls open the back doors of the hospital, my legs are so numb I almost stumble.

We walk along a beautiful area I never knew existed. Dr. Charles finally looks over at me. He says, "It's time to talk about Mama."

I know it's silly, but I can't help myself. "My mama or yours?" I ask.

He stops for a second and gives me the crooked eyebrow. I shrug and we keep walking. The sidewalk curls around, following the edge of the lake. He points to a park bench shaded by hanging branches overlooking a part of the lake lacy with shadows. I wonder how many patients he's led to the same spot in order to pry their secrets free.

"What do you want to know?" I ask, staring at a mama duck swimming with the cutest baby chicks you can imagine. The mama duck is watchful. She seems to love them. The ducklings *chirp-chirp* around her and I imagine I'm drawing the whole scene in my sketchbook. She loves them. It looks as natural as anything.

Mama could've learned a lot from that duck.

"Tell me: Do you want to go back home? With your mother? The way things were?" he asks.

When I snatch my head around to meet his eyes, Dr. Charles is staring at the water. I feel my features contort into a frown. The numbness migrating from my toes, up my legs, and into my heart vanishes. Pure fire takes its place.

"Why would you ask me that?" I snap. "No, no, I don't want to go back. I hope I never see her again!" Ignoring the fact that it's not even an option anymore.

"Are you sure?" he asks quietly. The muscles in my neck go

tight. My hands curl into fists. My heart is racing and I'm this close to either screaming or straight up slapping somebody.

"Why would I want to go back?" I am almost shouting. "Why should I ever go back? Mama wasn't good for us. I just wanted to take good care of Lilli and Lamar, wanted to keep everything nice and tidy so we could be together. But I messed up. If Mama could've . . . could've . . ."

I've been gaining momentum. Anger propelling me like a boat on flat water. Then my words catch air, tumble, and splash. I look up and see Dr. Charles watching me. His expression fills with more compassion than question.

Then I break open.

A flood.

I begin to weep and cry and rock back and forth. He produces a package of tissues from some hidden place. Tears and snot bubble on my face as I wipe and blow and make an even bigger mess.

He waits patiently, until my body shudders to signal an end to all the crying. Then he gives me a tap on the shoulder and stands. We walk some more and after a while, I begin to talk.

"I love Mama," I say, "but I don't understand her. I just don't understand why she can't love us back."

Dr. Charles sighs. "The sad truth is not everyone is capable of being a parent. Biology dictates who can conceive and give birth, but it takes more than making a baby to be a parent."

"It hurts," I say.

"Yes, it does."

I didn't know I had enough energy to be so angry. Dr. Charles says, "You should feel whatever you're feeling. There is no right or wrong way to be after what you've been through. The trick is how you handle those feelings. The hurt and anger are normal. Sadness, too. In a way, you are going to grieve the loss of your mother even though she's still alive."

I suck in air. I hadn't really thought about it, but he's right. It does feel like that, in a way. Mama may not be dead, but the life we had with her, the life we had as a family, is.

R.I.P.

Now, what I need to know is will there be life after death for me and my siblings.

~~

A few days pass. I fall into a routine at the foster home, helping out, staying busy. Mrs. Harris could use the help. She works—I don't know, somewhere. So, I start doing the family's laundry. She thinks I'm "such an angel," but I like their laundry room. Other than the room I sleep in, it's the only place in the house where I feel safe.

Not that anyone here has threatened me, besides LaWanda, who is constantly giving me the evil eye. It's just . . . how can I feel comfortable here? When I look at Michael and Jarien, I think about how much fun Lamar would have playing with them. I long to hear Lamar's happy clapping and singing, to see his smiling, chubby face again.

Don't even get me started on the little girl, Kyra. I can't even look at her without wanting to run screaming from the room! I don't want her to feel bad, though, so I do my best around her.

I stand to fold the sheets from Kyra's bed. Pretty pink ponies dance across a plain white background. I bite my lip, trying not to let myself get pulled under in sadness. Just looking at the sheet reminds me of Lilli. I wonder where she is and what she's doing now. I want to see her. I want to read to her. I want to hear her little voice.

"I know about your mama." The voice is ice on my spine. It's not Lilli, that's for sure. I turn slowly and see LaWanda in the doorway. Everything about her is hard looking. Her jaw is clenched tight enough to pop out a back tooth.

My body tenses but I don't say anything. I reach for another sheet.

"Is you deaf?" she says, taking a step toward me.

"What do you want?" I ask. I want my voice to sound strong and authoritative. The best I can do is sound annoyed.

She takes another step. Then another. I feel myself shrink away from her. Feel my body and mind curl away as this . . . this girl gets up in my face. I want to stand up to her and tell her I don't care what she's heard or what she thinks she knows. I want to tell her to beat it!

I don't, though. I stand there. Wide-eyed. A baby seal facing down a great white.

Her face is inches from mine. My throat tightens. I don't know where the rest of the family is. If I call out to Mrs. Harris, will that make things better—or worse?

"You act all goody-goody around here, doing chores and

playing with these kids. But you ain't no better than me or anybody else," LaWanda says. Her face is a snarl of anger and meanness that I don't understand. I want to reach out and draw a mustache in marker above her lip. "Your mama is in jail, just like mine."

She says it like a big mic drop moment. I just look at her with an expression that says, "So?"

My reaction is either not what she wanted or not what she expected. Her snarl stretches tighter, and I feel my body pull even farther away.

"What's going on in here?" Mrs. Harris calls out from the doorway. I want to call out, to say I'm doing laundry but I don't know what LaWanda's doing. But the words crawl into the back of my throat and curl up on their sides, choking me.

The snarl on LaWanda's face slips into a smirk. She turns away from me and marches out without a word. Mrs. Harris's face wears a question mark, but when Michael calls, "Mom! Mom! Come see!" she gives me one last look before disappearing beyond the doorway.

I feel my heart *thud, thud, thud!* I look around. Suddenly, the laundry room doesn't feel so safe.

In bed that night, I toss and turn. I'm mad. Angry at myself. After everything that's happened to me, I still didn't know how to speak up for myself. The book I read earlier, *Speak*, comes to mind. Would I ever find my voice like Melinda did?

I sit up in bed, knees drawn to my chest. I long for the freedom to go sit on the roof, like I used to. Instead, I rock back and forth in a fidgety motion.

Dr. Charles's words rush back to me.

How did I feel?

What did I want to do with those feelings?

My mama is losing custody of me and my brother and sister. How did I really feel about that? I'm rocking faster and faster. My foot is jiggling. I feel sick, that's what I feel. I finally stop rocking and curl into a ball on my side.

When I fall into sleep, I dream of deep waters, quiet and serene. Then sharks appear, hungry and dangerous. Part of me doesn't want to fear them anymore. I know they do good things for the environment. They are necessary creatures. But their flat shiny eyes chill me to the bone. And their teeth, razor-sharp, grinning at me as they open their mouths wide and inhale, and I feel myself being pulled, pulled, pulled inside. Will I ever escape?

I awake from the awful dream and realize, once again, I can't move. I can't call out. I can't scream. The grip grows stronger. The muscles of the great white's throat constrict, squeezing my bones. I'm awake, but unable to move or call out, I lie tucked on my side, heart hammering. Dying.

Then I see Bigfoot.

Well, Dr. Bigfoot. I remember his soothing manner as he told me how to fight the panic attack. Dr. Charles said the same thing about what they called "sleep paralysis."

But that couldn't be this!

Not what I'm feeling now.

It's a heart attack. A stroke. Something terrible. My head is a dull ache, and my neck muscles are more twisty than a soft-serve ice cream.

I feel sweaty, clammy. Knots fill my stomach. I can't breathe.

Then I begin fighting.

I'm not going to die in this dusty back bedroom in a house filled with strangers. I'm not going out like that.

A stabbing pain knifes through my skull. Tears wet my face. *Why fight it? Why not just give in?*

I won't give in!

No!

I want to live. I want to matter. I do matter. I deserve a life. I want to be a regular person. Be a kid. Could I?

Thrashing on the edge of the bed, fighting the invisible restraints of a nonexistent shark, I hit the floor with a thud. And it feels like tearing myself from the jaws of death.

I could move.

My feet.

My hands.

My legs, head, neck, body.

I could move. Except for the headache, the pain has vanished.

Relief.

I feel relief.

Not just to be free from the terror of the sleep paralysis. But to be free from Mama. It's bigger than the relief I felt in the hospital. I'm so scared to admit it, but I'm relieved I have a chance to try and be me.

Admitting that relief is mingled with my anger and sadness

had been tormenting me. It feels mean and wrong to think like that. It is like admitting I don't want my family anymore.

Not true.

I just don't want what Mama was doing to our family anymore.

THE NEXT DAY IS Halloween.

Miss Kadejah has invited girls from the dance teams to her house to pass out candy. With field season coming to an end, it's time to focus on dance team/majorette competition. Since it gives me a low-key legit reason not to be in the foster house, I'm down.

Most of the girls' mothers or fathers are going to drop them off. Miss Kadejah asks me, "Kita, you want to ride with me? Or are you going to catch a ride with Niecy?"

"I'll go with you, if that's okay," I say. Niecy told me her mom has signed her up to help with a church event before coming to Miss Kadejah's.

The house on Wickersham Road looks exactly like you'd imagine a house in a place called Wickersham Road should look: amazing!

Houses in Florida are bright, bold. Hers is no exception. Bright peach-colored walls, trimmed in white. She has a huge front porch with furnishings straight out of the design magazines.

"I've done some decorating," she says. Her arm sweeps around to indicate the fake gravestones in her yard, sticky spiderwebs strung across the porch and into the bushes, jack-o'-lanterns cut from real pumpkins, and a baby ghost flying across the lawn on a wire.

"You're really into this decorating and stuff, huh?" I follow her into the house. She is moving fast and occasionally tosses a look over her shoulder without breaking stride.

"Even though we weren't married long before he passed, decorating for any occasion was something my husband and I loved doing together. Halloween was one of our favorites."

We go deep into the rear of her house. The back room is filled with boxes but mostly plastic see-through bins that reveal decorations from Halloween to birthdays.

Then she tells me she's going to change her clothes. "Feel free to roam around or have a snack in the kitchen."

Then she is gone. I feel a little weird alone in her space, but I take her up on her offer and wander around, taking in the art and photos on her walls, until finally I find the kitchen.

I think I actually gasp.

Shiny white walls and upper cabinets that reach all the way to the ceiling. My heart beats faster seeing the forest-green lower cabinets with the bright gold pull handles. There's a waterfall granite island, with matching countertops. What would it be like to have a kitchen this beautiful?

Beyond the patio doors separating the kitchen from the outside world sits the most amazing, gorgeous pool I've ever seen. When I step outside, it's like entering another world. Huge planters overflowing with green vines or lush, colorful flowers stand in corners of the semicircular backyard.

A gentle breeze causes the water to pulse in a hypnotic rhythm. OMG! Lilli would love this so much.

I think of Lilli and how many times she begged me to take swim lessons with her. Wish I had. Picturing her in the pool, a perfect mermaid, makes my heart smile.

Then I feel a tug inside. I might want to learn to swim myself. Maybe. I wasn't going to go ask anyone for lessons, but it sure would be nice.

The doorbell rings, snapping me out of my daydream.

"Kita, would you mind getting that?" Kadejah calls from somewhere deep in the house.

I walk to the front door and it turns out Niecy is the first to arrive. "Girl, that church event was whack—they barely had any decorations! Took me ten minutes to put everything out," she says with an unimpressed *pfft*.

I ignore her and say, "Niecy, you gotta see this." I drag her into Miss Kadejah's kitchen.

"Omigod!" says Niecy.

"Understatement," I whisper.

The doorbell rings again and it's not long before everybody has arrived. Kadejah returns, changed out of her school clothes, wearing snug dark denim jeans and an oversized white shirt.

"All right, everybody. I've ordered pizzas and I have plenty of everything else in the kitchen ready to go. I'm so excited," she says, sounding like a little kid.

"Ma'am," I say. "I love your kitchen. I love everything about it."

She grins. "One day I'm going to learn to cook and put it to good use!"

We all laugh. I start to feel more relaxed. Nobody asked about Mama or the fire. For the first time in a while I feel . . . normal. Still, I can't help myself. While everybody rips open bags of candy, I run around cleaning up.

"Kita! Stop cleaning and come help us scare these kids!" Chasity says. A few girls laugh. I wrinkle my nose at Chas, but my heart races with worry over what else I could be doing to help. My natural guilty conscience, I guess.

Trick-or-treaters come and go. A few of the girls are in costumes. One has her face painted like a ghost. Miss Kadejah's neighborhood has so many little kids. I wish I had my sketch pad. They all look so dang cute in their costumes.

"Kita, are you coming back to twirling tomorrow?" asks a girl named Lulu. She's a dancer. A good one, too.

Words trip over a lump in my throat. "I . . ." clearing my throat, I start again. Exhale. Calm. "I don't know. My baton . . . I don't have one anymore." I'd dropped it in front of our town house the night of the fire when I went looking for Lilli. I have no idea where it ended up.

Lulu does an exaggerated jump back.

"*Guuuurl*, with so many of us on our team, I'm sure somebody has one you could use." I tell her I don't want to bother anybody like that, but she starts shaking her head. "We're sisters. I even have a baton. I started as a twirler. Not sure if it's long enough for you, though."

"If what is long enough?" asks Miss Kadejah, walking up to us with another bowl of candy.

"My old baton. Kita lost hers," Lulu says.

Miss Kadejah pulls a face. "We can fix that easily. I have only about a dozen different ones. Maybe more at my mama's. Come with me to the garage. Let's take a look."

Laughter and music follow us across the yard into the garage.

"Help me move these bins down here," Kadejah says. We stoop and grunt and both jump when a spider wanders into our path. Not long ago, the spider would have freaked me out and I'd have wanted to kill it. But Mr. Gavin has been talking to us about the link between organisms. Spiders are great pest control for other bugs. They're still gross to me, but maybe less gross.

We start going through a couple boxes, searching for Kadejah's extra batons.

"Are you doing all right, Sharkita? Are they treating you okay at the Harris house?" Her question catches me off guard.

It surprises me, her knowing my foster parents' names. She cares. About me. Did Mama know their names? Miss Kadejah's thoughtfulness causes the lump to return to my throat. Even though talking to Dr. Charles has made me feel better, I still have the urge to apologize:

Sorry I didn't take better care of the kids.

Sorry I couldn't prevent the fire.

Sorry for just being me.

Sorry . . . sorry . . . sorry . . .

I don't say any of that. Instead, I nod. She nods back at me, then sits back on her heels.

"Let's open this one. I think there are some old batons in here," she says. It's quiet as we peel back the lid on the bin.

After a minute or so, when I get my voice back, I ask something I've been wanting to since I woke up to see her in my hospital room: "Why do you care so much, Miss Kadejah? About me, I mean." I'm chewing at my lip like it's steak. Her eyes get big and round. She rises to her knees and does something APs are not supposed to do—she hugs me.

"Because you deserve to be cared for, Sharkita. You are an amazing girl. Not just because you were one of my majorettes— and we miss you, by the way—but because you're a good person. It absolutely breaks my heart to know the pain you and your family are suffering. To know that . . ."

Now it is her voice that breaks.

"To know what?" I ask, no longer thinking about the baton. I pull back so I can see her whole face. At first, she looks away, like she has to think about what to say.

"Sweetheart," she blows out her breath, eyes squinting like her brain was still searching for the right words. "Myself and a number of staff recognized that your family might . . . may have been in crisis. Even the elementary school AP gave me a call about Lilli and Lamar."

I feel my body jerk. *What?*

"We . . . I wasn't in a crisis! We were fine. Just like everybody else. Mama, Mama just . . ."

The words clogged in my mouth. Dry words that wouldn't be swallowed and couldn't be spoken. They were lies. Why? Why was my first impulse still to protect Mama? The band's drumline pounds in my chest.

Kadejah's eyes are wet. Mine too.

"Sharkita, baby, you are a twelve-year-old girl who was having to take care of two young siblings, one with a disability, and a mother who left you to deal with everything totally on your own," she says. "You don't need to downplay everything around me. That's a crisis!"

I stand, brush garage dust off myself. A billion bees buzz inside my skull. I need to walk it out.

When I look back at her, she sighs. Her eyes dip to the contents of the bin.

"Here, try this one," she says. She stands, too, removing a baton and having me measure it by placing the head beneath one arm and making sure the shaft extends to the palm. It does.

"All you'll need is fresh tape and to clean the tips."

I try the weight of the baton. It feels so well balanced. I do a few finger rolls up, and a low toss.

Miss Kadejah blows out another sigh.

"I'm sorry you've ended up in this position. I wish I could have done more for you. But every time I asked if you were okay, you said yes. Your clothes were clean, so were the younger kids'.

You all were clean, well fed . . . I'm guessing that was your doing. But I had no proof. I didn't know how to help beyond requesting a welfare check."

The well-balanced baton crashed to the floor as the realization hits me.

"You called the county on us?! Why? Why would you do something that?" Tears arose fast and hard. "I thought you liked me. I thought . . . thought you were looking out for me."

"I do like you, Sharkita! I did it because I was afraid of exactly what happened was happening. Of you or your siblings getting seriously hurt."

"Miss Kadejah, you should have asked. It was fine. Everything was fine."

"I did ask, sweetie." What she says next chills me to the bone. "We all knew your mother wasn't home when she was supposed to be," she says.

I shake my head. "How? How would you know that?"

"Grove City is a small community. People talk. Half the teachers and bus drivers here know your mother from high school. They would see her out when she should have been home with you three."

My face drops into my hands. I stand, trembling. All that time when I thought no one was watching, it turns out everyone was. It would seem like I'd gotten what I wanted, but it all feels wrong.

The horrible feeling of going numb, losing feeling, choking, and being squeezed, begins to happen. Right there in Kadejah's garage.

"Are you okay?" I hear her ask. I want to answer, but it is like I am choking.

Thank God the other girls can't see. Miss Kadejah goes to a mini fridge and takes out a small Gatorade. She hands it to me with a reassuring, "You're okay. You're safe."

I sip slowly, my mind whirring.

We're both sitting on a plastic bin. She sips from a blue sports drink; mine is bright red. After a few sips, she tries again.

"Sharkita, honey, I want you to know that people care for you. You're like the little sister I never had. You're a good kid in a tough spot . . ."

While she talks, I work the numbness out of my body. Once I feel comfortable enough to move my feet, I have to get out.

"It's not true!" I say, not even fully knowing what I mean. But I feel like I have to say something. People talking about Mama, about us, behind our backs. That isn't right. "We were not in crisis. We were fine!"

I'm shouting as I run from her garage.

Lately, I feel like all I do is run. Maybe I should quit dance and join the track team.

I don't get far. More tears streaked my face. I only get a block away before collapsing against someone's fence. Little trick-or-treaters across the street pause and look at me before moving on. Miss Kadejah stands at the end of the block, keeping an eye on me. Making sure nothing bad happens. Like a grown-up or parent should.

We were in crisis.

I knew it. I'm just mad it was that obvious to everybody else.

Then a thought hits me like a kick behind the knees:

Crisis was all I'd ever known.

And then another:

How much longer could I go on defending Mama?

I AVOID MISS KADEJAH at school the next day, walking through the halls like some kind of criminal watching their back. By the end of the day, I was actually excited to see that purple van. Didn't even care when LaWanda got on a few minutes after me and immediately started mean-mugging. After the van picks up the boys from the elementary school, we are rolling along.

We pass a road I recognize because Mama used to take it to get to the orange grove. When I inhale, I imagine I can smell the fresh, bright scent of the oranges. Wondering if I'll ever get to smell them for real again.

I get so caught up in the view and my thoughts, it takes a minute to realize my phone is vibrating in my pocket.

"Your phone is ringing," says Mean Mug. I look up to see her gaze raking over me. What is her problem, anyway?

I fish the phone out of my bag and turn it over. The number isn't familiar but I answer, anyway. What if it's Lilli or Lamar?

"Hello?" I answer, all hopeful one of my sibs will be on the other end.

"Kita, it's me—Mama." Hope crashes and burns. Replaced by the all-too-familiar squeeze of anxiety. "Look, I'm out of jail and I'm letting you know, Mama's getting her kids back!"

"What?" My response crackles in the mostly silent purple jelly bean. LaWanda whips her angry face toward me again. I turn my shoulder toward the window, away from her, and speak low into the phone. "Mama? Where are you? Have you seen Lamar and Lilli?" My hands have begun to shake.

"They're not with you?" she says sharply. "They put y'all in different homes? They've got a lot of nerve."

"Mama, what happened? Where did you go the night of the fire? Why did you leave the littles alone?" I ask, while what is left of my heart breaks with every word.

"Look, I don't have time for all that right now," she says, and for the first time I realize she must be in a car. "What's important, Kita, is that we put our family back together. And I can't do it without my partner!"

"Mama, Mrs. Grieves said—"

She cuts me off. "I don't care what that baggy clothes–wearing woman says. I have a lawyer now, and I have rights!"

My heart is beating so fast it feels close to bursting. I curl myself into a ball, arms around my knees, head pressed against my thighs, trying to keep the pieces of me from floating away.

"Mama—"

"Keep your phone nearby. Me or my lawyer will call you later.

It's up to us—up to *you*. I need you on my side. Now, I gotta go. Remember, you're my ride or die," she says.

"But Mama—"

She is gone.

Hearing Mama's voice feels like having lightning sizzle through my body. I'm not sure if it makes me feel better or worse. What she is saying . . .

Is it true?

Can her lawyer help her drag us back home?

How is she going to get us back together? What did she want from me?

And maybe the biggest question:

Did I even want to go back with Mama?

Nights and days, months and years of worrying and wondering. Planning meals when I was ten; babysitting when I was eight; left home alone and spending two nights in foster care when I was three.

After all that, how could I even consider helping her?

Lilli and Lamar. That's how. I love them so much. And I want nothing more than to be with them now, to know they're okay, to make sure they're taken care of even if I'm not the one taking care. How could I let them go? But in the same thought I ask: How could I let them go back to the way things were?

But . . . she is their mother! She is MY mother.

I let my head fall against the window as my thoughts swirl like a beige fog.

LaWanda is still glaring at me.

"I found out something about you today," she says. "They call you Shark Teeth on account of your mouth being so jacked up."

I look at her but my expression is blank. Is she for real right now?

The van stops in front of the Harrises' house.

I want to get out quickly, think things through in the quiet, dusty safety of my room. My bag is already on my shoulder, and I am heading for the van door. That's when LaWanda wrenches me around to face her.

"Oh, no, you didn't just roll your eyes at me!" she snarls.

I frown.

"You seriously need to chill," I say because I've had it with her.

I turn back to open the van door.

A terrible pain blossoms on the back of my skull. She punched me. The surprise force sends me falling out onto the dusty ground.

It happens so fast.

Van doors squealing on rusty hinges.

Me trying to roll away.

Her grabbing me, slamming my face into the ground. A tree root bubbles up from the earth. One of her blows sends me mouth-first into those roots. I hear my teeth crack.

Even as she is punching me, snarling, saying crazy things, all I can hear is Mama's voice. She wants us back. She wants us—me—back.

All the air leaves my lungs. I can't breathe. I can't move. Somewhere, deep inside my brain, a horrible little voice was telling me I deserve this. I deserved a good beatdown. Not sure whether the voice is LaWanda's or Mama's.

Or mine.

My arm gets tangled in the strap on my book bag. The other arm, the one I fell on first, aches so bad I think I might pass out. LaWanda pulls my hair, and as the van driver finally drags her away, she stomps my bad arm. A scream echoes and I barely realize it's come from me.

Mrs. Harris comes running, looking horrified.

"She started it! She started it!" screams LaWanda. The van driver is still holding her back.

My face aches, and my scalp is wet with what I guess is blood. My eye is swelling up and I don't even want to imagine what my already jacked-up mouth must look like. I don't bother trying to get up.

LaWanda keeps screaming about me "disrespecting" her, saying I started the fight. But the van driver, a Filipino man with serious brown eyes and soft black hair, almost growls as he tells Mrs. Harris what really happened.

"No! No! This one is lying," he says, gripping the girl tighter. "She attacked the other girl for no reason. No reason! I will be reporting this. She will not ride in my van anymore!"

That sets off Mrs. Harris, who seems determined not to report the fight.

She doesn't want the police involved. The van driver shakes his head, says something only the foster mom can hear, then he leaves.

"LaWanda! Get inside and go to your room. I will deal with you later!" Mrs. Harris says to the girl.

Then she turns her attention to me, turning me over, then shrinking back in fright from my bloodied face.

She pulls herself together and helps me to my feet. We go inside, and she cleans up my scalp and face with a warm towel.

"Let me see your mouth," she says, gently prodding my lips apart. In the mirror, I see my reflection. Split lip, swollen eye, and two bottom teeth that once stuck out were now chipped. The teeth that had seemed to form a second row were gone.

"My goodness, she did a number on your mouth, didn't she?" Mrs. Harris went on.

"I think she broke my arm," I manage to say.

But it is clear a trip to the hospital is not going to happen. If she showed up with a kid with a broken arm they'd ask questions. And Mrs. Harris clearly didn't want that. She gave me some Tylenol and patted me on the back. "Try to get some rest. I'll talk to LaWanda. I'm so, so sorry! But I think it's best that we don't make a big deal out of this. Now you be good and go to your room."

I stay in my room for the rest of the day. Mrs. Harris brings me a tray of food, but I'm not hungry—it would have hurt to eat, anyway. I am dizzy. As much as my mouth and face ache, my stomach burns even worse.

I lie curled up on the bed into the night. Maybe I nod off, exhausted from crying, from tossing and turning from the pain, but much later, when everyone else has gone to bed, I lie awake, mind trying to make sense of Mama, of being a foster kid, of getting smacked down by another foster kid for no reason at all.

How did I end up here? Why?

Everything just keeps replaying in my head:

Me deciding to hang out with my friends.

Mama leaving, then coming back drunk, then leaving again.

Lamar, that look on his face. The terrified gleam in his eyes as the house burned behind him.

Lilli trying to come find me alone in the dark, the responsibility too heavy for her little shoulders.

The good-good day I'd had before it all happened now felt like a mirage. Like it was something I'd imagined.

Every part of me ached. Even though Mrs. Harris made me brush my teeth and gargle, I still tasted the rich, dark earth that I'd inhaled when my face was in the dirt.

Lying here in the dark, the sharks come back. Lurking in dark corners. Attacking me slowly. Swallowing me whole.

The pressure in my chest, shoulders, and neck is so strong I try to cry out—only my mouth won't make any sound. My heart crashes over and over against my rib cage. The squeezing is worse than it has ever been.

I am definitely going to die. At least maybe then this pain will stop.

That afternoon, the little voice in my head had said I deserved it. Deserved everything that was happening to me. But now, a teeny-tiny part of me speaks—a part that sounds a little like Miss Kadejah, a little like Lilli, and even, at times like Dr. Charles.

It is a part of me that wants to survive, wants to live long enough to show people like Mrs. Wilcher and Chester Dunbar that I am smart and strong and better than they ever thought I could be.

Using everything I have, I finally begin to move one toe at a time. Then my foot, left one first, then right. Slowly rotating the ankle, wiggling my toes. The shark's grip is loosening. I have to keep fighting. Dr. Charles has told me it's okay to ask for help. That I don't have to deal with this alone. Even with the sharks letting me go, I still feel like I am having a heart attack. I have to tell somebody.

Little by little, I work to release myself of the pressure holding my body in place. I am able to move one leg, then the other. I still fear the sharks returning in the darkness. By the time I can move my arms, all I can think about is to turn on the light.

My arms and hands are still numb. I knock the lamp over. Heard myself whimper. Finally, the strangling feeling lets up. I have air in my lungs. I can breathe.

That is when the screaming begins.

I scream and scream—and *scream*!

(35)

I END UP CALLING Mrs. Grieves myself. Mrs. Harris sure wasn't going to do it, and I'm used to doing things grown-ups wouldn't.

She came and got me and took me to the hospital right away, even though it was the middle of the night. Mrs. Harris tried to talk to her, but Mrs. Grieves shot her the nastiest look I'd ever seen. She barely said a word to me on the drive over she was so mad—not at me, though. She made a point to tell me that, at least.

I must have fallen asleep in the hospital bed at some point after they got me all checked out, because next thing I know I am waking up to murmured voices. Once again, Miss Kadejah is the first person I see.

My head is throbbing, though, and I have trouble focusing on her. My throat feels scratchy, and my mouth feels even more sore than it did before. I try to speak but Kadejah stops me.

"You're okay, Kita," she says, coming over to grab my hand.

A cup of water appears on my other side. Standing on the

opposite side of the bed is Mrs. Grieves. She gives a sad half smile.

I take the biggest drink of water I've ever had.

"Better?" Mrs. Grieves asks. I nod and she continues, "Sharkita, I want you to know what happened at the Harris house is completely unforgiveable. Mrs. Harris should have made sure you got medical help immediately. You will not be going back there."

I nod. Another home, gone. It isn't even one I want or particularly like, but what is going to happen to me now? I take another sip of water. "Where am I going then?"

All of a sudden Miss Kadejah looks more nervous than she did for our first show. She releases my hand and grabs a chair, sliding it alongside the bed. Then she takes my hand again, this time placing it inside both of hers. I could feel that they were leading up to something, but I'm not sure what.

Then, after a deep breath, Mrs. Grieves makes her pitch:

"Kadejah recently got certified as a licensed emergency placement home. She would like for you to come live with her."

My head snaps around to face Kadejah.

"What?" I say.

"Only if you want to come," Miss Kadejah says. Her words tumble out fast, like she is nervous. "I really want you to stay with me. I—I . . . oh, Sharkita, I've been worried about you since the first day I met you. I recognized something in you, something I had inside me, too. I didn't mean to upset you the other day when I said your family was in crisis. I'm sorry that term upset you so much. I just—"

"We were in crisis," I say, cutting her off. "I just . . . I guess I didn't think so many people could see it. I thought . . . I thought I was doing a better job than that."

"Oh, Kita, you were doing the best you could, sweetie." She lightly touches my cheek, frowning. I wince from the light pressure on my face, still sore from my beatdown.

"As soon as you leave here, I'm taking you to see an orthodontist," Miss Kadejah says. "The doctors here gave us a recommendation. Once a good dentist cleans you up and fits you for some braces, you'll be on your way to recovery."

Braces? I think back to how many times I begged Mama for them, how she told me I wasn't worth the trouble. And with Miss Kadejah, I didn't even need to ask.

My stomach clenches at the thought of Mama, the call we'd had. Mrs. Grieves had instructed me not to speak with her and I didn't listen. Do I come clean now? I turn to Mrs. Grieves, who stands tall and wears a hint of a smile.

"It'd be nice to stay with Miss Kadejah," I say instead. Miss Kadejah lets out a strange little laugh next to me. It sounds excited. And I regret what I'm about to say next before it even comes out of my mouth. "But I want to see Lilli and Lamar."

The two women look at each other. Something exchanges between them that I can't quite understand.

"Sharkita," Mrs. Grieves starts. "Our biggest concern right now is finding you a safe space, a place where you can settle and feel a . . . connection. A place that, at least for now, you can call home."

"Yes, exactly," Miss Kadejah adds.

"Your brother and sister are in good homes. Truly, the best fits there could be for them. They're adjusting well. I know this is hard, and they are so lucky to have such a wonderful big sister, but you all need *time*. You especially need to relax and recover. Let the dust settle. There is a picnic next month, and if things go as planned, you can see them then. Okay?"

My heart soars at the thought of seeing Lilli and Lamar. My eyes even tear up as I nod vigorously. "Okay, yes, thank you."

"Of course," Mrs. Grieves says. "Now is there anything else you want to talk about?"

I think of Mama's call again. I think about telling Mrs. Grieves everything she said. About how she says she has a lawyer and is gonna try to get us all back. I know I can trust Mrs. Grieves—last night proved that. And I know I can trust Miss Kadejah, too. I want so badly to tell them what's going on . . .

But instead, I keep the memory of Mama's call tucked under my tongue.

What am I doing? I can't seriously want to go back to Mama, to drag my brother and sister back, too. Still, the words stay hidden.

(36)

THE NEXT MONTH FLIES by in a blur of moving boxes, tears, fears, and mouth pain. I move in with Miss Kadejah. I get braces—I picked out the pink rubber bands because I know Lilli would like them best. Getting my teeth fixed is pretty nice, not gonna lie, but the absolute best thing about living with Miss Kadejah so far has been having my own clean, non-dusty room.

She let me decorate it right out of a magazine.

I loved it.

Sometimes I hated how much I loved it. I shouldn't get too comfortable here—it's not like it was gonna last—even though part of me wishes I could.

Like everything else in my life that gets twisted, it's a call from Mama that sends me splash-landing back to earth.

It was past midnight. I had already fallen asleep.

Groggy, head fuzzy with the fresh scent of fabric softener in the pillowcase clinging to my nose, I answered the phone.

"Hello?"

"Kita? Kita, wake up. It's me!" Urgent. Demanding.
Mama.

"What's wrong? Why're you calling so late?" Brain scrambled. Was something wrong with Lilli and Lamar? Then: How would she know since the state is playing keep-away with her kids.

"Look, I can't talk long," she said, her voice rushed, frantic. "You going to that little picnic tomorrow, right?"

She was talking fast. The picnic? How did she know about that? An icy chill wiggled up my spine. My old friend, the great white, began circling.

"Yes, Mama, but . . ."

"I need you to listen to me. My lawyer says if you testify on my behalf—tell the court that I'm a good mother and I try hard—I have a chance of getting y'all back. But you have to make sure Lilli knows what to say. Her little grown butt. She could mess things up for all of us. Kita? You listening to me?"

I was fully awake by then, sitting up, rubbing my eyes. Mind whirring. Testify on her behalf? *What?*

"Kita!" she was yelling into the phone. I threw my legs over the side of the bed, back tensed like I was going to testify right then.

"Yes, Mama, I hear you."

"Do you understand? You have to tell that judge I'm a good mama, and you want to live with me. You want all of us to live together again, right? Be a family. And you got to get your sister to say the same. Can you do that Kita? Talk to your sister. I've gotta go."

She was gone. Like so many times before. Leaving me to figure it out.

I sit on the side of the bed, heart pounding in my ears, an ugly migraine peeling back layers of my brain.

My new braces feel tight inside my mouth. I squeeze my eyes shut trying to block out the thoughts in my head. Trying to see my way clear.

What am I going to do?

~~

The next morning before the picnic, I'm sitting in Dr. Charles's office. I've enjoyed coming to him more and more, even though I still don't tell him everything. Like, I haven't told him about Mama's calls.

But the way he's looking at me over the top of his coffee cup makes me squirm. I don't care what he says, part of me thinks he *is* psychic. He sips from his cup. Stares at me through the steam.

"So, are you going to tell me? Or do I have to guess why you look like you've been run over? I would've thought you'd be walking on cloud nine. Seeing your brother and sister for the first time in weeks, months. Are you nervous?" He takes another sip.

I gulp. Look away. I don't know how to say it—I don't know what to think or feel. It all makes my head hurt. Dr. Charles lets out a small sigh. He stands and goes over to his desk, and when he comes back, he's carrying a small photo. He hands it to me.

My voice is trapped behind a web of confusion. It's the same photo Mama showed me on her phone, that day when she washed my hair—a photo of me when I was three. I look so . . . small. And helpless. And sweet.

"Why, uh, I mean, what . . . um, why do you have this?" My voice cracks. My world tilts.

"Well, I had asked for photos of you. Especially younger photos, when you were around Lilli's age. Mrs. Grieves was able to find this one in your file."

"Why? I mean, why did you want photos of me from when I was little?"

He blows out a breath, then smiles. "Sometimes it's good to be reminded of our younger selves. Now, take a nice long look at that photo. Tell me, what do you see?" he says.

"I see me!" I state the obvious.

"Yes," he nods, opening his arms wide. "You see yourself. What else? Look closely."

I stare at the photo.

A little girl, happy to be wearing her sundress and sun hat. I also see my eyes in the photo glance to one side. I know Mama is standing there. Out of frame. Mercedes, her friend, took the picture, but my eyes were following Mama. Wanting her, needing her to smile at me; needing her to like me.

My heart thumps faster.

"I see a little girl," my voice says softly, fingers tracing the edges of the photo.

"What does that little girl want?" Dr. Charles taps the photo.

I chew my lip. The day we took that picture, Mama was having a good day. I'm remembering more now. She had been talking

256

about being a model. Mercedes said she was going to be a singer. They were giggling and clowning and having so much fun.

"It was graduation day," I say, memories rushing back at me. "Not for Mama. She graduated early. But for Mercedes and Mama's other friends. We went out to eat afterward. I don't remember where. But . . . I do remember how excited everyone was. I remember how safe it felt . . ."

Tears rush down my cheeks. The photo shakes in my hand. Dr. Charles gently takes the photo from me while I sob, not understanding what was happening.

"When I look at this photo, I see a little girl with her whole life ahead of her. A child who deserves to be safe and well cared for. A girl who is worthy of being a priority," he says.

I wipe my eyes with my arm, gulping back more tears.

"But when you think about it, Mama was just a kid herself. If I'm three in that picture, she's only eighteen. She was trying! She was trying!"

I stuff my face into my hands before folding into my lap. The room is silent except for my sniffles. I don't know why that picture is affecting me the way that it is, but the tears just keep flowing.

A little time passes. I finally sit up, wet-faced and sniffing.

"Sorry," I mumble. "I don't know why I'm so weepy." I try to push out a laugh, but it sounds more like a cough.

"You're crying for the girl in this photo, Kita. For the life you remember and the life you deserved all along," Dr. Charles says. "You don't deserve what's happened to you. All this hardship—it's not your fault." Dr. Charles locks his soft brown eyes on me. This time, I don't look away.

"But it is my fault." My voice is puny.

"Why do you think that?" he asks. Dr. Charles sits across from me. His legs were crossed but now he plants both feet on the floor. He leans forward, elbows on knees. Intent. Patient.

Another gulp. "Because—uh, um, because it just is! I know Mama. Know how she is. I should have known she wouldn't wait, that she'd leave the kids alone. I . . . I . . ."

"Look at the photo, Sharkita." Dr. Charles holds up the picture of me once again. "Look at that little girl. Would you tell her that she doesn't deserve a mom? That she doesn't deserve a chance to be taken care of and feel normal?"

"No, because I'm like three in that photo."

"Well, guess what? You're still a child, Sharkita. And you still deserve to be taken care of. You have a lot of people around you who want to help take care of you, whenever you're ready. I want you to keep that in mind today."

My thoughts shift from the tiny photo to Mama's call. Her command. She's expecting me to help her again. Be her ride or die.

The last time I didn't do what she told me, our entire lives went up in flames.

Could something new grow from the ashes?

(37)

A KNOT SWELLS IN my belly as I ride in the passenger seat beside
Miss Kadejah. Sunshine bright and warm pours over everything
in sight, except my mood.

"Excited?" she asks, glancing over at me.

"Yes, ma'am," I say, my smile pained. My session with Dr. Charles
replayed in my head. I still feel so much guilt—for letting all this
happen, for not telling Miss Kadejah or Dr. Charles about Mama's
calls. But mixed up in all that is exactly what he was talking about,
that need to be safe and cared for, too. I try to push it out of my
head for now, and concentrate on seeing my brother and sister.

The picnic. We are on our way.

We pull into a parking space. Ahead of us the park stretches
out in quilted shades of green and sky. Kids running and dancing
are like colorful polka dots, a pattern on the fabric of the world.

This is the moment I've been waiting for, but my butt stays
glued to the seat. I can't let Mama ruin this for me, too.

"Are you sure you're all right, Kita?" Miss Kadejah asks.

My gaze stays straight ahead. Looking at her feels impossible. Part of me wants to tell her everything. But I know if I tell her, that would mean saying goodbye to any hope I have of our family coming back together again. Is that what I really want?

My stomach burns. Heat fills my throat.

She lets out a small sigh. "Kita, you know you're family to me, right? I mean, of course, you want to maintain a connection with your siblings, maybe even your mother. And I want that for you, too. However, just know that I'm yours as long as you want me. I'm committed to you, Miss Kita. I . . . I love you. No matter what."

Her words wash over me in a wave.

Does she really mean all of that? I think she really does.

But for now, it's better if I don't think about it. She looks at me like she wants to hug me, but my head is too crowded. I'm not ready for all that.

So instead, I get out of the car and rush around, unloading the baskets and boxes we've packed to help out with the picnic. I need to stay busy, busy, busy. I try not to think about how hurt Miss Kadejah looks.

Inside the park, a purple bouncy house sprouts from the grass, while another jiggles like orange Jell-O. Groups of kids are arriving, racing through the grass, laughing. We tote coolers and pans to a table under the pavilion. Aluminum foil crackles. A fresh set of nerves arise as I look around. Are they here? Lilli and Lamar? I don't see them.

"Come meet some folks," Miss Kadejah says, her tone quiet and not quite as assured as before. She introduces me to the woman in charge of the group picnic, a nice lady with short hair and big glasses.

"This is Emily March," says Miss Kadejah. "She's the director of child placement for the county's foster care program."

I give her a little wave and want to drift away, but the woman says, "Sharkita Lloyd. How are you doing with your new home?"

She looks at me in a way that ticks me off. Like, "Ah-ha, I know you. Your mama's no good. Don't you like your new home? Isn't it so much better?"

I shrug at her—giving her the "whatever" look that grown-ups hate so much.

What if Mama's lawyer wins?

What if that's what I want?

Miss Kadejah and Ms. March are still looking at me so I say, "I'm going to walk around. I want to see if Lilli and Lamar are here."

"Of course. Go ahead. Enjoy yourself," she says, and I feel like a real loser because I'm being so mean and not looking at her or smiling. When I turn away, I walk—fast. I want to run. Run, run, run, run, run.

Heartbeats like thunder cause my bones to shake.

Pounding in my head reminds me how the sun gives me headaches sometimes.

I'm light-headed. Restless. Don't know what to do with myself. More and more foster kids fill the space. A banner reads

"Welcome Kids In Kare!" That's what the social services for family and kids is called. I'd read enough of Mama's mail to know.

I pass by long tables being filled with salads, fruits, cold cut sandwiches, chips, cookies, pretzels. When I see the pizza van arrive, I know it is a party.

I find my way to the playground. Kids are running around, screaming. One little girl plays princess atop the climbing gym. A little boy yells, "I'm a dragon and I'm going to burn down your castle."

The playground has a fort for climbing. The "princess" has claimed it. Now the dragon boy is blowing fire—really, he is roaring—and the princess is standing her ground, shouting, "Your dragon breath can't get past my shield!"

I blink. My head snaps around and I let my eyes zoom in on the little happy girl. My heart pounds. This time with pure excitement.

Lilli!

She looks so, so . . . different. I've never seen her like this—smiling, playing with other kids, laughing—outside of Mama's orange grove. The serious scowl she wears most of the time is gone. Her face is soft and relaxed. Serene. Like a mermaid.

Without even thinking, I shout, "Lilli! Lillieana!"

It takes a few tries before she hears me. I'm moving toward her by then. She turns slowly from her dragon. I can't wait to hug her.

But as soon as she sees me, a curtain falls over her eyes. Her face, her expression shuts down. And within seconds, the playful girl full of joy vanishes. She becomes the Lilli I know.

"I'm so happy to finally see you," I say. I bend to give her a big hug, but her body is limp as a wet noodle. I pull back. Suddenly, I'm terrified to see the look in her eye.

"Lilli? Aren't you glad to see me?" I'm holding my breath, waiting for her to respond. A familiar kick punches my chest.

"Did Mama call you?" she asks.

I flinch.

"Why do you ask?"

"Grown people be talking around little kids 'cause they think we dumb," she says, hand on her little hip. Funny and tragic at the same time. "I know she's trying to get us back."

She turns her face to look directly at me.

"And I know the only way she have a chance is for you to tell the judge-people she was a good mama. But that's a lie, Kita, and you know it."

My cheeks flare with heat. But I don't want Mama to ruin this moment for us. "Come on," I say, avoiding her comments, "let's go to the swings."

Thankfully, she agrees, and before long I'm pushing her high into the sky and she's transforming once again into a little girl.

When she swings back, she says, "I like your braces. I want braces, too."

"You don't need 'em, Lil." I give her a push and let her pump a couple times, going higher and higher, then slow her down for my next question.

"Lil, are you happy where you're at?" I ask.

She bobs her head up and down in an exaggerated nod. Her

long black hair catches the wind, ponytails floating, waving behind her.

Lilli digs her toes into the sand to stop the swing entirely. With the black leather swing at the top of her butt, she says, "I feel safe, Kita. The lady, her name is Miss Janey. She's nice. She works at the social service place. Her friends come over, they be talking. That's how I know Mama is trying to call you."

I sigh. I've been called out by a five-year-old once again.

"She did call me," I say. "You're right; she does want us to say she's been a good mama—"

"But Mama don't take good care of us." Lilli doesn't even let me finish. "I have a whole house with a mama and a daddy who don't drink stuff that make them act ugly."

Dang!

She slips off the swing and hugs me. I hug her back, hard.

"I love you, Lillieana. I love you with my whole heart," I say, feeling the warm tears trickle down my cheeks. My face is buried in her hair.

"I love you, too, Kita," Lilli says.

My whole body is about to start shaking with sobs, but I pull myself together. "Now tell me all about what you got in that whole house of yours," I say, changing the subject.

"Miss Janey bought me some books. And she bought one about sunshine. And I read it all by myself! She helped some, but I read the whole thing!"

"You mean *Ways to Make Sunshine*," I say. "High five."

"No," she says, "let's fist bump."

I laugh, wiping away my tears, realizing what's been in front of my face the whole time. Fist-bumping my baby sister, I realize it's time—time to make my own sunshine.

Thumb pad to her cheek, I sweep away her tear droplets.

"Let's go find Miss Janey and her husband. What's his name? Mr. Janey? I want to meet them."

Lilli giggles. "No, I call him Mr. Bernie."

"Come on, Lil."

She skip-stomps across the ground, fist held high.

I can't stop laughing. This girl is going to be a boss when she grows up.

Miss Janey finds us before we find her. She says to Lilli, "There you are! How was the playground, princess?"

"Good," Lilli sings with a grin. "This my sister, Sharkita."

"Just call me Kita," I say, reaching out to shake her hand. She takes my hand in hers and her smile beams.

"It is so nice to finally meet you! I absolutely adore your sister. Lilli is smart and funny, she . . ." That woman is loving on my little sis. She loves on Lilli so much, she actually cries.

I ask if Lilli can come with me to look for Lamar. Miss Janey tells me yes.

We found Lamar running in a field with a ball half the size of his body. Other boys were doing the same and sometimes crashing into each other. My heart dances when I see him. Much like with Lilli, it's like I'm seeing a different kid.

I want to yell out. Call to him.

I don't.

Instead, I just watch him for a minute. Something bubbles up inside me, a mixture of joy and sadness and loss and anger and happiness. Feelings that I've been burying, truths I've wanted not to see—now I can't look away.

My siblings are better off with grown-ups who can look out for them. Who care for them. I can see that now. They deserve to have lives without Mama. Without me.

"You looking for someone, girls?" The man talking to us looks like a gym teacher.

"Oh, yeah. I'm Kita, this is Lilli, and that boy right there is our brother."

"Ah, yes, Lamar!" The man introduces himself as Dan Cash. He is Lamar's foster dad. "We just love your brother. He's fit right in with our other two," he says, pointing to the boys. I can tell the other boys have similar disabilities as Lamar. "Let me go get him."

"Kita! Lilli! Kita! Lilli! Kita!" Lamar yells after Mr. Cash points us out. Then he races over and scoops both of us into a hug. Then he takes a good look at me, noticing my braces, and says, "Kita, who put them things in your mouth?"

Both Lilli and I laugh. It feels good to laugh together. Lamar has grown. So has Lilli. Seeing them, knowing their lives are improved, I want to be with them so badly. But it isn't fair for me to even think about helping Mama get us back when they are doing so well.

And you know what?

I look across the park and lock eyes with Miss Kadejah. Then it hits me: I'm doing well, too!

We eat and laugh and have a good time. The next hour passes so fast. Before we know it, Mr. Cash is calmly saying, "Lamar. It is time to go. What do we do when it's time to go?"

My brother starts waving, then sings, "You sing the Bye-Bye song. *Bye-bye-bye-bye-bye-bye . . .* "

With each "bye," he swings his head from left to right. Mr. Cash smiles and lets him sing, then he taps him again. "Lamar, my man, do you think you could give your sisters a hug goodbye before we go?"

Lamar stops singing and looks at me and Lilli.

"Kita and Lilli not coming with us?" he asks. He looks confused. If my heart wasn't already broken, it would be shattering right then and there. A couple hours together isn't enough time after months apart. Especially when I don't know when I'll see them again.

It is all too much.

Yet, I know it's enough. For now.

I hug Lamar and Lilli, managing to keep from crying. We hug till our arms hurt.

Miss Janey and Mr. Bernie come over and touch Lilli on the arm.

"Sweetheart, it's time to go," they say. Then Miss Janey looks at me. Her smile is soft and warm. "I know this is hard, but I promise you, my husband and I love this little girl with all our hearts. And as long as she's with us, you are welcome."

I'm overcome with emotion.

"Thank you," I say. "It means a lot, seeing her so happy."

Then Mr. Bernie taps my elbow and says, "I know Lilli would love to have you come over next month for the mermaid party." When I glance at Lilli, she's doing a little dance.

"I can't wait!" she screams. We all laugh.

"I would love that," I say.

Lilli gives me a bone-crushing hug before taking Miss Janey's hand.

Miss Kadejah is waving to me. I turn back and see Lilli looking over her shoulder at me. She looks so different from when she first saw me today.

I see a little girl at peace.

"Come on, preteen, help an old assistant principal out!" Miss Kadejah says with a laugh. I help her and several others clean up paper and chip bags, soda cans and water bottles, paper plates and utensils. Cleaning helps keep the tears from flowing.

Throughout the day, I'd caught Miss Kadejah watching me from across the park, checking on me, making sure I was okay. Even as we clean she is cracking more jokes than usual, probably knowing I am feeling down after having to say goodbye to my siblings and trying to make me feel better. Can't say it totally works, but there is a speck of happiness sitting next to all the sadness inside me.

Guilt, too, when I think of how I behaved earlier.

Once everything is cleaned up, we heap her coolers and everything into the back of the SUV.

Before we get inside, I stop her.

"I'm sorry about how I acted earlier. I . . . I . . ." The words won't fall out.

She opens her arms wide. I'm not sure if she pulls me in or if I jumped into her, but we hug and tears roll down our cheeks.

When she releases me, I quickly wipe my face.

"You are one of the best people I've ever met. I—I'm happy to be here," I take a breath. "I've just had a lot on my mind."

Miss Kadejah nods, smiling, but her eyes are sharp and intense. She says, "I know you have a lot going on inside that head. I want you to know, when you're ready, I'm here to listen. You don't have to worry about being judged or punished or ridiculed. But I can't help when I don't know what the problem is."

"Yes, ma'am," is all I manage to say.

"Whatever you choose, Kita, do it based on what you know is real, not what you hope can *become* real," she says.

We buckle up inside and she starts the engine. Before I lose my nerve, I make a decision. I say:

"I have something to tell you."

(38)

BACK HOME, MISS KADEJAH makes iced tea. We go sit out back by her pool. The sun is going down but the day still feels warm. If you listen, you can hear birds in the trees, frogs croaking, and insects buzzing in the garden.

She kicks off her shoes, leans back on the lounger, and I do the same. The whole truth about Mama is no longer a barrier between us, but something uniting us. The tea is icy and tastes like peaches. I take a long sip before speaking again.

"When did you last hear from your mother?" she asks, turning to look at me. "Mrs. Grieves thought she'd probably tried to get in touch with you, but you never said anything so we couldn't be sure."

I look down, embarrassed. "I know I should have said something, but I was so confused. Everything with Mama is confusing. She called last night."

Miss Kadejah tenses. "And what does she want you to do?"

I take in a deep breath. "She wants me to go to court and tell the judge that she is a good mama and we want to come home to her." I sit back, take another long sip. Listen to the ice cubes clink.

Silence sits between us for a moment. Then she asks, "Is that what you want to do?"

Big sigh. At first, my shoulders droop. But I pull myself up straight.

"No." The tiny word sticks to the tip of my tongue. It feels wrong, but I say it anyway.

I take in my surroundings—grass so green it looks right out of a paint box, a patio and deck like something from the home channel, and a pool. A real pool. The water dances in the breeze while dark orange and stripes of gray lace the sky.

"Did you know I don't know how to swim? Like, I've thought about it but didn't believe it would ever happen. Not for me, at least. I kind of convinced myself I didn't like pools because the water made me think of sharks. Crazy, right?" I lower my head.

Miss Kadejah's voice is soft but urging when she speaks again. "I can hire a one-on-one swim instructor to teach you right here at the house. But I need you to learn to ask for what you want. Now, it may not always be possible—I might not always say yes. Sometimes I'll have to say no. But that's how life works. Doesn't mean you shouldn't try."

I nod. Life works in funny ways.

"If I say no to Mama, she'll be so mad," I say, sounding like some little kid. "But . . . I can't say yes. Not after today. Not after seeing Lilli and Lamar. Seeing how much better off they are.

I can't take that from them. I can't do it. No matter how much I want to have them back."

Miss Kadejah bobs her head. "And what about you?" she says.

"What about me?"

"You just said 'I can't do that to Lilli and Lamar.' What about what's best for you? Do you think you're better off with Brittany or . . ."

"Don't even finish the question," I cut her off. After a moment, I raise my head, and the strange feeling of a weight being pulled off my body overtakes me. I feel so light, like I might float away. "I don't want to go back to Mama. I think I'm right where I need to be!"

"So, swim lessons?" she asks. We both laugh. When she reaches for her iced tea glass on the ground, I reach for her hand. We sit there for a bit, sun setting, shadows growing large around the yard. Me and my AP turned dance coach turned foster mom. Swinging our linked fingers together, like kids on a swing set.

She squeezes my fingers and something surges through me with such force, it takes a moment to recognize:

It's love.

My mind is still racing to catch up to where my heart has already landed—I love Miss Kadejah. The way she has supported me, stood by me. Thinking about her standing at the end of the block on Halloween, watching to make sure I was okay; how she'd added pictures of me at our twirling performances amid photos of her mother and father, her sorority sisters and friends; or the way she got me braces no questions asked, and now the same with the swim lessons.

Or the way she always encourages my twirling and dancing. And the way she has been introducing me to all different kinds of movies for movie nights because she knows I never let myself have favorite movies because I was only concerned with what the littles liked.

It didn't seem possible that a few months with this woman who was not a blood relation had taught me more about myself—my true self—than a lifetime with the woman who birthed me.

A scent touches my nose. Something soft and sweet. Familiar.

Not the tangy bite of oranges in the sun. Different. I sniff. "What's that smell?" I finally ask.

Miss Kadejah smiles. "I believe that's my lilacs. The bushes are over there. My mom had them in our yard growing up. It reminds me of being home."

Home.

~~

Mrs. Grieves gives us an official update the following week. Mama's hearing date has been set. I have three weeks to prepare what I'm gonna say.

At my next appointment with Dr. Charles I ask, "Do you think she can ever change?"

"Who are we speaking of?" he says, but of course he knew.

"Mama. Can she ever be better at being a mama than she has been so far?"

"Well." Dr. Charles spins around until he is no longer lying on the leather sofa but sitting upright. "What do you think?"

I roll my eyes. I might not be the most experienced at therapy, but I knew one thing: they didn't like answering questions. They asked them or answered your question with a question.

"Can you just answer the question? For once!" I say with a sigh. "Do you think my mama can change her ways enough to actually care for kids the way they—we—would need to be cared for?"

Today he is rocking Tampa gear—an old Tom Brady jersey from the Buccaneers. Light wash jeans. A Tampa Bay Rays baseball cap. A different pair of J's.

He raises his hands and shakes his head. "I don't know your mama. Never met her. What you're asking is impossible to know." He draws a deep inhale, sighs. "What I can tell you, based on your file and the files of your siblings, your mother has had her fair share of challenges. Becoming a mother at such an early age, losing her father, it sounds like she found herself drowning in a world she wasn't ready for."

"I've known since I was three that something with Mama just wasn't right," I say absently. I don't mean in the ways that made Granny send her to that therapeutic unit, or the ways she always said would get me admitted to one. I explain how Mama was constantly agitated about things like taking me to day care or making dinner for me. Ordinary things.

"Sounds like she was overwhelmed," he says.

"I guess." Something about knowing the court date is coming up and that I'll have to make a decision for real makes me want to continue, to tell Dr. Charles everything. So I tell him about the first time I was taken from her and placed in foster care. He listens, nodding and taking notes, saying little. I tell him the whole story of how she left me alone because Granny was coming back home, only Granny sent the cops instead.

We talk more about Mama and Granny. How they were always playing games with each other—games that led to suffering for me and my sibs. Like Granny refusing to take us in to teach Mama a lesson of some kind. He and I also discuss the toll of becoming a teen mom with limited support.

"It sounds like your mama didn't have a good example of what it means to be a mother," Dr. Charles says, talking about Granny.

I shake my head. My voice is tight when I speak. "But I didn't have one, either. And I still stepped up."

Dr. Charles leans forward. "That's because you saw something wasn't right and instead of playing into the game your mother and grandmother created, you put a stop to it. You are breaking the cycle, Kita. You know how to create change. And I have no doubt you'll continue to do just that."

I give him a shrug and an eye roll. Even though it is kinda nice to hear all that.

"You ready for the hearing?" he asks. A nervous knot has begun to claw its way into my gut. "Has she tried calling you again?"

I nod. "Three times. I didn't answer. She left messages. She was really mad."

Dr. Charles takes in a deep breath. "Kita, just remember,

275

when you walk into that courtroom, you are there to tell the judge what you know is true, not what your mom says is right."

In my head, the picture of what I wanted was becoming clearer. There was no turning back.

My phone feels heavy inside my pocket. Silent for now. My stomach gurgles. I do the deep breathing Dr. Charles showed me. He waits, a small smile playing at the corner of his mouth.

"It's hard, right? Standing up for yourself, doing the right thing? It's hard."

I look at Dr. Charles. A fist twists the nerves in my gut even tighter.

My voice when I speak is tiny. I can feel myself aging backward, becoming younger and younger until I'm the three-year-old girl Mrs. Grieves led away all those years ago.

"I just want it to be over, Dr. Charles. All of it. I want it to end so me and my siblings can have some type of life."

Inside my head, a small voice whispers:

A better life!

(**39**)

THE COURTHOUSE IS A large building downtown—the largest I've ever been in. It's hard to believe Mama worked here. I wonder if she still does. Miss Kadejah's high heels click on the marble floors, sound echoing off the walls, ceilings.

I'd had a choice to come to the courthouse or not. Mrs. Grieves said they were getting recorded testimonies from Lilli and Lamar, and I could have done the same. But I wanted to say what I needed to say in person.

"Remember, you don't have anything to fear," Mrs. Grieves says once we join her outside the judge's office. Miss Kadejah says the offices are called "chambers."

"I'm okay," I say.

"I'm glad. This won't be like on TV. You're not going to be in a big courtroom. There's no jury. You and I, along with Miss Kadejah, will be on one side of the table. Brittany and her attorney will be on the other. The judge will . . ."

"I know, I know. The judge will ask me a series of questions, and I'm supposed to answer as truthfully as possible. Then the judge will decide if and when he can make a determination. Right?"

We've gone over this about a billion times. I know what I plan to say.

Even so, I'm not prepared for seeing Mama when we walk in. But the even bigger shock is seeing she brought Granny along with her. So much for Granny saying Mama has to figure out her problems all on her own.

At first, when Mama catches my eye and her beautiful face lights up, it almost breaks me. She looks so different. Her hair is longer than usual. She is wearing minimal makeup. She looks younger.

Granny sitting beside her looks serene and respectful. No hint of the woman who fights regularly with her daughter and enjoys it. Who is as much a part of this terrible cycle as Mama is.

Then I see it. The two of them. Banding together to gang up on me when they've put me in the middle of their fights for years.

The more I think about it, the angrier I become. I won't be intimidated. Not this time. I will never go back to being Mama's "partner." I am no longer her ride or die.

"My name is Judge Josiah Rush," says the tall Black man in the long black robes. "You may refer to me during these family court proceedings as Judge Rush or Your Honor, and I will have absolute order in my chambers. No hysteria, no outbursts. Am I understood?"

He slams his little hammer on a thing that looks like a plaque on the table. He reads the petition from *Department of Children and Families for the State of Florida v. Brittany Lloyd Ambrose in the matter of termination of parental rights of the minor child(ren) Sharkita Lloyd, Lamar Ambrose, and Lillieana Ambrose.*

Once he finishes reading and repeating all the legal business, he talks to Mama's side of the table. Her attorney, a skinny white man who looks more nervous than me, answers most of the questions.

While all of it is happening, Mama keeps stealing looks across the table in my direction. At first, I want to look away. Then I realize I can't keep turning away from Mama, running, running, running like she so often did.

I face her.

Not mean-faced like LaWanda.

Not sad like I used to be.

Just me.

As the judge talks and discusses Mama's charges with the county for child neglect, it hurts me deep inside to hear that ugly phrase spoken in this important room. Because he is talking about me—*I* am the neglected child. And for some reason still hard to accept, I wish I could snatch the words out of the air and make them disappear. But the whole reason I am here today is because I am tired of hiding, tired of pretending. Mama has been neglectful. To me. To Lilli. To Lamar. And I am not gonna let it happen again.

When it is Mrs. Grieves's turn to speak, she tells how her

office made repeated attempts to work with Mama and offer her services. She tells the judge about us being temporarily removed in June of last year. Then she explains the action plan she created to allow Mama one last chance.

Mrs. Grieves, in a soft but clear voice, avoids her notes, instead looking directly at Mama, while she describes the incident in October when Mama left Lilli and Lamar alone at home, resulting in the house fire.

Through all this, Mama cries softly into a tissue and Granny sits at her side, rubbing her arm. When it is finally my turn, I am dry mouthed. One glance at the judge and you can see he's thinking bad thoughts about Mama. It feels mean for me to say messed-up stuff about her, too.

"Now, I'd like to know your feelings, young lady," Judge Rush says.

I shut my eyes for a moment to calm down my internal earthquake. I tell myself, "Stop running, stop running, stop . . . running . . ."

Miss Kadejah squeezes my hand and when she does, I see Mama flinch a little before going back to dabbing her eyes with the tissue.

"I love my mother and brother and sister very much," I say, taking a long exhale. "Granny too. But Judge Rush, I have visited Lamar and Lilli. They are doing so well. And . . . so am I. I didn't know how I would feel about it at first, but I love living with Kadej—um, Dr. Sapperstein. As much as I miss my brother and sister, I don't miss staying up late at night to try to help Lamar through his nightmares; I don't miss showing up late for school, unprepared and dead tired because I'd spent the night taking care of the kids—"

"Your honor!" Mama cries. Her face is red. Her Princess Jasmine eyes are ablaze. "She's making it sound like that happened all the time. It didn't! I love my children. I love my children!"

BAM! BAM! BAM!

The little hammer bangs and bangs. Judge Rush's face, dark as it is, flushes a reddish purple.

"Order! Order! Young woman, you will refrain from speaking unless you are spoken to, do you understand me?" The judge glares at my mama.

Mama, who's standing, seems to remember that she is supposed to be trying for sympathy. Her skinny lawyer pulls at her arm.

"Your honor, my client deeply regrets her actions and—"

"Save it, counselor. One more outburst from Mrs. Ambrose or anyone else on that side of the table, and I'll cite you all for contempt."

After that, the judge asks me some specific questions—some hard questions about Mama, about Lamar's disability, about me.

When Judge Rush finishes asking questions, he tells us all to wait for an hour "recess" and he'll return. The bailiff dude who'd been standing so still in the corner I'd barely noticed him leads our side of the table into one conference room and Mama's side into another.

Before I can even think of sitting down, Miss Kadejah is

wrapping me up in another big, tight hug. "I am so proud of you, Kita. I know that was so hard, so impossibly hard for you, and you did it. I am in awe of you, my strong girl." You bet I hug her right back.

And you know what? I feel proud of me, too.

We didn't say much for the rest of the break, and before I know it, the recess is over. The bailiff is taking us back into the judge's chambers. I notice Judge Rush wiping mustard stains from his tie. I try to hide my smile, but he catches my eye and looks sheepish.

"Nothing like a pastrami on rye with mustard to help an old man understand himself," he says with a wink.

Then . . .

"In the matter of *Department of Children and Families for the State of Florida v. Brittany Lloyd Ambrose*, I am ordering that the county agency of child protective services take custody of the minor children herein. Order for the plaintiff. Case dismissed!"

Mama has lost.

I hadn't realized how much I'd been holding my breath until the words are spoken. I wasn't sure how I'd feel once it was all said and done. Now I do:

I feel peace.

Still, I want to talk to Mama. To let her know that I wish only good things for her. That I'd like to hear about her life once in a while and talk the way we used to.

She rushes out of that room like she's on fire. When we enter the hall and I call out to her, she looks around, says something to Granny, and they both put their heads down and walk quickly away.

Even though she doesn't have power over me, Mama's total ignoring of me hits like another punch in my gut.

Thanks to Judge Rush, though, it will probably be her last.

(**40**)

NIECY RACES UP TO me the next day in the hallway. We don't walk to school together anymore since I live with Miss Kadejah.

"It's over! No more Britt!" I had texted her the news last night and I thought she'd gotten the celebrating out of her system, but apparently not.

I shake my head with a laugh. "No more Britt." Niecy wraps her arms around me. The next thing I know Chasity and several other girls from our dance team come over and hug me, too. A rush of tears threaten to spill, but I know if the tears start to fall I might drown us all.

"Dang, you guys!" I say, laughing and crying at the same time. "Thank you so much!" We all pull apart and I notice several of them wiping their eyes.

Quintin pops up then. We hadn't talked much recently—he texted every once in a while, but I'd had so much on my mind I usually forgot to respond—but he still comes over and gives me a hug.

"I'm happy for you, Kita," he says before pulling away. "Hit me up some time, okay?"

All I can do is nod.

When I look at Niecy, she's wearing a wide grin.

It's a perfect moment and I realize I'm not waiting for the bad thing to come and kill the mood for once.

Then the bad thing comes along and tries to kill the mood. But with everything that's happened to me over the past several months, I feel different. Stronger.

Mrs. Wilcher glowers at all of us.

"Ladies, the bell's about to ring. I know you've got some place to go. And I happen to know, Sharkita, that you have an early math class. You definitely don't want to be late," Wilcher says.

"I'm doing really well in math, actually, Mrs. Wilcher. It's been nice having a math teacher who cares." I say it in a soft, unassuming voice. But when it comes out, the girls swoop around, eyes big, gulping back the urge to tell her, "In your face, Wilcher."

Mrs. Wilcher's face goes red and she uses the last bit of power she has over me to tell us once again to get to class. Then she stomps off.

I'd stood up for myself and I knew it'd feel great. Eventually. Right now, however, my lips are numb and I might be having a heart attack.

But no, it's just good old-fashioned shock.

I mentally add another goal:

Practice ways to stand up for myself.

Today is Lilli's birthday party. We've been invited.

I bought her a cute gift with my allowance—I still can't believe someone is giving me an actual allowance. Miss Kadejah has been amazing. We're still getting to know each other, but we're both trying, both doing our best.

Several cars line the block in front of the Millers' house. It's a butter-yellow craftsman with black shutters, window boxes filled with bright red geraniums, and a wraparound porch.

Cheers and laughter, pure joy, fill the atmosphere surrounding the house. I can clearly hear my sister's giggle. Splashing sounds perk my ears. Is Lilli in the water?

"I think everybody's back here," says Miss Kadejah. She heads around the side of the house clutching two large, glossy shopping bags. I try to take them.

"Let me," I say, reaching out. "I'll carry it for you."

She gives me a look.

"Kita, I've told you, I am perfectly capable of doing things myself. Thank you for offering, though." She gives me a wink. My cheeks sting with nerves, then I puff out an exhale and smile.

"Okay," I say. What I don't say is it's still hard not stepping in and trying to do everything or fix everything. Sometimes I wonder if that feeling, like I always need to be doing more, will ever go away.

When no one answers the door, we head around the side of the house to the back. Bouncy castles and inflatable pool toys lounge on emerald grass and turquoise water. Colors as plentiful as confetti sprinkle the greens and blues of the backdrop.

Pointy birthday hats, at least ten little kids in swimsuits, moms in capris and sandals, tables filled with food. Primary colors blend with shades of pastel and my eyes water trying to take in all the vibrancy, while the brightest shine of all comes from my little sister's brilliant white smile.

"Kita!" Lilli squeals soon as she lays eyes on me.

I feel nervous and giddy. Like I said, I bought her a gift. But I made her one, too.

Then there's the surprise I've been planning.

"Lil!" I squeal back. We run toward each other like we're on TV. I bend to scoop her up and make an "*Oomph!*" sound. I want to raise her up and snuggle her, ask how she's doing, but realize Lilli's legs are dang near long as mine.

"Put me down." She giggles, beginning to squirm. I let her slide off me. "I'm too tall." She's right. The truth of it hits me with a strange sense of pride, like I had something to do with her growing taller—and the gut-punching reality that the littles could continue to grow and change without me.

"I have a surprise for you," I sing out.

"What is it? What is it? What is it?" Lilli is insistent. I shrug. For the first time, she notices I'm wearing a swimsuit under a pair of shorts. I quickly kick off the shorts and my flip-flops.

The family has their own pool, and I know they hired a swim coach to teach her, like Miss Kadejah did for me. She looks at me and says, "I know how to swim like a mermaid. Lamar does, too! Did you see him in the water, too? I wish you could be a mermaid like us."

"We'll see. Let's go play with Lamar." My little brother is being monitored in the shallow end of the pool. He smacks the water with his hand. He's making a plastic shark dive into the tiny swells that cover his ankles. He's playing with the shark I bought him at the Florida Aquarium.

"Mar-Mar!" I say. He looks up briefly but is more enamored with his shark. "Are you ready for your surprise, Lilli?"

She screams, "YES! YES! YES!"

I grin.

Then I take a deep breath, eyes wide open, and I jump in. The pool is heated. Warm water holds me in an embrace that lifts my heart to heaven. I'd give anything I ever have or will have for the expression on my sister's face.

What's bigger than joy?

Bliss?

Has to be bliss.

"Kita! You can be a mermaid, too!" She dives in while other grown-ups and kids look on. No one else gets in. Not yet. I'm grateful. Lilli takes my hand and we dive beneath the folds of the turquoise waves. Beneath the water, we can't smell orange blossoms or hear tractors in the background. The water pulses against us as we go deeper, then rise, never breaking the surface, listening to our hearts beat in rhythm with our movements.

I look over at my sister and smile.

We pop up for air and her little goggles fog over. She pulls them on top of her head. We make our way over to Mar-Mar. He looks at me closer now and knits his brow.

"Kita, you look different," he says. He's squinting at me, dark brown eyes assessing every inch of my face. I brace myself because there's no telling what that boy is about to say. After a minute, he says. "Your face looks happy, Kita."

For a moment, I am stunned. Then I reach out and grab his tummy and tickle him. Another boy from the same home giggles and soon the two of them drift into their own world of make-believe.

I look at Lilli in her adorable mermaid-inspired swimsuit of blue, green, and silver.

"To Chocotopia!" she yells.

I glance at Miss Kadejah, who sends a big smile our way, and shrug. Then I shout:

"To Chocotopia!"

The two of us dive under once again. The only sound that penetrates the dense silence of the water is the sound of Lamar singing, "Swim! Swim! Swim! No let the shark get you, get you, get you-ooo-ooo!"

More mermaids join us. It doesn't matter. We have a bond that will never break, whether we're in a make-believe underwater city, or a yellow craftsman across town, the three of us will always be bound together. No matter where we live.

Family.

ACKNOWLEDGMENTS

I would like to acknowledge my mother. The mama/daughter relationship can be fraught with missteps and hidden injuries. And while the absentee nature of the good-timing mama in this book is in no way indicative of my own mother's style of parenting, my mama brought a level of tough love that was known to leave bruises, particularly on the psyche of her sensitive daughter. For all the mothers who loved their girls so hard because they wanted to make them grow up tough and strong, hey, I salute you. Mama was right: once I had my own daughters a lot of her messages became clearer.

Now, for all the daughters who, unlike me, were forced to navigate life without the strength of a good mother, the same way Sharkita is forced to step up and be there for her siblings, I say to you, don't give up. You are worth the journey and the fight. So keep fighting.

I'd like to thank my editor, Alex Borbolla, for her encouragement and optimism, not to mention her deft precision in cutting through the noise and helping me shape this into the story I envisioned. For an author, it's a rare treat to recognize that the book between the covers is the same as it appeared in your dreams. Thank you, Alex. And as always, my agent, Laurie Liss at Sterling Lord Literistic, who has always got my back. I'd also like to thank the rest of my incredible Bloomsbury team: Kei Nakatsuka, John Candell, Oona Patrick, Briana Williams, and Lex Higbee.

This story is for those young people who feel invisible, overlooked. You are seen.